Kane Unleashed

Wolfwere Series Book 2

Dick Wybrow

Dee Dub Publishing

Copyright © 2023 by Dick Wybrow

All rights reserved.

No portion of this book may be reproduced in any form without written permission from the publisher or author, except as permitted by U.S. copyright law.

Chapter One

Specialist Ian Flemming shrugged off his parka and laid it on the back of the chair in the tiny dinette. He knew the rule was to always hang the coats on the coatrack. Hell, he'd *made* the rule. Their four-room border security annex had little space for being untidy. One errant Tim Hortons wrapper and he and his partner Jack would be bumping into each other.

However, when he'd seen the fogged glass of the empty coffee pot, smelled that burnt sludge baking at the bottom of the carafe *again*, well, he could break rules too.

Ian stared out the window facing the US border. The slash separating the two countries cut wide enough for two cars to ride side-by-side as their drivers traded "yo mama" jokes out their open windows.

Not that anyone drove through the slash. Not without bringing down the defense forces of both countries.

"Some big international hubbub stop you from making coffee, Jack?" Flemming rubbed the gray-black stubble of his face, still not used to working third shift even after two years. He used to think of it as black-gray stubble, but the house hadn't been the only thing he'd lost in the divorce.

And, since then, his apartment bed felt too cold at night to sleep, so he'd decided he might as well get paid for being up at all hours. "First in, you drop some grounds, eh?"

Their security outpost, a converted cabin dating back to sometime early last century, had been built by hand. Some Canadian frontiersman who'd had a family of four, a sharp ax, and a sociopathic dislike of trees that stood upright.

And the old porous wood soaked up everything.

Coffee steam, Jack's meat-themed body odor, and the stank of whatever their boots might drag in from the slash outside.

In the spring, when the woodland carpet of British Columbia seemed permanently damp, the converted cabin felt like sitting inside some yawning giant's open mouth. Still, Flemming had grown accustomed to it. Even liked it.

Except when there wasn't any coffee.

"Sorry, Ian," Jack said, shuffling in from the monitoring station that, decades earlier, had once been a kids' bedroom. Fading gouges in the door's frame told the story that "Mandy" had grown taller than her older brother "Graham" between the ages of nine and ten. Must have been a blow to little Graham.

When Jack elbowed the door wider, the harsh light from the six screens inside bit into his partner's peripheral vision. Flemming wasn't eager to jump right into the room and get bathed in that electronic wash. Probably was giving him cancer.

Ian's fingers probed a lopsided shelf stuffed with three different bags of coffee, four tea tins, countless napkins, and one cellophane-wrapped Danish that bore no expiration date. He gingerly pulled out a filter so all the other stuff didn't topple out and end up on the floor. Jack had once called the stacks "Coffee Jenga," and to Ian, that seemed about right.

What *wasn't* right s being the second man in and having to play it. "'Sorry, Ian' don't really give me the jolt I need in the morning like a shot of java, yeah?"

"*Morning?*" Jack said, shuffling into the room and slumping onto the chair next to the cloudy window, using Ian's coat as a comfy backrest. "Someone forgot to tell the sun!" He chuckled, watching his partner scoop a bent steel measuring cup into a giant bag of dark grounds like a tiny front-loader digging through rich, Columbian dirt.

The coffee-making man shrugged. "Easier to think about it as morning. Gives ya some normalcy to the day." Flemming nodded toward the room Jack Shred had just come from. "Anything on TV tonight?"

"Oh yeah," the other man said with a weary grin. "They got the tree show on tonight."

"Again?"

"Season two," Jack said, scratching his brown birds' nest of a beard. "So I been binge watching."

Flemming pushed the decanter under the Coleman water cooler and thumbed its worn rubber blister to fill the jug. All the way to the top.

Jack nodded toward the pre-coffee. "She's a ten-cup night, is she?"

"Gonna be. I can feel it already."

"You must be part First Nations or something, hearing whispers on the wind." Jack crossed his arms, grinning. Then his face turned more serious. "Or did somebody call you too?"

Flemming flicked the coffee maker's on button with his knuckle and dropped into the only chair in the kitchenette not draped with a coat, waiting for his younger partner—younger by a year, but Jack was always happy to make something of it—to finish the thought. Ian lifted his hands toward the other man. *Well?*

"Got rung up by McClarsky about twenty minutes ago," Jack said. "Says he had to spend two hours resetting his maple taps after some*one* buggered them up."

Ian groaned.

Stan McClarsky's family had run an impressive syrup outfit for generations. It had started up back before there were electronically monitored borders, armed patrol guards, and chronically empty coffee pots.

The McClarsky domain covered thousands of hectares, but its main moneymaker had been the area west of British Columbia's Kootenay River and south of Crowsnest Highway. That's where the maples had been at their thickest.

Stan's grandfather had pitched a fit when he'd first been told they'd wanted to cut the slash right across his property's border, but it had been explained that this had been a matter of national security. The security of two nations, actually. A proper line of designation between Canada and the United States.

Grandfather, a Canadian patriot, graciously agreed. And would shoehorn his graciousness into casual conversation—as well as the tacit gratitude of not one but two countries—any chance he could. Some would say he dined out on that story until he died. Others might say he gorged.

Previously, a central border station a few thousand kilometers to the west, near Vancouver, had monitored the slash. However, years back, the new fella in Ottawa wanted to impress his southern neighbor and had "beefed up" security, repurposing the cabin where Jack and Ian had been stationed a few years now.

Before then, Stan McClarsky's paranoid calls about intentional interlopers had gone to Vancouver.

These days, they came to Jack and Ian.

Flemming stared dully at his partner, waiting for the news, too tired to offer up a conversational prompt. Had there been coffee, maybe he'd have been more accommodating. But there hadn't, so he wasn't.

"Lines all twisted up, some knocked down," Jack continued, yawning and stretching. Ian watched as the man's lazy spasms shifted his coat on the chairback, nearly knocking it to the floor. Nearly. "I dunno how he can tell whether they're messed up or not, strung around the trees like a maniac cat's cradle."

"Old bastard's got maple syrup running through his veins, not blood. Probably puts his hands out and can just sense it," Flemming said, laughing softly, too tired to stay mad about the coffee. "He think it was kids or something? He should just ring up RCMP."

The coffee pot beeped. Jack began to lift himself up but then caught the expression on his partner's face. Cowed, he slowly put his butt back into his folding chair. Flemming stood, grabbed the two coffee cups which had been left to dry on a tea towel, flipped them over, and poured the black ambrosia inside.

"Not kids," Jack said. "He says the way the lines were snapped and twisted—What?" His proffered coffee cup hovered in front of him, just out of reach, like some mirage hanging in the air. When he looked at Flemming, he noticed the man was staring past him into the next room.

The monitoring station.

"What?" he repeated then stood, spun around, and crossed the threshold into the next room.

Jack dropped into his rollaway chair, and a moment later, blissfully, his steaming cup of coffee appeared atop the dried moisture ring next to his keyboard. Scanning the screens, he heard Flemming's chair squeak.

"You see something, Ian?"

The other man pointed, blowing on his steaming up. "Cam two. Ten seconds ago."

"Crosser?"

Flemming shrugged. "On all fours, so an animal. Big one too. But weird."

That got a long exhale out of Jack, which rolled into a deep chuckle. "There ain't nothing weird for about a hundred clicks other than you and me."

"Hey," Flemming said, sipping his coffee. "Don't include me in your odd-man circus. You're the only man I know who likes honey in his joe."

Jack smacked his lips and grinned, delighted that his partner hadn't forgotten. "Better than sugar. All that processed shit." He pointed at the screen. "Cam two, yeah?"

A nod.

When he banged away at the keyboard, the image on the second screen stopped then reversed. The timecode ticked back as the trees waved unnaturally in the backward breeze. They watched and waited.

"You sure that you—?"

As time's arrow reversed in front of him, Jack saw the strangest thing. And, he agreed, *weird* indeed.

The top third of the screen burned in the deep oranges of the setting sun, playing some havoc with the camera's iris. Just below the horizon, in darks a bit too dark, he saw the tiny image of what looked like a woodland creature on all fours. In the dim light, it was hard to tell if it was a wolf or a bear or... what?

With the thunk of the space bar, the image froze.

Crossing the slash was what looked like an animal, but its limbs were long, bent high up on the front and back legs. People don't walk like animals and on all fours; they can't help but arch the back.

"That is weird," Jack said. "But the way it walks, it ain't human."

Flemming sipped his coffee again and put it down next to the monitors. "Didn't say it was."

"Color's jacked up because of the light," Flemming said, leaning in close. In the day, the images were clearer and sharper, of course. When the sun went down, they had night vision and heat sensors that could help discern flesh from flora.

But at dusk, that's when it was a trickier read. Still, it didn't explain that smear of color on the creature's back. Flemming tapped the grainy image on the second screen.

"Could just be a reflection of the sunset."

Jack snorted. "Pink? Purple?"

A shrug.

"Maybe it got into some clothesline on the American side," Jack continued. "Dragged down some supermodel's G-string on accident."

Flemming rolled his head toward his partner. "You need to get out more."

"I get out plenty," Jack said then hit the space bar to get the image moving. He pointed at the screen once again. "The purple almost looks like hair the way it splits."

"Damn thing moves fast."

And it had. Between the timecode 8:43:14 and 8:43:16, the whatever-it-was crossed the slash from the US side to the Canadian. Then it was gone. Too fast for a human, *especially* on all fours.

Both men sat silently, sipping their coffees, slurping in stereo, as they watched the pleasant sunset colors on the tiny screen.

"You wanna call it in?" Jack asked, turning to his superior.

Flemming tilted his head lazily and finished his mug in a gulp, enjoying the burn of it. He stood to get another and crossed back into the kitchenette. He poured another cup, black, as always, then stood at the cold window of the cabin-turned-security-annex and stared down at the slash, which ran for miles and miles and miles.

Part of him wanted to set the cup down, put on his coat, and run to the end of it himself.

Ah yeah. His coat.

Pulling his parka from the back of the chair, he lifted it onto one of the two hooks on the wall, right next to their steel-reinforced front door.

Back at the window, he said, "You know as well as I do what got into McClarsky's maple lines."

The dual-toned squelch of a rollaway chair told him that Jack had spun around to look at him. He could hear the grin in the man's voice as he spoke.

"Smokey, yeah? Out there looking for dessert."

"Had an old aunt, ancient. She always ate dessert first in case she died before the main course came." Flemming cracked a grin. "Smokey's an old timer, so my guess, he first got his fill of maple syrup. And whatever that was running across the slash?" He turned to his partner, raising the fresh mug to his lips. "I'd say that's gonna be dinner."

Chapter Two

Despite how many layers I'd wrapped myself in, I was shivering. Freezing in July. But, of course, this was Canada.

I'd strapped myself to Kane's back like a toddler clinging onto its lululemon mama training for the half-marathon. Of course, my French-Canadian boss was six-foot-seven, and I was, um, not. I hung there, my arms and legs wrapped around his torso, as he ran through the forest, dodging left and right around trees and brush.

Every now and then, he'd stop, and I'd hear him suck in a few deep breaths. I knew he was sniffing the air. Then, boom, off like a rocket again.

At least he'd stood upright after we'd crossed the border.

Initially, he'd dropped to all fours to masquerade as an animal. Wrapped as he was in a massive black parka with matching hood, he'd galloped across the cut in the trees, which, he'd told me before our trek, would mark the border between the US and our neighbors to the north.

It took all my strength to hold on. I'd thought the backpack would serve as a cushion between me and my man-ride. Instead, at every bump and turn, it just punched my sternum.

The going hadn't been much easier when he'd switched from four legs to two.

Not that he had four legs—at least not at the moment. That, of course, would change if he got even the slightest wink of moonlight onto his skin. This was why he was wrapped head to toe in thermal gear that would make an Arctic explorer sweat bullets.

Big furry gloves. Ski mask with no mouth opening. The only thing that made him look slightly less animalish were the wraparound sunglasses. He'd picked a pair with a rainbow tint.

Standing in the sporting gear store seventy-five miles south of the border, Kane had snatched them off the spinning rack with a huge grin.

Gazing at the reflective lenses, he'd said, "They remind me of the aurora in the dead of winter. When the cold night air opens the heavens so that you might see to the beginning of time."

"No, you think they make you look cool."

After strapping them on, he bent low to look at himself in the tiny rectangular mirror at the top of the sunglass display.

"Yes, Emelda, also because they make me look cool."

I'd looked markedly less cool after I'd snatched up the dark navy backpack. Far from my preferred color, the blue one was the only one that had all the extra pockets I wanted. We were likely going to be on the road for days, and I needed the storage.

Two hours later, we'd parked the jeep we'd gotten from Miss Florida on the far edge of a small used car lot. A sign on the front door said the owner was in the middle of a two-week vacation. I figured it could sit there for a few days without drawing too much attention.

My head banged against the thick muscles of Kane's back as he, apparently, leaped over some downed tree or boulder or rusted Volkswagen. Even through the padding, I felt like I'd face-planted on a wood floor.

"No more jumping!" I said, spitting out bits of down feather, pretty sure the bang had misaligned some vertebrae in my neck.

Good thing we were heading to a doctor.

George Fineman had been let in on Kane's secret shortly after my friend had made the transition from wolf to human the year before. Fineman had been the family doctor and our only potential lead to find Cal Davis.

John and Linda Davis—or Père and Mère, as Kane called them—had taken him into their home after he'd changed. I suppose they might have felt some responsibility since it had been their biological son, Cal, who'd bitten Kane and started all this chaos.

Hospitals had been out of the question. You could tell Kane's biology was a bit screwy when he laughed, not that he ever did. But I'd seen him yell once or twice, and he had a few extra teeth jammed in there. Incisors that could probably dent a car fender.

Kane's adoptive father had known the doctor from their army days and trusted him with the family's *unusual* secret.

That must have been a hell of a conversation: "Hey, doc! Long time. So my kid bit a wolf and that wolf turned into a human, so we named him after our other son who died. Can you give new Kane a once over?"

However that conversation had gone, it had been the doctor who'd first noticed Kane's rapid aging. Last year, the newly minted human had been estimated at about fifteen. At times, I'd seen him look at least twenty years older than that.

That said, Kane had discovered a rather macabre fountain of youth. As long as that fountain spewed blood now and then—so gross—he'd revert to a man in his mid-twenties.

Thanks to a few stray cats the day before, he didn't look much older than he had a month ago when I'd first met him. Of course, when I had first met him, he'd been a little yappy dog.

Yeah.

And, points to me, I'd figured out the moon phase thing. Tiny sliver of moon in the night sky, tiny dog. As it got bigger—waxing, they called this, I googled it—the larger the dog. I'd only seen a pug and Rottweiler.

Well, not only.

When the moon had gone full, he'd become something else entirely. Not a monster because he wasn't that. Instead, I came up with a name for it that I thought was kinda clever.

Kane wasn't technically a werewolf because that's a human who becomes a wolf with the full moon. My thumb-powered research discovered "were" actually means man. He was a wolf who became a man, so the opposite of werewolf. The new designation, well, it just came to me.

A wolfwere.

Hmm. Maybe a bit on the nose.

My head snapped back as the big man made a right-angled turn at speed.

"Okay, okay!" I shouted, but he didn't stop. "Whoa, horsey! Stop! Sit! Play dead!"

Finally, he slowed, twisting his head toward me. "What is it? Do you sense danger, Emelda?"

"Only to my consciousness. Can I get off you now?"

The big man swiveled his head left and right then looked ahead. When he spun around quickly, I nearly barfed.

In my dizziness, I wondered if this had been his life as a wolf. Running, halting, checking for dangers, running again. It seemed exhausting.

"Is this what it was like?" I said, my words muffled into the down jacket cocooning his body. "Always looking for some threat?"

Kane stood straight—I hadn't even realized he'd been crouching as he ran—and I yelped, fearing I was about to tumble off his back. I just hung there like a fat tick, arms and legs waving in the air. He'd lifted himself with ease as if I hadn't been there at all. Kane tugged at the straps of the navy backpack, and it fell from his back. So did I.

Thankfully, I landed on my feet. I unhooked the front Velcro straps that had kept me secure then slung the pack over my shoulder.

"There is a scent in the air," he said, eyes cutting between the thick trunks of the British Columbian forest. "I cannot place it."

"Huh," I said and put a hand on his shoulder. Well, I couldn't reach his shoulder. I put a hand on his back. "I thought you had some of those wolfy senses even as a human? Not so much? Maybe you're becoming more and more people-like."

Kane spun on me like I'd punched him in the gut. Then he softened. "No, but human nose not like wolf nose. Yes, I can pick up more than you, but reading the scent... I am not yet so good with this."

I scanned the woods and took in a deep breath. Sure, it was probably a balmy fifty-five degrees, but it chilled me to the bone. That said, the earthy aromas were intoxicating. Alive and rotting at the same time.

Faint birdsong in the dying light, last call for avian lovin'. The chatter of crickets.

The loamy soil beneath my boots. I knew that in a few months, this would all be frozen and covered in snow. Or at least, I thought I knew. I'd never been to Canada before. Mainly because I'd never had a reason to go.

Secondly, I didn't have a passport, which is why Kane had to sneak me across the border.

Cal Davis was the only one with the answers Kane needed to become a wolf again. For him to return to his wolf-wife and his pack. Cal had ditched us after a near-deadly encounter at a shuttered mall in Minnesota. After that, his trail had gone cold.

It had been my idea to head back to his human parents' hometown.

"My grandfather was kind of a drunk, but when he wasn't blasted, he was actually kind of smart. Still an asshole but a smart one," I'd told my big friend. "He used to say, 'When you lose your way, you go back to the beginning and start again.'"

Of course, we couldn't go back to the home once owned by his human parents, where he'd "grown up." It had been burnt down in a fire on a night that Kane didn't like to speak about.

So, we had to find Cal. And our only possible lead to find him was Dr. Fineman. Hopefully.

Walking through the forest, I found it difficult to see in the dark. There were a few clouds above us, some with a faint glow. I knew what lay behind them.

"Moon's playing hide-and-seek with the clouds, man," I said, pointing up to the canopy of trees. "You think there's a cabin or cave or HoJos around here?"

Kane turned to me slowly, his face covered by cloth and rainbow sunglasses. Even through the material, I could sense his frown.

He said, "There is something out here in the woods."

I blinked, took a step back, and looked around. "What do you mean 'something'?"

Kane dropped into a crouch and once again sniffed the air.

"We are being hunted."

Chapter Three

I've always loved the night and used to think I'd be best suited for shift work.

Until I got a job at a 24-hour diner and realized, nah, not for me. Lots of boozehounds, burnouts, and drug addicts. The customers weren't much better.

I'd worked since the day I'd turned sixteen. Mostly in bars and restaurants. My last boyfriend always had side jobs when money was tight, and money was always tight. Roy had taught me the ropes and, ironically maybe, hung himself on them.

Not literally, of course.

He'd had me join him to break into a warehouse with *surprisingly* lax security. That should have been a red flag. Turns out, the owners felt their reputation would be all the security they needed.

Roy hadn't gotten that memo.

Despite it supposedly being a "simple job," as Roy had said, the bonehead tripped the warehouse's alarm.

The only reason I didn't get busted was because I'd been in the car, waiting. Getaway driver, right? Roy hadn't put me out there for my protection. Driving all fast and furious had always just been one of those things that came naturally to me.

Once the big floodlights came up and the metal gate came down—the owner had installed a portcullis-type device, how nuts is that?—I'd hit the gas and never let up. That had been the plan, although I doubted Roy ever thought it would come to that.

When he'd been out on bail, a crew from the rival gang tracked us down. Fair enough; it had been their warehouse we'd busted into, and they wanted to convey their displeasure with long steel pipes.

It hadn't worked out so well for them.

After that, Roy went to prison, and I went to bar jail. No sentence or cage for me, just a job I had to take or starve. That's just a prison of a different type.

I worked ten-hour days. No lunch, but I did carve out time to scarf down whatever some group of tennis ladies hadn't finished. Humiliating, sure, but when you're damn-near starving, pride is the first thing you eat.

"Where the hell are we going?" I shouted up to Kane, who was dodging and weaving through the dark forest ahead of me. There wasn't any trail except, I suppose, the one he was carving out. Dude was big, so I just followed in his wake.

"Kane?"

Instead of answering, he let out a low growl, something I shouldn't have even been able to hear as fast as we were hauling through the bush. But he wanted me quiet. I'd gotten the message.

We weren't *going* anywhere. We were running away from something.

I turned my head to look behind us, but with the thick ceiling of trees above us, it was like looking into the black void of space. I'd only just started to swivel my head back around when I smacked into him.

Bouncing off the big French Canadian, I fell back on my ass.

On the ground, the cold's icy fingers began to reach up through me, and I shivered.

"Scent on the breeze," he said, legs bent at the knees, feet pointing in two different directions. His arms were out, hands splayed, like he was using them to taste the air.

"What kind of scent?" I didn't dare blink as I scanned around us. "People? Animal?"

Kane shifted his weight, left and right. Then he spun toward me, held out a hand, and lifted me to my feet.

"Maybe you should climb tree."

"What?"

He pointed at a large knotty maple. I'd done a bit of panicked tree climbing back during those summers on my uncle's farm when my older cousins had chased me down with their paintball guns.

The memory reminded me that I hadn't come wholly unprepared. I spun my backpack off my shoulder and reached inside. I dug out the slingshot with its rubber loop-and-cup contraption, untangling the snaking tube.

In the cone-shaped cup, I could load a steel arrow about as long as my forearm. A few days earlier, I'd put one of those darts into the neck of a monster. It hadn't killed the thing. Kane had done that when he'd used the arrow to twist the creature's head off.

Kane scanned the surrounding forest, sniffing the air and growling in frustration. When he saw what was in my hands, he grimaced.

"That will not help."

"My slingdart helped before," I reminded him.

"Your aim is terrible. Put elastic wishbone away and climb tree."

His face covered in a ski mask, his eyes just two dots of dim light—the reflections off his sunnies—I couldn't tell if he was serious or not. Didn't matter. There was no way I was climbing a tree.

Before I could inform him of my decision, I heard the *huff-huff-huff* and thudding of massive paws shake the ground. In the next moment, a throaty exhalation of damp breath, the smell of rotting meat, and Kane shot sideways

My boss, my friend, was huge. The beast that had leaped at him was easily twice his size.

In the strobing light from the slits in the canopy of leaves above, I watched him tumble end over end with the creature. Not just any creature.

I'd seen animals like this before. In YouTube videos that carried red-band warnings and ended poorly.

But never for the animal.

Chapter Four

Kane

I had heard the grizzly approach, and had it not been for Emelda standing there, I would have leaped away to dodge its attack. However, had I done that, she would have made a squeaky sound then been consumed.

Bad way to go. Not that there are many good ways.

The bear is massive, its large paw wrapped around the back of my neck as we tumble down the hill. I reach up with a gloved hand to grip its long claws, avoiding their tips. They are sharp and would easily shred the fabric of my hand coverings.

And strip my fingers to the bone.

Rolling end over end, I have enough time to curse myself. I should have recognized its scent when I first picked it up. Alas, the things I remember as a wolf do not translate well to my human mind. It is like the same words but an unfamiliar language, so I cannot easily interpret them.

Will I ever be able to knit those two worlds together?

The grizzly roars as we tumble, face to face, and its spittle splatters my rainbow sunglasses.

For as powerful as I am in human form, I concede I am no match for a grizzly. Even as wolf, I would have never taken on such a massive creature. In a pack, maybe, but only out of desperation and with little hope of victory.

Halfway down the rise, we smack against a boulder as big as a two-car garage. Not that I've ever had a two-car garage, but I have seen Emelda looking at magazines with houses. She shows me pictures.

The grizzly twists and bucks, incredibly agile for a beast so large. A thousand pounds of flesh, fat, and muscle, it's trying to get on all fours, so it might tower above me. I have dealt with these bears before, usually by running in the opposite direction.

I try to roll away, and it strikes out, hoping to hold me in place as it finds its feet. With both hands, I punch upward, blocking its arm, but can only deflect it. The impact gives me leverage to slip away.

Back on all fours, I search my surroundings for a path. With grizzly, there is only escape. My former alpha learned this, and while it spared the rest of the pack's lives, it cost his own.

He'd been a better alpha than I, this is undeniable. And he'd lasted no more than a half minute with such a creature. One-on-one combat will end quickly. And badly.

The grizzly roars, its mouth twisting, spittle flying.

I am wolf but not wolf. Larger as a man, I lift myself to my full height. My hands high above my head, I roar back. The grizzly tilts its head to the side and blinks.

He is unimpressed by my animal call. Insulting bear. I would very much like to kill him now.

For once, my advantage is that I am human. I have rarely seen this as any advantage. Clothing, for one, is very troublesome. I do not like to match. However, black, Emelda has taught me, matches everything. And it makes me look cool.

Focus!

The bear lunges toward me, in its lumbering, leaping gallop, and I turn to run. After a few paces, I tear sharply to my right, a cut to my left, then another to my right. I will not win a footrace with it, only buying time to formulate some plan of escape.

As I make another juke to the left, I hear the snap of its jaw behind my head, feel the burst of damp exhalation at my neck. Far too close!

I have seen the bite of a grizzly split a tree in two. Despite my powerful torso, *so powerful*, I do not think I would fare better.

I run perpendicular to the slope of the hill, but the ground covering is damp from rain and rot. If I lose footing, the beast will be on top of me. The creature's paws slip and slide as it pursues me on the uneven terrain.

Pulling slightly ahead, I try to devise an escape.

Going up a tree is an option. However, it's only a few seconds behind me, and I would just get up half the height before it plucked me like ripe fruit.

Ahead, within a few spotty pools of light, I see what I need. Not a solution, but it will buy me a few precious seconds. Leaping forward, I grip the fallen tree trunk with my hands, but it's difficult to hold on. However, I cannot remove the gloves.

The grizzly only a few strides away, I spin around and flip the jagged length of the trunk upright. No time to swing it, I instead drop to a knee and press an end of it into the ground.

Wood splinters burst as it connects to the animal's neck, and it howls. The mass of the creature replants the tree, and for a moment, it is suspended in the air as if its head were the top of a totem pole from cowboy western movies.

Back on my feet, I turn to run and see it swipe away at the log, leaving a red gash across its throat. The blood buzzes a hunger, a need within my brain, but I ignore it.

Once again, I hear the terrifying *huff-huff-huff* of the creature as it pursues me, unfazed by the injury.

Running down the hill now, I hear the beast pick up speed, its exhalations growing louder and fiercer with every grunting step. Careful about my footing, I juke left and hear it groan and howl as it tries to make the same turn.

Damp leaves and mud are my allies. The grizzly slips and stumbles, going end over end as it tumbles down the hill. However, once it reaches the bottom, it's back up once again.

Running along the hill is difficult, one leg lower than the other, but it is my best chance of survival. The bear will struggle even more than I with the uneven gait.

If I can get far enough away, it may lose interest.

I chance a glance over my shoulder and see that, yes, I am widening the gap. When I turn and look forward again, I notice strange-looking skinny trees. Sideways trees? However, I notice these too late and smack into them.

"*Ooof!*"

Bashing through the first, blue plastic shards fly everywhere. I hit another, which catches me waist high. Slowed, I do not break it and instead flip over top of it and land on my back.

I stare up at a long tube connected to a tree.

What foul magic is this?

Chapter Five

I hadn't gotten very high up in the tree, but I didn't need to climb far. The grizzly saw Kane as a much better meal than me. Me, I'm more appetizer size. Grizzly potato skins to Kane's nacho platter.

Hanging onto a low branch, I watched Kane run, twist, and jump away from the bear, easily three times his size.

Despite Kane giving me grief about my slingdart, I'd pulled out a few steel arrows and jammed them into my back pocket. I clutched the slingshot's handle with my sweaty hand and secured the rubber loop onto the wrist brace.

Seeing the six-foot-seven French Canadian dance and prance in the dark forest would have been comical had it not been for the eating machine chomping the air at his heels. Twice, the damn thing got so close, I thought he was toast.

Kane began sprinting sideways on the hill after the bear tumbled ass over teakettle to the bottom.

"Nice move, boss."

That said, he'd also been running *away* from my location. I didn't need to be left alone in the Canadian hinterlands if he just kept on running. Kane hated cellphones, so I carried the one we had. Not like I could text him if he ran off.

Note to self: get Kane a cell. Who knows? Maybe there's a wolf Tinder or something?

When I'd lost sight of him again, I took a gamble and jumped down onto the ground. I'd gotten up the tree pretty fast, and grizzlies don't do trees. Too fatso. At least, that's what I'd hoped. I think I'd read somewhere that black bears are good with trees.

And by "read somewhere," I mean I saw it on Instagram. Whatever.

I chased after the prey-and-predator show ahead of me, considering options as I ran. If the grizzly bear even winked at me, I'd scoot up to the top of the nearest tree and hold on like some cartoon owl until dawn.

The echo of Kane's voice rolled over the hills: "Ooof!"

Oh shit!

Did the grizzly…? No, it was still coming up the hill.

Kane was nowhere to be seen. Had he fallen?

My hand on a tree, I arched up on my tiptoes to see better. I hissed and snatched it back when I felt the bite of jagged metal.

Stepping back, I sucked at the gash on my palm. Dammit, I'd have to get a tetanus shot.

When I looked at what had cut me, I saw a rusted sign nailed to the tree. Squinting in the twilight, I read it aloud.

"McClarsky's Maple Syrup."

Chapter Six

Kane

I have been befouled by skinny plastic snakes!

No, not snakes.

For I have dealt with their kind in the past, not many, but enough to leave a lasting impression. They are moody creatures prone to long, disquieting stares and, it would seem, too much reflection. Whether this is self-indulgence or self-doubt on their part, I do not know.

In the animal world, there are no mouth words. A twitch of fur, a furrow of skin, a flicker of the limb, this is our language. And each species has its own, their communiqués directed at their own kind. However, some facial expressions are universal.

The grizzly standing over me on its hind legs, mouth distended in an ear-splitting roar, talons extended from its paws slicing through the air. I am very clear on what he is saying.

"I'm eatin' you!"

It is in this interpretation of the situation where we differ. I will not be consumed only to spend the remainder of my days on Earth laid out across the forest in damp clumps of bear turds. Not a fitting end for an alpha wolf.

Not even one who is second best.

I spin away before the beast can drop its weight upon me and lift myself to a knee. From the crouching position, like I have seen runners on television, I burst into a sprint.

The roar behind me electrifies the hair on my body, making it ramrod straight.

My eyes should have adjusted to the dark but still so difficult to see, I am not sure—

The rainbow sunglasses.

As I run, I reach up and strip them off, stuffing them into the front pocket of my new parka jacket. It takes a little effort, but they cost me twenty dollars. I am a frugal wolf.

The fussing with the pocket's zipper distracts me as I run, and I once again run into a horizontal blue plastic tube, snapping it in two. A sticky, gooey substance splatters across my clothes. Normally, I would not concern myself with such things. Mud, grass, and leaves, these are the clothes of the forest.

However, being pursued by the bear, which sees me as its dinner, I realize I have just slathered myself in sauce.

As Emelda would say: "Not ideal."

Thankfully, the grizzly is also struggling with the snaking tubes and pauses to lick at the liquid dripping from its jagged breaks. A shimmering on my left catches my attention—unnatural in the deep thicket of forest. I slow my pace, ducking under the blue tubing as I run, and look over.

A large tank. Something human made out here in the middle of the forest. There is writing on the side of it, but human writing vexes me. I have learned their mouth language, both English and French. However, their written sounds I struggle with.

This is why I have Emelda's help. To drive their confusing vehicles and read their even more confusing writing.

The tank is cylindrical, laid upon its side. Mère and Père had something similar on their property which they'd used to make the cooking fires on their stove.

"*C'est du propane,*" my human father once told me of that tank. "*S'il y a une fuite, vous pouvez sentir le gaz.*"

Père had taken opportunities to teach me about the human world, since he knew it was alien to me. In the conversation about the propane tank, he'd said an odor was added to the tank so that leaks could be detected by scent. However, even as a human, I could smell both the propane and the added rotten-egg smell.

Stopping for just a second, I sniff the air and smell neither. Only the sickly-sweet aroma of tree sap.

The bear is huffing once again, running toward me, and with no other options, I run toward the tank. I have no plan for when I reach it. It is shimmering in the light, and strangely, this calls to me. When I am just ten feet away, the ground gives out below.

I tumble into a hole, and my knees land hard, scraping against the damp ground. Rocks and broken branches scratch at my black jean pants. Above me, I hear the bear stop its charge. When I look up, I can see that the silvery tank sits upon a concrete slab.

Unnatural in this habitat, water runoff has trickled around the slab and created a gully where it now flows down the hill. I have fallen into that crevice.

The grizzly is stalking slowly forward, and I hear its halting breath as it sniffs the air. My own scent must be masked by the maple, um, gravy that is slathered across my chest. This will not fool the bear long. From a crouching position, I see the gully carved out by the rainwater runoff tilts downward, and I begin to follow that trench.

My plan is to run along the gouge in the earth, hoping it will lead me to safety.

Foolish plan!

The earth shakes around me as the grizzly leaps down next to me, and I know that deadly swipe is coming, so I waste no time and leap toward the silvery tank and out of the hole. I feel its claws dig into my boot, stripping it away.

It pulls the footwear to its face, throws it to the ground, and buries its nose into it, chewing. Then it growls in frustration. I am also frustrated because it was an expensive boot, despite the discount for buying more than fifty dollars' worth of products at the store.

I reach up to grab the tank, hoping to pull myself up. But my gloved hand just slips across its shimmering surface. I strip it away and toss the garment at the bear, hoping it will distract the creature for a moment. The glove smacks it in the face, which elicits a grown then a growl.

Reaching up once again, my fingers grasp a thick metal tube. I pull myself up, but the massive tank shifts, and I notice it's only resting on the concrete, not bolted down.

I slide backward.

I feel the bear grasp my leg, pulling me downward back into the hole. Desperate, I strip off the other glove and reach for the concrete slab, glowing with promise of escape.

But when I grab the edge, I realize my mistake.

My bare hand is in the moonlight.

Chapter Seven

When I saw Kane get swallowed by the earth, I'd started running. If he got eaten by a bear or fell into a deep cave, I'd be dead. I had no idea which direction I needed to go to get out of the forest.

Note to self: get a compass.

Note to self, addendum: learn how to use a compass.

Stopping half behind another tree, I tucked my slingdart under my arm and just stared.

Squinting, trying to make shapes out of the dark, I was only about a hundred feet away from where Kane and the grizzly had fallen into some gouge in the forest floor. Next to them, I could see a tank with the same label as the one I'd seen on the tree.

"McClarsky's Maple Syrup," I muttered.

Seemed a bit on the nose for my first foray into Canada. Next, I'd be sitting at a Tim Hortons, eating poutine, watching the hockey, and complaining about a beer strike.

But at least I felt there would be a next.

Minutes earlier, in the crosshairs of one of the largest apex predators in the world, that had been up for grabs. And just seconds ago, it looked like Kane was about to be grizzly chow. Panicked, I'd lifted the metal arrow up and aimed, but it was impossible to tell what bobbing lump was bear and what was wolf-turned-man.

Hitting the bear wouldn't register much more than a bee sting. But I couldn't just stand by and watch my friend get chomped.

Then, I didn't have to fire.

A flash of pale fingers. Kane's bare hand had come up into the moonlight.

With the moon full, I'd seen him transform into a nightmarish hell-beast only a few days earlier. The wolfwere.

But before then, he'd been lesser threats.

Holding my breath, I waited to see what would emerge from the ground. Half hidden, the bear was growling and snarling, then it stopped. I could see just the top of the grizzly, and it looked like it had scooted back.

Then, in the light of the moon, I saw a long snout. As the head pushed up, damn, just more snout.

Before the entire head appeared—*zoom!*—the new creature leaped from the hole in the earth, sleek and slender.

And, good God, he was moving!

Chapter Eight

Kane

I am the wind.

No, I am faster than the wind. I have never been so fast.

And agile!

I cut left and, *huzzah*, look at me being so fast.

First time using "huzzah." This is a word I learned from Mère's television show with swords and dragons and very many naked people. They said huzzah a lot, whether naked or not.

This is the joy I feel at running so fast. Look at me go, I am the wi—

"Ouch!"

Trees hurt much more when running fast. A little dazed, yes, but I can go fast again. But maybe I will not go so fast.

But I could!

I turn back to see if grizzly is chasing now, but he is not. Probably because I can move so fast! I feel like running, sprinting, racing, and, strangely, chasing rabbits. That part is weird.

A tiny voice calls out from far away. "Kane?"

It is Emelda. She sounds worried.

I will return to her so that she is not too worried.

Also so that she sees how fast I have become.

Chapter Nine

I watched as the greyhound rocketed through the forest like a quicksilver dart fired from a rifle.

The bear's growl morphed into a roar as it tried to pursue. But the mud and bramble just fell away each time the grizzly reached up to pull itself out of the hole.

For a moment, it disappeared. Jesus, was it going to burrow under the ground? Could grizzlies do that?

When it lifted its head again, I was almost relieved. I had images in my mind of a thousand-pound burrowing bear, teeth like a beaver that propelled it along underground until it burst up, chewed the tree I was hiding in from root to tip in big beaver-bear swallows, and took me along with it like the gooey bit at the center.

Sure, a totally implausible, impossible scenario, but I've just spent nearly a month with a French-Canadian dude who turns into dogs.

Lately, I'd become more open-minded.

The bear wobbled its head in the direction Kane had run then looked back to the large silvery tank. My new farm friend, Denny, whose units of measure were defined by various kitchen appliances, might have said the bear's head was as big as an oven.

I watched as one of its arms came up, reaching for the shimmering tank. The grizzly wrapped its claws around some vertical piping and, for a moment, was able to pull itself from the pit. Halfway out, though, the massive tank tipped and rolled.

The bear fell back into the hole, and the tank rolled once, the stainless-steel legs jamming into the dirt on the opposite side, trapping the grizzly beneath it.

I crunched across dead leaves and branches toward the overturned tank, waiting for it to burst away like a champagne cork but instead of fizzy bubbles exploding out, just claws and bear teeth coming at me.

But the big cylinder didn't move.

Even so, I grabbed one of my steel darts, pulled it back in my sling, and pointed at the gap between the tank and the darkness of the hole.

In the moonlight, I saw the reflection of two eyes. Staring at me.

The grizzly didn't growl or lunge or even blink.

Just stared.

"Kane?" I shouted, not taking my eyes off the creature. I called again but got no answer. "Jesus, how far did that damn—?"

The impact knocked me off my feet, my arrow went flying, and I heard it *plink* off the tank. The grizzly roared, out of fear or frustration, and I hit the damp dirt. A second later, a thin, angular gray face hovered above me.

"I am sorry, Emelda," Kane said, his tongue lolling and flapping. "But I am very fast and cannot judge braking distance yet."

I pushed his head away, lest I get covered in self-satisfied doggie slobber. "It's fine."

When I stood, I picked up my slingdart and glanced at the tank. It hadn't moved. Below it, again, I saw the bear just watching me.

Doggie Kane wound around me a few times, which was very not Kane-like.

"What are you doing?"

He circled me one more time, stopped, lowered his head, tilted it sideways, then looked up at me.

"I have a lot of energy." The dog shuffled its feet as if the forest floor were hot. "This form is very…"

"Greyhound."

"Yes," Kane said, lifting a paw in front of his face to look at it. "It is very gray but also so much energy. And speed! Did you see how fast—?"

"Saw that. You're very fast," I said and took a tentative step toward the hole. The grizzly growled, sounding less menacing than before. Out of an instinct born from an exposure to countless horror movies, I looked around just in case another bear was about to burst from the shadows.

Kane picked up on my expression.

"Grizzlies hunt alone," he said, spinning in a tight circle. "Antisocial. Maybe because no one likes them."

"Harsh."

He looked up at me again, the angular mouth on his thin face hanging open.

"No, not harsh. They eat *everyone*," Kane said, hooking his snout back toward the trapped creature. "You know how judgy vegans like to say they do not eat anything that has a face?"

"Huh?" I said, taking another step forward. Sure, it was a fierce creature, but trapped, it seemed pitiful. "Yeah, I've seen the bumper stickers."

"With grizzlies, it is the opposite. They *only* eat things with a face," he said, inching back away from me. "And they eat the face and ears and nose and tongue—"

"I got it."

"They would eat *many* vegans. All the vegans," he said, hopping—yes, hopping—from foot to foot. "I think that is irony."

"No."

I circled around to the left side of the gouge in the earth, and when I did, a massive paw poked through the gap. I nearly swallowed my own damn tongue when I saw the tank lift slightly. But it only raised a few inches then came back down again.

The paw retreated into the dark void below but not before I spotted a massive gash across the top of it. The skin split and soaked the mottled hair around it red with blood.

Making a wide arc around the other side, past where the concrete slab lay, I saw one end of the tank, at least partially filled with maple sap, resting on the ground. The space for the bear couldn't have been much bigger than the animal itself. Then I realized something.

"I think the tank is on top of the bear."

"Good!" Kane said, spinning in a circle. "Then we go. Leave the bear."

I cocked my head toward him. "Won't it die down there?"

"Possibly. But what of it?"

I crouched down to get a better look. When I met the bear's eyes, it just stared back. I knew the thing would love to chew me up and use my bones to clean its teeth given the first chance. But it seemed cruel to let it just die in a pit.

"What if we, you know, freed it and ran like hell?"

"What? No, this would be a terrible idea. Bears are very clever. The moment it jumped out, it would eat both of us. Maybe not me because I am so fast, though."

I spun toward Kane. "Hold on. I specifically remember you saying bears were dumb."

Until that moment, I'd never before seen a sheepish look on a dog. It was totally bizarre.

"They are not," the greyhound said. "I was being..."

"Racist?"

Kane took a few steps back and raised a paw to his mouth. I laughed and told him I was kidding.

"I get it," I said. "Ones like that probably ate a few of your friends."

He stepped up next to me. "My old alpha, yes."

"Well, you got a wife out of the deal. Didn't turn out all bad."

The greyhound lowered its head and then closed its eyes. He turned slowly, opening them again, and stared deep into the forest.

"Do you think that is what my wolf-wife has done now that I am gone?"

"I—I don't know anything about your world, Kane," I said then went to a knee and petted his head. "But you didn't die. She'd know that, right? A girl can hold a torch a pretty long time."

He nodded, then his bulbous eye shot upward at my fingers.

"Why are you stroking my head?"

I snapped my hand back. "Sorry. Habit."

"Make this an un-habit. I am not a dog."

"Clearly."

For the next minute, I went over some ideas about how to free the bear and run for the hills. Or the woods, whatever. At each suggestion, Kane reminded me how dumb this was. But I am an animal lover. It's because of that trait that Kane was even alive. I'd found him being beaten by some stupid kids that first night when he'd been just a tiny thing.

I didn't bring that up, though. Kane's a proud guy. Or wolf-guy. Dog-guy. Whatever.

Two minutes later, I'd tied some rope that had been holding up the maple sap lines to the end of the tank pointing down the trench. It had been carved out by rains and rushing water, pointing downward. I reasoned that if I could yank it just a little, it might start to move on its own. Enough so the grizzly could slip out.

"Right, yes, this is good plan. For *bear*!" Kane pranced around, shaking his head. "And then the chasing begins all over again!"

I'd grown tired of his complaining, despite knowing, sure, he was probably right.

"Listen, here's a human lesson." I tugged on the rope to check the tension. "Life is precious, and unless something is killing you, it's a good policy not to kill it."

"This from girl who eats Quarter Pounders all the time."

"Not all the time."

"A lot of the time."

I held the rope in one hand, my other on my hip. "Some of the time. And that's different."

"How?"

"Because those cows are, you know, vicious."

Kane tilted his head, eyes wide. "*Quoi?*"

"In captivity, cows get very aggressive. Dangerous. When those beef, um, people try to work with them, they can attack, so…" I said, digging myself in deep, "the ones that do get violent, they have to kill. Once a cow gets a taste for human flesh…"

The wolf-turned-man-turned-dog spun in a circle, looked up at me, then down at the earth. I got a small kick out of how I'd kind of rocked his world.

"This sounds ridiculous," he said.

I tugged on the rope, testing it out. "It's important you know more about the human world, so I'm trying to teach you."

"Why? Why is this important? I will be wolf once again and leave this world behind."

"It… Well, you know, that might take a while. Would it really be so bad?"

The greyhound nodded its head vigorously. "Yes."

"Fine," I said, wrapping the rope around my palm. "Until then, I'm learnin' you stuff, son."

Kane spun slowly. "This is new information to me. I had been in much danger and did not know. I must rethink cows."

"Well, while you do, get ready to run when I pull this," I said, waving Kane forward. "A greyhound can outrun a grizzly. Fastest dog in the world. They race them, you know?"

"I would like to race!"

Tugging the free end of the rope, I walked a few feet and wrapped it once around a tree. Then I braced my boot against the trunk.

"Here's your chance," I said. "On your mark. Get set..." I grunted and pulled as hard as I could. The rope went taut then snapped loose, and I stumbled backward. I was sure I'd snapped the rope.

Instead, I had shifted the tank down the slope. Just enough to free the bear.

The grizzly roared.

"Go!" I shouted and chased after the greyhound, which was pulling away from me like I'd been standing still. "Don't go so fast!"

Kane looked back over his shoulder at me. "Are you joking?"

Chapter Ten

The grizzly had bolted in the opposite direction, likely in search of less troublesome dinner.

After the sheer terror of being on the bear buffet menu, the next few hours were boring and cold. Much of it I'd spent walking by myself.

Kane the greyhound had tons of energy and would disappear through the forest then run back. It was comical to see the brooding guy I knew bounce when he approached me.

"You having fun?" I said as he bounded through the underbrush for what had to be the tenth time.

"I am doing reconnaissance," he said, sidling up next to me and trying to match my pace. "Up ahead is only more forest for miles and miles. To the east"—he motioned with his snout to my right—"there, more forest. Also to the west."

For a moment, shivering, I stood there, waiting for more greyhound intel. It didn't come.

"And?"

"And nothing," he said, shrugging his slick dog shoulders. "Just woods over much uneven ground. Holes from rodents. Running could result in broken ankles."

"So no running."

"For you, I would not recommend, no."

"Kane, I assumed you had a plan to get wherever we're going?" I spun in a circle and raised my gloved hands. "This isn't a plan!"

"It is plan," he said, glancing around. Although, I got the feeling he was avoiding my eyes. "Early stages of plan. More plan is coming."

"How about now?" I wrapped my arms around myself. "Can more plan come now?"

Without another word, Kane shot off once again, hopping through the dark forest and disappearing between trees.

For a city girl, it's crazy disorienting to be surrounded by forest in all directions. In Minneapolis, you can just look up at a street sign and get an idea of where you are.

Out in the suburbs, they've got big water towers with the names of their towns and cities. Don't know who came up with *that* idea, but they look like giant-sized pushpins jammed into the earth.

Here, no water towers.

No cross streets.

In the forest, I was standing at the corner of Maple and Oak. Which was the exact same address I'd been at a hundred yards back. Left on my own, I'd be lost and never get out again.

Finally, Kane came back, walking at a brisk pace but no longer bopping and bounding like some cat-dog.

"Well?"

"I have found what I need," he said then lowered his head and sniffed the ground. "But we will wait until morning."

"Morning?"

"This is why we have tent in your pricey backpack," he said. "We camp for the night and in morning catch ride."

I blinked, my jaw hanging down slightly. "What are you talking about?"

He nodded to a cluster of bushes. "There is a small clearing just beyond the hedges. Good spot for us to put up the tent."

I took a step back and looked him up and down. Then pointed at his sleek gray body.

"*Us* put up tent?"

The dog grinned at me. Creepy. He held up a paw. "Well, you will have to. Alas, I have no thumbs."

"Helpful."

"I will stand guard."

Trudging toward the clearing he mentioned, I said, "That's just a cool-guy way of saying you'll watch me do the work."

"Ah, you are right." He chuffed, staring up at the stars. "I am finally learning the human ways."

Chapter Eleven

The tent had been simple enough to set up. I'd remembered putting tents up being so much more complicated when I'd been a kid.

Digging into my backpack, I pulled out the device I'd dubbed my slingdart. Basically, it was a wrist rocket-style slingshot with a cup on one end that you could notch an arrow into. It was my favorite possession in the world. However, it didn't have a lot of competition in that regard, because I didn't have shit.

In fact, most of what I had was Kane's stuff.

Technically, he was still my boss. At least in the sense that he was paying me, so hauling around his crap didn't bother me. I'd had worse jobs.

I had gone back for his clothes after the grizzly run-in because he'd been carrying his passport wallet in his down jacket. Without that, we'd not have his bank card. Can't do shit in the world without money.

At least in the human world you can't. That must have been such a queer disappointment to Kane when he'd become a dude.

All his life as a wolf—about five or six years was his best guess—he'd never had to worry about buying food or shelter or any of that stuff. He hunted for what he needed to eat and bedded down in the forest.

Now, like the rest of the humans, his life was controlled by little bits of green paper we traded around. On the very long drive to the Canadian border, he'd asked me about it, holding a twenty up to the interior light.

"How does this tiny piece of cloth have so much value?" he'd asked.

"Because it's got a twenty on it." I laughed.

This hadn't satisfied him.

"But twenty cloth is exactly the same as the one cloth. No difference in weight or smell. There are slight differences in material, but these are not more valuable materials." He pulled a one-dollar bill out of his wallet and held both up, leaning on the dashboard of the jeep. "How can this one be twenty of these?"

"Because..." I started then faltered. "It... Well, because it's got a number twenty on it."

"Then you could draw a number twenty on this one and it is worth same?"

"Ha, no. It doesn't exactly work like that," I said but then remembered a scheme my ex, Roy, had gotten into. "Although, there was a time when you could bleach the color out of the ones and print twenties onto them."

"Then they were worth more?"

"Yeah."

Kane shook his head. "Is too confusing. Because it is printed with this number it is more valuable." He clutched both bills, crinkling them. "Because someone says this one is worth more than this one, it is more valuable. No other difference."

"Right."

"What if people stop believing the numbers written on the paper?"

I sighed. "Then the whole system collapses, and we're basically feral animals all over again."

"You should be so lucky."

After I'd gotten the tent set up, Kane insisted I put our meager food supply in a plastic bag and walk about fifty yards into the bush to hang it from a tree. On the way back, I'd chewed through a protein bar and nearly stuffed the wrapper into my pocket. But Kane had warned me of that too. Animals could smell it.

So I'd had to turn around and stuff the shiny wrapper in the bag.

When I got back to the tent, Kane was gone.

That hadn't floored me—he had a habit of disappearing, although he'd have never called it that. He always knew where I was, so in that sense, he was still there.

After I hung Kane's clothes in the tree for him, I slipped into a sleeping bag and put my head on my backpack. Checking my phone for the time, I saw it would be about six hours until dawn. The simple cell phone that Denny had given me had internet capability, but out here, it didn't even have phone capability. No bars.

Damn phone didn't even have old-school *Snake* on it.

When we got closer to town, I'd have to download something to keep busy for when Kane went on his disappearing runs.

I didn't fault him for it. It would be nice for him to be back in the woods.

Chapter Twelve

Kane

As dawn breaks, I breathe in the cool air, happy to once again walk through the forest.

Nature's soundtrack wraps me in its warm, comforting embrace. The birds and insects—predator and prey—enact a brief armistice to create a beautiful morning symphony. War will return, but for now, only music.

Sadly, other animals look at me queerly. Maybe it's the pants.

Only when I became a human did I start wearing trousers and jean pants and, more recently, Denny sweats. They are not called that as far as I know, but I name them such to honor my casual-wear benefactor, Denny Newman of Pine Valley, Minnesota.

They are comfortable and, strangely, make me want to eat snack foods and watch college sports. I do not give into such basic urges.

Once the sun rose and I felt the greyhound form fade, I became a human once again. I quietly returned to the camp and retrieved my clothes from the tree. I would prefer to not wear them, but doing so makes humans uncomfortable.

Is it my nakedness or is it that they see perfection they could never attain?

Either way, I am now in jean pants and lumberjack shirt and motorcycle boots. The grizzly tore at my parka, so this I have discarded and am wearing jean jacket coat. I miss my rainbow sunglasses very much.

I had protested the purchase of the motorcycle boots because I do not ride a motorcycle. Emelda insisted they looked cool on me, so I relented. When I then suggested I attempt to drive a motorcycle while wearing them, she protested. And nearly returned the boots to the shelf.

This, I stopped her from doing. Because they did indeed make me look cool.

Even dressed in human clothes, the forest calls to me, for I am her child.

Out here, somewhere, is my pack. My wolf-wife who awaits my return. Unless she has "moved on." This is a possibility. Of course, if she had a social media profile, I could have checked her relationship status.

Alas, wolves do not have Facebook.

However, from what I have read there, a few may have X-Twitter. Of this I cannot be certain.

When dawn returned and I became a man once again, I longed for my animal form. The greyhound, as Emelda called it, was new to me. Fast, agile. Also a bit hyper. But preferable to this dense, meaty form.

I spot a deer drinking from a brook, and it lifts its head in panic and worry. Stepping back and then crouching, I convey to it that I am not its predator. Merely another inhabitant of the British Columbian countryside.

This is more difficult to convey as a human. When wolf or even dog, I can express my intent with furrow and frown, twitch and nod. My large body troubles this creature, so I slowly lower to the ground and wrap my arms around my legs, making my form smaller.

The deer blinks and tilts its head. It then begins drinking once more. For a moment, I do not move so that it knows my intentions are true. I am rewarded by a subtle gesture. Ears flicker, eyes dart. One of her rear hooves stomps lightly.

My heart glows warmly at this creature's grace. With this final gesture, she has gifted me a warning of a danger in these woods.

Yes, I know of the bear, I attempt to convey but do not know if I can as a human. Then I hook my arms, hoping to convey gratitude for the guidance she did not have to give. This deer is braver than most, and I honor her by leaving her to her drink in peace.

I am searching for a white tree that flakes. My human father told me this is called birch. Père had known my time with him and Mère was short, and he taught me what he could of the world of people. My greatest ability may come from combining the cunning of wolf with this human intelligence.

I also expect I could be a very good dancer. But that skill has never been tested. One day, I will drop it like it's hot, and the world will rejoice.

In the distance, I hear a faint echo. The call of wolf, many miles from here. It is not the song of my pack nor any that I know. This is not a warning but the sound of longing. It is a sound I know very well.

It is the sound my heart makes, endlessly.

I spot the birch tree and carefully begin pulling away strips of thick bark.

Once we reach the highway I spotted a few hours earlier, we will head north to find an old friend of my human parents. The kind doctor Fineman.

But we must get to the highway before midday, and it is across difficult forest terrain.

As the greyhound, I covered this distance quickly and easily. Now, it will be less simple as a human and less so for Emelda. She is capable but small. Or more accurately, if the grizzly *has* returned, bite-sized.

To get to the highway safely and quickly, I will need to make a call.

Chapter Thirteen

When I woke up the next morning, the first thing I noticed was that Kane was gone. Again.

Well, not the first thing. I first noticed that I had to pee like crazy. That urge more often than not had served as some sort of whizz alarm clock for as long as I could remember. An alarm that doesn't really have a snooze button.

Oh, you can think, nah, I'll just sleep a few more minutes. But as you do, you can almost see your bladder pointing at the door, going, "Really?" In my mind, the animated bladder—a slick purple thing shaped like a kidney because I didn't know how a bladder was shaped—looked at a wrist watch and tapped its foot.

After a minute, Bladdy started making whooshing noises like you would hear from a faucet.

"All right, all right," I said aloud and leaned up, my body aching all over. I'd had a sleeping bag, but it had to be thin to fit into my backpack, so essentially, I'd been sleeping on the ground. I could feel dents and divots in my back from the poking rocks and branches that had elbowed me as I slept.

Grabbing the zipper, I dragged it up in the half circle to open the flap.

Despite my insistent bladder, now gurgling and sputtering like it was drowning, I smiled at the sound. When you're camping, the first *zzzzt* of a tent zipper announces the day has begun. It's incongruous against the birdsong and faint echoes of random animal cackles.

Maybe that's why I kind of liked it. That sound.

As if, yeah, I'm here in a place I'm not supposed to be, but *zzzzt*, there's still a bit of the human world around me. Like a canvas cocoon.

Or whatever they make tents out of these days. Probably something that'll survive ten thousand years in a landfill.

But so comfy!

I grabbed my boots and pulled out my socks. The first year I'd gone camping with my uncle's family, I'd left them outside the tent. That just seemed like the thing you were supposed to do. I woke up to damp socks and, hidden underneath those, a spider the size of a half dollar.

Naturally, I'd thrown those socks into the fire.

I'd regretted that, but you know. Spiders. They must burn.

Slipping on my socks and then my ankle-high leather boots—I'd slept in my jeans and shirt—I crawled out of the tent, reborn unto the new day.

"Kane?" I shouted but got no answer. That hadn't been a surprise and was kind of a good thing. If I were going to heed the call of nature, I didn't want nature boy anywhere near me.

Guys have it easy.

They can just pull out their release valve and, well, release. Anywhere, anytime. In dark alleys behind bars. The side of a road on a long stretch of highway. I once drove with Ray from Minneapolis to South Dakota for some shady deal of his, and he'd used empty beer bottles.

It had grossed me out, but if I'm honest, there was a tinge of jealousy there.

For girls, it's more of a production. You can't just unzip and poke it out. If you can, you probably need to see a specialist about it. Or, hell, start a page on OnlyFans.

Nope.

It's pants down to midthigh at the very least. Any higher and you've got washing to do. You can double-door drop it on the side of a road too. That's where you open the car's front door and rear door, which creates a bit of a side-of-the-road bathroom stall for you.

If anyone's watching, they'll see a pair of shoes and a stream. And if they are watching, they're creeps. Whatever.

I found a tree to duck behind and unbuttoned my pants. When the button popped, I saw the head of a squirrel jut out of some leaves and give me the side-eye.

I scowled at it. "Get away, creeper." Once I took a stomping half step toward it, it ran off, but I'd also nearly peed myself doing it.

When I finally unzipped, I could almost hear my bladder doing a slow clap. What a dick.

Of course, moments later, I heard a rustling.

"Emelda?"

I closed my eyes, trying to concentrate. The bladder in my head was rolling its hand, eyes wide. *Come on, Come on.*

"Emelda?"

Growling, I shouted over. "Gimme a sec, Kane. I'm busy."

"Busy?" he said, and I heard more rustling. "This is forest. How can a human be busy in the woods? You are not chopping trees or—"

"I'm trying to pee, Kane!"

That silenced him. But only for a few seconds.

"Marking territory," he said and grunted his approval. "Very smart. Very animal."

I growled again. "If you keep talking, I'll show you animal."

Squinting as I coaxed the water from my body, I heard him trudge away. Finally, I got the beginning of a stream.

"Emelda, I have—"

"Kane! Stop talking."

"Okay, sorry," he said. "Once you are finished, we need to go. I have some birch bark to help us catch a ride."

None of that made sense.

Nope.

Not a bit.

Didn't care, didn't think of it. Just let the flow begin, and when it finally did, just utter bliss. I didn't even care about the sound. Hell, he was an animal, he wouldn't think twice. I just enjoyed—

"Do not use leaves for the wiping," Kane called, his voice a bit farther away. "Some are irritating."

I slapped my hands over my ears, trying to just enjoy my moment.

Through my laced fingers, I heard him say, "Drip dry is best."

Chapter Fourteen

When I'd finally finished, I crunched across the uneven carpet of leaves and branches while buttoning up my jeans. I nearly stumbled trying to do these two simple things at once.

My brain hadn't slipped out of its sleeping bag as early as I had. That's the thing about camping. If you don't bring coffee, there is no coffee.

That said, my mood lightened as I looked around and drew in the crisp morning air. The windows of my old basement apartment in Minneapolis had been right at the level where car and truck exhaust would billow against the glass like an angry spirit looking to get in.

Even with the windows shut, wispy tendrils of diesel fumes would snake through the cracks.

I got used to the ever-present smell of oil and carcinogen. If the Devil got into the Glade PlugIn business—and hell, he probably had—I think he'd have made one that smelled just like that.

Other hell-borne offerings might include scents like Fish Flatulence and The Tears of Ed Sheeran.

I definitely needed coffee soon. I was struggling to focus.

Kane had pulled out what little stuff I'd had in the backpack and laid it out on a dry patch of ground. When I rolled up, he was staring at the tent, rubbing his beard.

"Is a confusing cave design," he said. "How did something so large fit into your puny backpack?"

"Magic, obviously."

He frowned. "There is no such thing."

"Says the guy who turns into little dogs when the moon comes out." I grinned at him and got the obligatory scowl in return. That felt like a win. Almost better than coffee.

I noticed something that looked like a wooden scroll in the hand resting on his hip. I went to reach for it, and without looking, he lifted his arm. I went around him, and he raised it in the air, out of reach. His eyes never wavered from his examination of the tent.

I went on my tiptoes trying to get at it, but the dude was six-foot-seven. I'm somewhere in the vicinity of five-six. Well, as much as Columbus, Ohio, is in the vicinity of Chicago.

As he stared at my confusing canvas cave, I reached to his armpit and wiggled my finger.

Kane's arm rocketed down, and he swore in French. At least, I think he swore. When I hear him speak French in an angry tone, it all sounds like swearing.

Shielding his sensitive underflesh with his upper arm presented the scroll of wood right in front of me, and I snatched it.

Seeing it in my hands, he scowled. "That is a devious way to get what you want."

"Not my fault the big, strong man-wolf is ticklish."

"Stupid human body. What purpose does tickling have?" He reached for the roll of bark, and I yanked it away.

Ignoring his question—because my answers in that department were very NC-17—I examined the roll of bark. I ran my fingers over its outer surface, the white flakes I'd loosened drifting gently to the forest floor.

Turning it over in my hands slowly, I looked closer at it. I couldn't work out why he'd had it, but if nothing else, it frustrated the hell out of him that I had it now. So worth it.

"You didn't sleep last night, did you?" I asked.

"Not in tent cave, no."

I looked up at him. "Why not? Worried I might try something?"

"Try what?" Kane knitted his thick, dark eyebrows together. "You would choose now to turn on me? You are too weak and tiny."

"Ha," I said, kind of relieved he didn't get my meaning. I held up his treasure. "I did get this from you. And don't forget I've got my slingdart."

"It is a puny child's weapon."

I shrugged. "Saved your life with it."

"True. But your aim is terrible."

"I'll practice," I said and sighed. I held the roll of bark out, and he snatched it back. "Okay, what the hell is that for?"

Kane couldn't help but hide his grin. Even wolves who turn into men sometimes act like little boys. He had his toy again!

When he saw me looking at his smiling face, he held the bark up to hide it.

"Return the canvas cave to your backpack," he said then began rubbing his hands over the bark roll. "We need to go."

"Go where?"

Kane nodded north. Well, I assume it was north because I knew that was the direction we were headed.

"The house of my human parents was close to a town near of Kitimat."

I peeked into the tent, brushed out some dirt and leaves, then stepped out and zipped up the entrance. I reached down and pulled a fiberglass rod out from the base, and the tent tilted at an angle. I unhooked the other rod and slid both out from their sleeves.

As he busied himself with his bark, I snapped each rod into its segmented four pieces, connected by thin elastic rope. I folded each branch onto the next and then did the same with the other rod.

I knelt to brush the tent skin flat as Kane tramped a few feet away and dug at a tree with a knife we got at the sporting goods store. Once I got the tent flat, I folded it into thirds then rolled it all up into a tube, as tight as possible.

He returned as I stuffed the roll and the two folded rods into my pack.

Kane blinked. "Where did cave go?"

"Magic." I laughed then saw he was rubbing sap onto one of the sides of his birch bark roll. "I like your squirrel hat."

"Is not hat."

"Fine. So how far away is this Kitimat?"

Kane looked out into the forest. "About fifteen-hundred kilometers from here."

"What? I know you're used to tramping around the forest, but that sounds way too far to walk. At least for me."

The big French Canadian grinned and held out his birch bark. He'd rolled it into a tube, one end flaring out, so it looked a bit like a long funnel.

"I ain't gonna fit in that," I said.

He frowned, and I felt a little bad because I'd taken the wind out of his wolf sails. Just a little.

"Not for riding." He pointed at the bulge in my jacket pocket. "Is like your phone."

"You're going to make a call?"

The grin was back. "Sort of. You have a circle on your phone screen that does same as this."

I blinked and shook my head from side to side. None of those words made any sense to me, so I rolled my hand, indicating I needed a little more.

He took a few steps forward, sniffing the air. "Are you ready to go?"

"Uh, yeah!"

"Good," he said and held the tube up to his mouth. His grin grew as he shifted his eyes toward me. "I am calling Uber."

Chapter Fifteen

Kane said weird shit all the time.

In part, I put that down to him only being human for about a year and to the idea that, somewhere along the way, whatever he'd intend to say got lost in some wolf-to-person translation.

I also think he took advantage of this "your world, it confuses me so" persona he had, which allowed him to say crazy stuff and get away with it.

I'd also realized he would hold back stuff he knew.

Like when we'd first been looking for the "biting man." I'd been a bit thrilled to discover his real name was Cal Davis. But Kane had *known* that—Cal was a child of Kane's human parents. My big friend had kept that to himself.

Kane boasted that animals don't lie. That did not mean, however, they always told the truth.

It's a small distinction. But one with enormous ramifications.

What other *truths* had he chosen not to share?

He'd insisted I pack up all my gear because, depending on how long it took to do whatever he was about to, we might have to go quickly.

I stood there in the middle of the lush British Colombian forest, breathing in the clean air, enjoying the feel of the soft earthen carpet beneath my boots, and just waited. In the ten minutes it took for him to ready himself, I'd switched my backpack from shoulder to shoulder twice because it was putting my arm to sleep.

Of course, I could have just looped both arms through, but I had gone through the American high school system. Only people looking for ridicule and the occasional bruising wore backpacks with both straps in place.

Kane rolled the birch bark in his large hands, trying to get it into what he felt was the perfect shape. When he'd finished it, it didn't look much more or less conical than when he started. But he was the expert, I suppose. Or just showing off.

"Ready?" he said, twisting his head toward me, the corner of his lip curling upward. For as big a man as he was, the expression made him look like a little kid. Even with the bearded face.

Holding the cone up to his lips, he produced a call that sounded like a wheezy, past-his-prime tuba player with a respiratory infection.

Bah-eu-ahh!

Kane pulled the cone from his lips slightly, blinked, and sniffed the air. Then tried again.

Bah-eu-ahh!

He went silent, not moving a muscle, just listening. I did my best to keep quiet until I couldn't any longer.

"You'll never make first chair if you don't practice," I said, stone-faced.

Ignoring me, he twisted the cone of bark in his hands, examining it. Even for a part-time wolf, Kane was such a dude. Of course, it wasn't anything he was doing wrong. Must be the tool. Whatever.

Then he groaned and began muttering to himself in French.

I asked, "What? Too much sap?"

"Wrong call," he said, looking sheepish. "That is male. Wrong emphasis."

"What-the-who?" I said and shook my head. Again, I couldn't tell if he was just impossible to understand or screwing with me.

He put the cone to his lips once more.

Baaaah-eu-ahh!

Baaaaaah-eu-ahh!

Kane pulled his bark tube away from his mouth and listened. One minute went by. Then two. My shoulder was aching again, and I made the tiniest motion to switch arms but stopped when his hand flew toward me, palm up.

Don't. Don't move.

Whoa.

That had caught me off guard. Not that uber-woodsman Kane wanted absolute silence from me.

But I swear I had heard his voice in my head. I hadn't, of course, but it *felt* like that.

When I'd met Kane, one of the things that he'd said frustrated him was using spoken language. He found it cumbersome. He'd told me that wolves, maybe all animals, conveyed intention more through gesture and expression.

In the few weeks I'd been with him, increasingly, I'd begun picking up on some of those non-verbal cues with him. Sure, that could be wishful thinking, that I might tap into some animal way of communicating.

But there have been occasions...

Like when he'd extended his hand moments earlier. I knew he'd wanted me to stop moving. But in my head, it was like I could hear him say *Don't. Don't move.*

Maybe I was picking up on those cues, or maybe my mind was scattered sans coffee at 7:00 a.m.

I watched as Kane slowly moved his arm up to his mouth, but this time, he didn't lift his bark cone. Instead, he put a finger to his lips and looked at me.

Yeah. I didn't need any animal senses to work that out. Shut yo trap, girl. Got it.

Ahead of us, a rustling of leaves drew my attention, and as images of grizzly danced in my head, I fought the urge to run. Kane remained stone still. I did the same.

Just on the other side of a busy ridge, I saw movement.

Then, a moment later?

Antlers.

Chapter Sixteen

"Kane," I said, taking a step back. Before I could take another, I felt his hand on my shoulder, holding me in place. I looked down at his big meat hook on me. At first, I got pissed, then I remembered this was his world. I stopped moving.

"Yes," he whispered. "Be still."

"I am."

He cracked a tiny grin, eyes never wavering from the beast about a hundred feet away. "I wasn't speaking to you."

"You're *talking* to it?"

I felt a squeeze at my shoulder and waited. After a minute, he spoke in a low, gravelly voice.

"Speaking but not with word sounds." His head dipped slightly then tilted a few inches. "Difficult as a human. He fears me."

"How could he be scared of you? He's three times your size." I looked back at the massive creature, which had tilted its antlered head slightly. "And how do you know it's a 'he' anyhow?"

Ever so slightly, he raised the birch cone. The animal shuffled its hooves slightly and looked as if it might bolt away. Kane stiffened, unmoving.

"First call, mistake. It was one to attract females. I have been away from the forest for too long." He sighed. "Second call, different intonations, that was to attract a male. Now one stands before us."

"Oh."

"Also, there are his *couilles*."

I frowned. "Right."

"Balls," Kane clarified.

"I got that."

He nodded. "They are quite impressive."

This time, I tilted my head at him. "You feeling insecure because of the *huevos* of a... what is that?"

"It is moose, of course."

Right.

This was Canada. They probably had moose running around like we have squirrels in the US. I mean, not like squirrels. I can't imagine they jump from tree branch to tree branch and get stuck in chimneys in the winter.

But who knows.

Canada is a weird place.

Kane was quiet for another minute, which was making me antsy. Especially because all I had running through my brain was packs of moose jumping from eves, searching for nuts.

My brain is a weird place.

I asked him, "You gotta whip your coolies out and have some dangle showdown to see which of you is the alpha?"

That earned me a grunt.

"Moose do not have alphas. They are lonely, majestic creatures who do not hunt other animals." Kane stifled a chuckle. "You might say they are the vegans of the forest."

"Good to know. I'll avoid any conversations with Moose Boy, then." I looked back to the moose. "If he doesn't eat animals, and hell, he's too big for anything to eat him... why's he so skittish?"

Kane's eyes slid toward me. "You. Your kind. They are hunted by humans. This makes them wary."

I stared at the beautiful animal. "Oh. That's kinda sad."

"Why? They are good source of protein," Kane said. "Père taught me how to hunt them, which is how I know about birch phone."

The large creature dipped its horns and put its snout to the ground. It waited for a moment, eyes glassy. Recently, I had to forcibly stop myself from anthropomorphizing every animal I saw, which was tough. Just interacting with Kane, by definition, was anthropomorphizing.

However, to me, it looked as though the moose had dipped its head as a test. To see if the two strange humans would lift a rifle or leap for an attack. I wanted to ask Kane, but now that it looked like it was calming, I didn't want to spook it.

A moment later, it began gnawing at the forest floor.

Kane nodded and let out a slow *"sssh,"* which I knew had been directed at me. So I shushed.

The big man crouched, arms crossed over his knees. Then gracefully, he slid back, rolled onto his rump, and extended his hands. Laying the birch cone on the ground, he straightened his arms.

The moose looked at him curiously, watching as it chewed.

Once it lowered its head, my friend then lifted his backside off the earth so that he was on all fours facing upward. I stared down at him, trying to work out what the hell he was doing.

"Kane," I whispered, "What are—?"

I stopped speaking when he tweaked his head at me.

The moose had returned to grazing, but its eyes were locked on Kane. Slowly, the big French Canadian crawled forward. It was bananas to see. Like a four-legged spider flipped over with its tummy to the air, tramping forward through the leaves and sticks.

Using his hands and feet, he moved toward the moose. After he'd closed half the distance, I'd lost sight of his face. But the entire time I'd seen it, he'd never once blinked. It made my eyes water just watching him do that.

When he was just a few feet away, one of the moose's rear legs shifted backward. Kane slowed, moved a few inches to the side—opposite of the leg that had moved—and continued forward.

"Holy shit," I mumbled to myself as Kane came up next to the moose, splayed out and vulnerable. If Moose Boy charged forward, he'd have no way to protect himself. For two minutes—maybe five, it was hard to tell because I wasn't moving to check my phone—he waited there. I could see the slightest tremor in his arms, which had to be screaming with the effort.

The moose crunched away at the twigs and leaves, and I saw it blink. I hadn't noticed it do that before.

A moment later, Kane pressed his body slowly forward. Onto his knees, then he straightened his thighs. He lifted his hand in front of the moose's face.

Another blink?

Or had I imagined the second one?

Kane leaned forward and stroked the creature's shoulder, slowly, slowly, slowly. When his hand traced along the animal's back, caressing it in long, gentle sweeps, I realized my friend had stood. I hadn't even noticed the moment he'd done that.

After a minute, Kane drew a hand between the creature's antlers, held it there for a moment, and traced his fingers down its haunches.

I watched as he bent down, and for a moment, I thought he was going to try to pass under the creature. But then his leg came up, and when he straightened his arms, I gasped.

Kane was sitting on top of the moose.

Continuing to stroke its neck with one hand, he waved me over with the other. The entire time, the moose nibbled on the forest at its feet.

The big man didn't have to tell me to go slow. I was shitting myself, so moving toward it at all was an absolute force of will. When the creature looked to me, I did as Kane had. I met its eyes as I took small steps toward it.

But it didn't stare me down as it had Kane.

Maybe I didn't seem like a threat? Had I just been insulted by a goddamn moose?

Keeping my feet close to the earth but not rustling leaves too much to startle the animal, it took me about a minute to walk up to the side of it. I held my hand out above its skin and looked to my friend, got a smile and a nod, and stroked the animal.

The hair was rough, coarse, and I could sense the powerful muscles hidden beneath. Feel the breath as it huffed once, then one more time. I pulled my hands back, and Kane smiled again, shaking his head.

I returned my hand, stroking it gently. Feeling the heat of its body, the strength and power of it. Life coursing through this beautiful, amazing creature.

Despite not having to stare it down, I found my eyes watering nevertheless.

Gently clearing my throat, I looked up at Kane.

"What was with the upside-down crab walk thing?"

He shrugged, still stroking and caressing. "Impossible to explain, different every time. I felt this way, the moose doesn't see as threat. I respond to his move words."

"Move wor—" I said then thought about the shifting of the hooves. "Okay."

"But so much more. As I have said, furrow and frown. It is a purer way to communicate. Your expressions, movements… all these betray your true thoughts. If I had intended to harm him and made the same moves, exactly the same, he would have seen that."

I nodded. I'd heard of that. "Microexpression."

"No." Kane shook his head. "It is a moose. Very large."

Frowning, I looked at him. Sometimes, I just didn't know when the guy was screwing with me.

"So you put on a happy face, and he just let you get on?"

"This position I chose, crab-style, as you say—"

"Naw, didn't say it that way," I said, being a pain in the ass because I felt like it, "but go on."

"It also... presents me to the moose."

"*Presents?*"

Kane rubbed his dark beard with his hand, wiping his mouth as he thought. Nodding, he said, "One's scent is strongest at the top of the thigh. Um, in between."

I raised my hand. "Got it. Yep."

"Those scents also communicate intent. To animals, they see them as you might see colors. Those colors each have meaning. The shades and ribbons of scent are a language, but again, much like human world, some phrases are universal, some specific to species."

Nodding, I was beginning to understand. "Like if a hot Spanish boy was speaking to me, smiling, even though I didn't understand the words, I'd pick up on what he was saying."

Kane shrugged. "I don't wholly understand your analogy."

"But if a German guy was speaking, who knows, right? It all sounds like angry *eins-zwei-itchenstein* to me."

"Is that racist?"

I smiled, ignoring the question. "So in the end, it did kind of come down to your coolies. You probably need to bathe soon."

"Maybe when we get to town," Kane said then nodded behind him. "Climb on."

"What? What do you mean climb on? I thought you were just, you know, showing off," I said, gritting my teeth together. "You want to ride this moose into town?"

"Not into town. Just to road. About ten miles"—Kane looked around then pointed—"that way."

"Is that what all this was? The birch cone and all that? You were *actually* calling a ride?"

Kane smiled and stroked the neck of the moose. "Canadian Uber."

Chapter Seventeen

I held onto Kane as the massive creature beneath us trotted through the forest like it was going out for a Sunday stroll. I weighed a bit over a hundred pounds, but my big friend was tall and muscular. Huge. The moose ran along as if he didn't even know we were there.

He'd temporarily joined our merry "pack of two," so it didn't feel right just calling him "the moose" the entire time. I had named him, which, bonus, kind of annoyed Kane.

"He does not look like a Bruce to me," he said.

Grinning into his back as I held on, I couldn't help but laugh. "Come on! Bruce the Moose makes total sense. There's something about alliteration that makes it totally valid."

That got a grumble out of him. "I thought alliteration was the repeat of first word sound."

"It... I dunno. And *not* the point." I reached down to stroke the creature's flank. "Is it, Bruce?"

For his part, Bruce just continued trotting.

I was surprised how easy the ride felt. Not that I thought a lot about moose—mooses?—but for some reason, I pictured that when it ran, it would be a chaotic, loping, rocking back-and-forth. I was wrong. Bruce gracefully glided through the bush, stepping expertly to avoid holes or fallen trees.

I accepted that I knew nothing about moose—meese? Like geese?—other than they hung out with flying squirrels and had an affinity for bad magic tricks. Not primo intel, mind you.

Twenty minutes later, Bruce slowed to a walk and then stopped at the edge of the forest. He just stood there, waiting.

Looking around Kane's big shoulder, I asked him, "Everything all right?"

"We are at our destination."

I stared at the strip of grass and low brush, which raised up to a blacktop highway. On the other side, a similar strip of grass then more forest. Glancing to the left, just a long ribbon of black-gray road. To the right, the exact same.

"This isn't a destination. This is isolation."

"Must be valid," Kane said, looking back over his shoulder. "Since it rhymes, yes?"

I straightened out and leaned back a little to stretch my back. It had been a surprisingly easy ride, but my spine had gotten jostled around some, and I just needed to stretch. Kane reached back and put a steadying hand on my calf. I hadn't been sure if he was making certain I didn't fall off or didn't want me to move lest I upset Bruce the Moose.

So I stopped moving. And was a bit curious as to why his strong grip on my leg sent a bit of a buzz up my body. Must have been more of that nonverbal communication stuff.

He was focused on stroking the creature's flank with his other hand. Then he leaned forward, slipped his leg around, and ended up back on terra firma. Despite how far from the ground the drop had been—the moose's shoulder came up to my forehead—Kane hadn't made a sound.

I looked at him as he came around and faced Bruce. Not uttering a word, just small, smooth gestures. Not like hand signals, of course—just little hitches to the head, a tilt of an arm, the shift of a foot. I had no idea if this was one creature speaking to another or if he was getting the kinks out of his back and legs like I needed to do.

Apparently satisfied, Kane looked at me.

Smiling, I extended my arms out like a little kid being asked to be picked up. He laughed at me and walked toward the road. Walked *away* as I sat on one-and-a-half tons of moose meat.

"Nice," I muttered, and Bruce shifted slightly. Okay, no more talking.

Slowly, I lifted my knee up and slid my foot over the animal's back, trying not to scrape against its coarse hairs. Mimicking Kane's movements as best I could, I rolled onto my side and slid down to the ground. Me, I landed with a thump but, thankfully, got no reaction from Moose Boy.

I looked up to see if Kane had seen my dismount, the marvel of it, but he was just glancing up and down the road.

Stretching, I stifled a groan and adjusted the backpack. During the ride, it had rested on Bruce's hindquarters. Now, I was back to lugging it around, and my shoulders were not happy about the change in circumstance.

I made a wide arc around the animal then turned to face it. The moose regarded me with big, beautiful onyx-black eyes. It blinked a few times then slowly dragged its head to the left then once again back to center. Was it trying to communicate? Probably not. My guess was that it was just happy I'd gotten off its damn back.

Unsure what to do in response, if I needed to give it a response, I simply said, "Thanks, Bruce. You're a good moose."

It chuffed, took a step backward, then another. Then the animal turned into the woods and trotted away. Going home?

That spurred a question in my mind, so I tightened one of the straps on my pack and walked up to Kane.

"That was fun in a weird, impossible way," I said and got a grunt in return. The big guy looked up to the sky, a few wispy clouds making a run at the sun. "Bruce wouldn't cross the road, then?"

"He may have if I'd asked. But we are where we want to be."

"You wanted to end up in the middle of nowhere?"

"This is British Columbia," Kane said, squinting down the road. "To foreigners, everywhere will feel like middle of nowhere."

He drew in a deep breath and exhaled. Then he returned to the shoulder, and right on the side of the road, he sat down in the gravel. I looked down at him.

"Did you ask Bruce to bring us here?"

The big man struggled with how to respond. "Not so much ask. But this is where we needed to be."

"Did you steer when I wasn't looking?" I chuckled and pulled the phone out of my jacket pocket. No signal. I held it up to the sky and didn't even get a tiny letter R, so I shoved it back in. "Grab onto the antlers and turn left at the shrub. Turn right at the big rock."

Kane looked at me like I'd ripped out a fart in front of him.

"Never touch the antlers. They are... um... sacred? Not right word. But personal and important. It would be insulting to do so."

Letting go the fact he'd basically ignored my question, I walked to the middle of the two-lane highway and stared in both directions.

"You wanted to be here?"

He nodded and closed his eyes, taking in deep breaths.

"Why?"

Kane glanced up and got to his feet.

"Transport will come in the next two minutes," he said and looked up to the sky once again. Squinting, he bobbled his head from side to side. "Maybe four."

I walked over to see what he was looking at. All I saw was the sky above, chewing away at the thin clouds against an ocean-blue sky. I shot a look up at Kane.

"What time do you think it is?"

He shrugged. "About 11:17. Give or take."

I dug into my pocket and grabbed my phone. It read 11:18. I blinked as I stared at it.

"What? You can read the time by looking at the sun? No way."

Again, he shrugged. Then I caught the hint of a smile.

I frowned. "You saw my phone."

"When you checked for bars, yes. But I can read the sun time as well."

"Really?" I slipped my phone back into my jacket pocket. "And what does it tell you?"

With a dead-serious face, Kane looked up to the giant golden orb in the sky.

"It tells me... it is daytime."

* * *

We stood at the side of the road for the next few minutes, and I avoided asking Kane any more questions. Was he hoping to hitchhike? I mean, who would pick up a guy as big as him? Me, I could probably get someone to stop, but anyone who might stop could be the sort to eventually stuff my dead body in their trunk.

Maybe.

I think I had trust issues.

When I saw Kane stiffen and shuffle his feet, I turned and caught a vehicle coming up the road toward us from the south.

As it got closer, I could see it was a long-haul bus.

"Did you know that was coming?"

Kane smiled. "Transit system in Canada is much better than where you are from. The TrailMaster buses cross here in the morning and just before midday. They keep a very good schedule."

I nodded. "Is that how you got around before I became your driver?"

"Sometimes, yes."

We watched as the bus approached. Kane took a half step forward and lifted an arm in the air. Not waving it around—there would be no way the driver would miss him.

A moment later, the carriage flashed its hazard lights and began to slow down.

Events were so out of my control. Or maybe just in Kane's control, which didn't make me feel much better. I chewed on a thumbnail and spoke in a low voice.

"We don't have a ticket."

"Is fine," Kane said without looking at me. "We get on here and pay at the next stop. This bus will continue on and bring us to Kitimat."

"They'll take us to the next town without paying? What if we got off and didn't pay?"

He looked back at me and frowned. "Why would we do that?"

"People do shit like that all the time, Kane."

I heard the whistle of air brakes as the big carriage slowed to a stop. Kane began walking toward it, and I followed.

"If someone did get on the bus and get off without paying, it could be that they did not have the money to pay," he said as the bus hissed, lowering slightly at our approach. "The bus would be going that way already, so no harm done. And it may help someone who needs a break."

The sleek silver door folded back into the frame briefly before rotating on a hinge and opening. Three stairs extended out.

I laughed. "That's not how the human world works. You don't pay and they toss you in jail."

"I prefer animal world, then."

"You eat each other!"

He shrugged. "And what you describe is different?"

"Just get on, wolfy."

Kane spun around to me and spoke in a quick, harsh whisper. "Have you traveled on a coach bus before?"

"Like a long ride?" I shook my head.

He looked over his shoulder and smiled at the driver, who nodded and returned the gesture. When he looked back at me, his face was deadly serious.

"Once we are aboard, there is very important rule you must follow."

"Okay."

"This rule must never be broken. Do you understand?"

I swallowed hard and nodded. Kane gave the driver a kind wave, then the grave face returned when he looked at me once more.

"Promise me you will abide by this rule."

"Y-Yes. What is it?"

"The most important rule of long-haul transit," Kane said then exhaled. "No number twos on the bus."

Chapter Eighteen

When we pulled into the Kitimat depot, it was roughly nineteen hours after we'd been picked up by the side of the road. We'd stopped three times. At the first, I'd paid for our tickets. Well, I'd used Kane's debit card to pay for them. I held onto his passport wallet because he tended to lose his clothes from time to time.

Turning into yippy dogs when you step into the moonlight can do that.

The next two stops along the way had been stretch-your-legs-and-pee breaks. I had done both, just happy to be off the bus for a few blissful minutes. Nothing against buses, but sitting on my butt for hours and hours had been torture.

Kane had slept the entire time.

At one point, I'd used the phone Denny had given me to google: *Do wolves hibernate?* I'd never seen anyone sleep for that long in a single stretch. However, when we'd been at Denny and Florida's farmhouse, the big guy had done something similar. He'd spent the better part of two days sleeping.

He'd been injured then, so I thought he'd just been recuperating.

By the way: wolves do not hibernate.

Except maybe wolves who become humans. At least mine did.

We'd sat in the back of the bus for two reasons. One, we could stretch out a bit more. Two, we only had to worry about our set of blinds to cover the windows. Last thing I needed was for the moon to peek in and suddenly, I've got a Great Dane chillin' next to me.

No thanks.

Thankfully, as we rolled into Kitimat, dawn was just warming the sky. I punched Kane in the shoulder, and when he didn't wake, I bopped him again, a bit harder.

Without opening his eyes, he said, "Why are you tapping me with your puny fist?"

"Time to get going. We're here." I threw my hand out as the bus came to a bit of an abrupt stop as the overhang of the depot cast a shade throughout the carriage.

His voice didn't sound like someone who'd just come from a half-day sleep. Not craggy and woozy.

As people began to file off the bus around us, I stuffed my sleeping bag back into my pack, staring at him as he rubbed his face and looked out the window.

I asked, "Were you sleeping?"

"Did you see my eyes closed?"

"Do you know it's rude to answer a question with a question?"

He nodded. "Then I will forgive your rudeness."

"It... No, you didn't—" I said then got banged in the head by a woman who'd been sitting in front of us. The fat orange cat inside the pet carrier bared its teeth at me, but when it caught sight of Kane, it slid back deeper into its soft-side cage, eyes wide.

After the woman left, I hoisted my backpack to my shoulder and pointed at the carrier—two kitty eyes still locked on us as it drifted farther up the bus. "I should get one of those pet bags for you."

"I would not fit," he said, standing and stretching.

"There are times you would." I flashed him a ridiculous grin. "Maybe get you a few sweaters so doggy Kane don't get cold."

He watched as the few people who'd been nearby grabbed their gear and passed out of earshot. Then he turned to me.

"If you ever put dog sweater on me, I will fire you."

I shrugged and stepped into the aisle. "It would be totally worth it."

Chapter Nineteen

Kitimat, British Columbia, was the first town I'd stepped in outside of the United States. The streets were impossibly clean and lined with leafy green trees. The shops around us were tidy—older but well maintained. A low fog hugged the tops of the hills in the distance, which, depending on your mood, might feel like a comforting blanket or a pillow stuffed over your face.

The tops of the mountains lining the horizon were lopped off by the white void of the mist. It was as if someone had drawn the snow-lined peaks on a piece of construction paper and then torn the top of the page off, leaving jagged edges behind against a white table.

And, weirdly, this part of Canada smelled like pancakes and bacon grease. I decided I could live here.

Some of the people exiting the bus met with friends and family who'd been waiting in the parking lot. Others hiked bags of various sizes higher up their shoulders, ready to run toward whatever adventure might come next.

Or running from one that didn't work out.

About a third of the bus people stumbled toward a small restaurant with dirt-colored brick and red awnings. The name Tim Hortons was written across the face of it, each of its letters as tall as I was.

"Looks like a Waffle House," I said as Kane stretched his legs.

My friend grumbled. "Is much better than the Waffle House."

"Better?" I squinted at the building as travelers went inside, a man in a puffy jacket holding the door for strangers. "How could anything be better than a Waffle House?"

I hadn't slept much on the bus but nothing a few carafes of coffee couldn't take care of.

For a moment, Kane just watched the people around us, scanning his head from left to right. He tilted his head and sniffed the air, scrunching his nose as he did.

"Human smell is terrible."

"Especially if you're downwind," I said.

"No, I mean the ability to smell. So feeble."

"What is it?"

"Familiar scent. But cannot place it."

I pointed at the restaurant, my stomach growling. "Is it pancakes? I bet it's pancakes."

"It is not pancakes."

Kane took a few steps away from the restaurant, smelling the air again, then cursed under his breath. Actually, I realized I'd never heard the big guy curse. Of course, he could be cursing in French, and I'd never know it.

He could be a bubbling curse factory for all I knew. At some point, I'd have to learn a little bit of French.

After a minute of my friend taking a few steps, sniffing, then moving a few more steps in another direction and sniffing again, I pointed at the restaurant once more.

"Let's grab some breakfast. You can dance and sniff much better on a full stomach."

He looked at me intensely, then his bearded face split into a grin. "Actually, this is not true," Kane said. "Sense of smell improves when hungry."

"Then I am at maximum olfactory efficiency," I said and got a blank stare. "Dude, I'm starving. You wanna go in?"

"Yes. We are here to find someone." He nodded. "He will be inside."

"Great," I said then realized what he'd said. "*What?* Who?"

* * *

"What do they look like?" I said as we stepped inside, the beautiful aroma of coffee, frosted sugar, and waffles wrapping me in a loving embrace. The heat had been jacked up, too, which was fine by me. Crossing the threshold of the restaurant almost felt like stepping into a dry sauna.

"Old. White," Kane said, shrugging.

He had just described ninety percent of the clientele and one hundred percent of the staff.

"Who is this person?" I whispered, waiting in the short line at the host station. "Do they work here?"

"No, George Fineman does not work at the Tim Hortons," Kane said then nodded to a clock above the front door. "Each day, he comes here for two cups of coffee, eggs, and hash browns."

"Hash browns."

"Sometimes toast."

"Helpful. Who is—?"

"Two for breakfast?" a woman in a gray cap and shirt with red piping said, the corners of her smile nearly reaching each ear. Her name tag said Shelly.

"Hi, Shelly," I said since Kane was looking around the restaurant. "Do you know if a George Fineman is here this morning?"

She put a hand on her hip and, impossibly, smiled wider. "Dr. Fineman is here every morning." She tilted her head toward the kitchen area. "He's sitting at the breakfast bar. Should be a few seats over there."

Without a word, Kane snapped his head toward the far side of the restaurant and began heading that way. I trailed behind him.

I called after Kane, "Doctor Fineman is *here*?"

Apparently, I'd spoken louder than I intended to, because a rail-thin man in his late sixties turned from his folded newspaper, pulled his wire-framed glasses off, and looked up at us. As we approached, his face was open and inviting. This was a man who met strangers every day and had a practiced expression to greet them.

When his eyes drifted from me to the six-foot-seven man walking just ahead of me, his eyes got big. Then the arm holding his glasses fell to his side. He stood, dropping the folded-up paper next to a bottle of syrup with a label that read *McClarsky's*.

My heart rose into my throat because Kane was moving so quickly toward him. I looked around the restaurant to see if anyone else had noticed us. They hadn't. At least, not yet.

"Kane," I called out, but my friend didn't slow.

I held my breath as he walked up to the man but let it out when I saw them embrace. Dr. Fineman's face buried into the other's shoulder, and he gave him a warm squeeze. Then he pushed Kane back from him, his hands remaining on his arms.

"Look at you, my boy," he said, his eyes misty.

"Hello, Doctor Fineman. You look well."

As I came up, the doctor slid his glasses back on.

"And you look much younger than I would have guessed by now, Kane," he said, then his face darkened. "I expect there's a story behind that I'd rather not know about."

Chapter Twenty

We stood in front of a long row of shops on what I'd assumed was the main street of town. I'd looked for a street sign but hadn't seen one. Maybe they didn't have them in Canada.

I did notice, however, that many of the road signs were both in English and in French. When we'd rounded the corner from the Tim Hortons one block down, the red octagon sign above me read both "stop" and "arrêt."

Despite the chilly morning, Dr. Fineman wore his coat open as he walked. After we'd passed a bakery, which smelled amazing, I was reminded that we hadn't taken time to eat.

The moment Kane had started to speak back at the restaurant, the good doctor patted him on the shoulder and said, "Let's go find some privacy, yeah?"

That privacy was his office just a few blocks away. However, when we'd gotten to the door, the key wouldn't fit into the lock.

"I don't really hold regular office hours," Fineman said. "Not of late. It's"—he grunted as he tried to jam the key deeper—"a bit stuck."

Kane reached down and turned the handle. There was a *ping!* within the knob, and the door opened.

"I should keep you around," he said, shouldering the door wider. "You'd save me a fortune on locksmiths."

"I am sorry." My friend shook his head. "We cannot stay long."

Standing at the open door, Fineman looked at me. "He still doesn't really get humor, does he?"

"He's catching on." I smiled up at my friend. "Hey, Kane. Knock, knock?"

The big man looked between me and the doctor. He pointed to the door, cocking his head to the side. "Door is already open."

I pushed passed him, following Fineman inside. "Yeah, still needs a bit of work."

Despite allegedly being summer, the front office felt colder than it did outside. It smelled like dust particles had been floating happily through the air then, when the temp dropped, held them there suspended in space.

The doctor chucked his keys into an oversized iron ashtray sitting at the reception desk. A coffee cup with a broken handle held an impressive collection of pens and pencils. Next to that was a desk lamp sitting atop a small stack of faded green folders.

Against the windows was an L-shaped collection of seats. Red vinyl backs and cushions all linked together within a metal frame. Three against the front store window and another three down the wall.

The doctor noticed me looking at them.

"This office is older than I am," he said, rubbing his hands together, which sounded like low-grit sandpaper. "Before I came here, it was a bakery. Took about a year before the place didn't smell like frosted crullers. Before that—"

"An abattoir," Kane said, frowning.

Fineman looked at him, surprised, then smiled sadly. "Not quite so dramatic. Just a butcher." He waved a pink hand in the air. "You can smell that?"

The big man nodded, his frown deepening.

The doctor jammed his hands into his pockets and pursed his lips. "Must be hard for you. Would you like to go somewhere else?"

Kane ignored the question, walking past the doctor and heading toward the back.

The office was just the two spaces. A reception area and the examination room. Kane opened the door to the second room and went right inside.

He'd been here before.

"Make yourself at home, Kane," Fineman called back. "They're in the second cupboard from the left. Top shelf."

Before I could ask what the hell he was talking about, he had a question of his own.

"How'd you get tied up into all this, young lady?"

"Emelda."

He grinned sweetly. "How did you get tied up into all this, Lady Emelda?"

The guy was an old-school charmer and impossible not to like. But I'd met many, many charmers in my short twenty-five years. They weren't always what they pretended to be. Despite his warm smile, I was wary.

If for no other reason, then because he obviously knew much more about Kane's story than I did.

I sighed. "Superman can't drive, so that's me."

"But," the doctor said, staring out the fogged window. "You guys said you took the bus up here."

Smiling, I said, "He still pays me."

We went into the back room, which was a combination of an exam space and office. Fineman clicked on the florescent light, which *tick-tick-ticked* to life. Then he grabbed what looked like a white television remote and thumbed an orange button. Above his desk, a long rectangular wall unit came to life, a bottom louver opening like a mouth.

"It'll take a minute or so for it to heat up, but it gets pretty cozy fast."

I looked over at Kane, who was leaning against a counter with his arms crossed. Next to him was a tall glass jar with a rainbow of lollypops and sticks. One of the white sticks was poking out of his mouth, bobbing up and down like a conductor's baton.

Fineman laughed. "Don't chew it, my boy. You're supposed to suck on the darn thing."

"Takes too long," Kane said then stripped the stick out, dug into the jar, and grabbed another.

Fineman rounded his desk and went to a three-tiered shelving unit. He struggled to get the top drawer open for a moment, and when it popped free, a roll of gauze bounced up and nearly hit his face. Old dude didn't even flinch.

"How much do you know about…?" I said, nodding at the big lollypop junkie.

"I've known Kane since he was just this high," the doctor said, digging in the drawer with one hand, holding the other out just under his ribs. "Which, of course, was only about a year ago."

"Growth spurts," I said with a grin.

Fineman slammed the drawer, holding a plastic tray. I saw a needle, vial, gauze, scissors, and a bunch of other stuff I didn't recognize.

"Can you pop up on the exam table, please?"

I looked between Kane and the country doctor. "Me?"

Nodding, he pointed at my hand. Damn, I'd forgotten about cutting it on the metal sign. When I looked at it, it began to sting. As if my body were saying, *"Yeah, duh. Hello? Ow, right?"*

As I hopped up on the padded table, as if on cue, the heat pump clicked to life, and I felt its warm, dry breath on my face. The doctor laid the tray next to me and gently grabbed my hand. He lifted it to the light, twisting my palm left and right without a word, as if he were listening sympathetically while the cut appendage told him how mean I'd been to it.

Unnerved by the silence, I asked, "So you knew what he was back then?" I looked over at my friend, who was stuffing a cellophane wrapper into his jacket pocket.

"I knew. Jacket off, please." The doctor leaned forward, his glasses resting on the tip of his nose. "Impossible to believe, but it didn't take long to work out what John and Linda had told me was true. Bizarre as it sounded."

Kane's face darkened at the mention of his late parents. He turned toward the wall, where a calendar hung. It was dated four years earlier.

Slipping out of my leather, I tucked my grandmother's locket under my T-shirt so it wouldn't bang the doctor in the head. I pointed at the calendar with my good hand. "You don't have patients anymore?"

"Retired, so I do a lot of fishing. My neighbor has a seaplane, and we take it out a few times a week. Our secret spots." Fineman winked at me and released my palm. "But I do the occasional treatment when the new place gets backed up. Or"—dampening a small wad of cotton balls with alcohol, he nodded toward Kane—"when an old patient wants someone familiar and needs a more specialized service."

"This is why we are here," Kane said, stepping forward. It would have looked more menacing if he hadn't had a lollypop hanging out of the corner of his mouth.

Fineman gingerly drew the damp cotton across my cut, cleaning it. It stung, but I bit down against the pain and gave no reaction. This drew a smile from the old guy.

"I don't really practice anymore, my boy," he said. "And, so we're clear, I don't have any blood to give you."

I nearly fell off the table. "What does *that* mean?"

Kane crossed his arms and looked down at the tiled floor. "I do not need that. We seek Cal Davis."

This time, I watched the doctor try not to react. It was only a second of hesitation, but I saw it. He balled up the cotton, did a final wipe with a bit of gauze, and then wrapped some fresh material around my hand.

"Haven't seen Calvin for some time now. Last time *he* needed, um, blood work." The doctor secured the bandage with a clip and snipped away the remaining fabric.

"He's still your patient?" I said and moved to hop off the exam table. The doctor gently put a hand on my shoulder to stop me as he grabbed a small vial of clear liquid. "You did blood tests on him? Why?"

The doctor chuckled as he rubbed a damp cotton ball on my upper arm. "No, not like that. And if you've been around our wolfman long enough, I expect you know exactly what we're talking about."

I looked at Kane, but he avoided my eyes.

"The participants in that god-awful program were stricken with a nasty side effect," Fineman said, his voice tired. "Kane inherited that in spades when Cal infected him. But it's that side effect, I suspect, that may have had something to do with why the program got shut down."

My head was spinning. I held my arms out, trying to get the world to make sense. When I did that, the doctor poked me with the needle in the shoulder and pressed the plunger.

I didn't even feel it. I asked, "What program?"

Chapter Twenty-One

As Fineman spoke, Kane kept quiet. I'd long suspected he was far more aware of what had happened to him than he'd told me. Was he worried what the doctor might say?

"Like his father, Cal has always been someone who loved walking up to the edge and poking his toe over the side. I think Linda tried to cure John of that some, which probably explains why they came way out here to the middle of nowhere."

"A family of adrenaline junkies?" I asked.

The doctor shook his head. "No, risk for the sake of risk. Or whatever high he might get from the attempt. For Cal's part, he liked to do things others said he couldn't. Or things that he'd been told couldn't be done."

"That sounds dangerous."

"Ha, you have no idea," Fineman said. "I think I patched up or stitched every inch of that boy's body by the time he was nine!"

The doctor crossed the room and sat at an old desk, cluttered with papers. He pulled a ring from his pocket, pushed a small key into a drawer, and removed a thick folder—of the same faded green as I'd seen out on the reception desk. He flopped it open and paged through old notes, a wistful smile on his face.

"Calvin loved action movies. The American ones. We don't really do action movies in Canada. We're more suited for dramas. And comedy because we're far funnier than the Americans."

"Action movies," I said to get the guy back on track.

"*American* action movies," he said. "Both his mum and dad were old Canadian armed forces, so I suppose it runs in the blood. As it were."

Fineman pulled out a photo and slid it toward me. It showed a boy who looked about thirteen sitting on his exam table, holding out a green sucker. I looked up at Kane, a lolly stick poking out of his mouth.

"That's...?"

The doctor nodded toward Kane. "About a year ago. He's grown, hasn't he?"

"And that... I mean, that somehow makes sense to you?" I stared at Kane, who crunched the candy and grabbed another. "You're talking about it like this is all normal."

"Ha, no," the doctor said, sliding the photo back into the folder. "But it always surprises me how our definition of normal can change. What seems impossible or strange quickly becomes routine."

I nodded and glanced over at my friend, who was not looking our direction. I sat on a stool with wheeled feet.

"You were talking about Cal."

"Right," Fineman said, nodding, paging through his old records. "So he goes down to the US and tries his hand at Los Angeles. He loves Arnold Schwarzenegger and wants to be an action star just like his hero. But the city spits him out. It does that, I hear."

"An *actor*?"

The doctor shrugged. "A young man's dream, and one that eluded him. He wanted to be an action star, so he did the next best thing."

I nodded. "He joined up."

"Right. Like his parents, he signed up for the military but the American one. It can be a fast track to permanent residency." The doctor closed the folder and sighed. "They ran him through a battery of tests and found something. Maybe in his physical makeup or psychological profile, probably both, and then suddenly, he's part of a program."

I had a sudden thought that ran a cold shiver through me.

"Were you involved with that?"

Fineman busted out a bark of a laugh. "Oh, heavens no! I only know what I'm telling you because Cal told me."

This caught Kane's attention. "When? When did he tell you this? Recently?"

"No, only a short time before..." The doctor sighed, and a sad smile drew across his face. "Before I met you, young man."

That made sense to me. "He'd come to see his parents, and after he attacked Kane—"

"Right. They brought Cal to me here, and a few days later, this newly minted human boy."

"How did they know they could, you know, trust you not to go to the authorities or something? If you believed what they'd told you, that seems like a no-brainer."

"Is that what you would have done, Emelda?"

"No, but I'm a criminal. Part-time, mind you," I said and gave him a small smile. "But you're a doctor."

"And they were my best friends," he said, the wrinkles around his eyes smoothing slightly. "Cal was out of control. He didn't understand why, just that he was losing his mind."

"Which is why he attacked Kane."

A nod. "When he'd first left town, he'd already grown into a young man. But when he returned last year, he was at least a foot taller. No color in his eyes, all pupil. His limbs long, lean, and powerful. His jawline looked like when body builders take steroids or GHB. Like they tried to swallow a small frying pan and it got stuck there."

I spun in my chair and faced Kane. He looked at me, frowning.

"So, they'd given them stuff like steroids? That's what happened?"

The doctor paged through his file again. "I wish it were that simple. No, not steroids. But I didn't know, so I thought I should do a few tests on Cal. That was a big mistake."

"Oh?"

Fineman stared off and shivered slightly. "I drew some blood, and when Cal caught sight of it, he went crazy. He had a modicum of control—I think in part because his dad was holding him in a bear hug—and we realized he was *craving* blood."

"What, like vampires?" I said with a wry grin.

"No, is not like vampires," Kane said, frowning at me and scratching his beard. "Vampires are make-believe. Who could believe in such a stupid thing?"

I stared at him and waited for his own words to sink in. They didn't.

"You don't really get, you know, irony," I said, rolling my chair over noisily. I stared up at him. "Do you?"

Kane crossed his arms. "I understand irony."

"Fine." I crossed my arms, too, and leaned back. A bit too far. I forgot there wasn't a seat back and nearly fell over. "Give me an example."

"This is like," he said, "rain when you have your wedding day."

I put my hand up. "Uh, no."

"It is getting to ride without paying—"

"Stop."

"—but, alas, you did pay earlier."

I frowned at Kane. "Bad dog."

Not surprisingly, that earned *me* a frown, so I scooted closer to the doctor's desk.

Fineman thumped the folder in front of him. "I sent Calvin's blood off to have it worked up then waited for them to email the results. The lab didn't email. They called me."

"Is that unusual?"

"It is at one thirty in the morning, yes."

I blinked, my mouth going dry. "W-What? What did they say?"

"It wasn't what they said but what they asked," Fineman said, leaning over the file. "They wanted to know where the patient had been because he had a virus."

"Virus?"

The doctor nodded. "That's all they told me, really. And only did because they'd wanted to know more about whose body I'd drawn the blood from. Of course, I didn't tell them that."

"Why not?"

He looked between Kane and me. "Because labs are forbidden from even asking. That's protected information."

I felt like I was missing something. The look on Fineman's face was like a professor giving some oral exam, patiently waiting.

It took me a moment until I got it. I said, "That call didn't come from your lab."

The doctor smiled at me and tapped his temple.

I jumped when my boob buzzed. Then I realized it had just been my phone on vibrate. I'd forgotten I'd even had the damn thing on me. When I looked at it, the screen showed me a text. It was Denny.

Mom wants to speak to you.

Chapter Twenty-Two

I stuffed the phone back into my leather jacket because, while I appreciated how sweet Miss Florida had been with us, this was no time for a catch-up.

Finally, we were getting some answers. Sort of.

The doctor told us that when Cal Davis had come home a year earlier, his parents had been desperate. He'd just attacked a wolf, which they'd set up in their barn to heal. That following morning would be Kane's first as a human, but even before that, their world had been upended.

Cal was in big trouble but had refused going to a hospital. He said the people he'd been running from would find out.

John and Linda Davis had known George Fineman since they'd all been in their twenties. When Linda sought somewhere quiet to raise their son, it had been George who'd suggested his neck of the woods. They'd settled just north of Kitimat near a city called Terrace.

After that late-night call from someone seeking information about whose blood had been tested, Cal had gone into hiding. Without anywhere else to turn, the terrified couple had asked their friend to do the unthinkable.

"I was able to get Cal a supply of blood for a time," Fineman said, putting his hands behind his head and leaning back against his wall. "We had a few butchers in town, and I'd switch between the three of them every few weeks."

"That didn't raise suspicions?" I shuddered. "A doctor coming by and picking up blood deliveries? They probably thought you were building Frankenstein's monster."

"Like many folks out this way, I've got a plot of land and do a bit of farming. A lot of locals have switched up to cannabis now that it's essentially legal, but there are plenty of us growing boring old vegetables." He nodded up to a chart on the wall that showed the food pyramid. "Some of the best fertilizer in the world is blood meal, which is made from animal blood. Tons of nitrogen and better than most of the store-bought stuff."

I looked at the chart but didn't really see it. My mind was elsewhere. "Cal couldn't pick the stuff up himself because he was too, um, erratic?"

"Right, and the alternative was far too grizzly," the doctor said with a weary smile. "Cal never came to town, and I told him if he ever did, I'd turn him in myself."

That got a frown of out Kane, and Fineman raised his hands up in *surrender*.

"No, no, I wouldn't have done that, but Cal was, by all definitions, manic," he said. "For his safety, and for the safety of everyone, he couldn't be around people."

"How'd you get the blood to him, then?"

Fineman stood slowly and walked to a map of Kitimat on the wall. He pulled his glasses out of his pocket and strapped them on.

"There's an old barn on a property three or four kilometers out," he said then looked at me. "That's about two-and-a-half miles in the old money."

He tapped on the dog-eared map. "Right around here. Last year, every few weeks, I'd drive out and drop the blood into a barrel. Sometime later, Cal would come by and pick it up."

That had gotten Kane's attention. "And go where? This was when I was at the home of Mère and Père, and I know he did not stay there."

Fineman looked between the two of us, his face a jumble of emotions. He nodded to himself then said, "Years ago, John helped Cal build a place of his own. Every kid wants a clubhouse, but not every kid has an engineer for a dad. They built a one-room cabin way out in the middle of nowhere." Before I could ask, he raised his hands. "And no, I have no idea where it is. You won't find it because that's what Cal wanted."

I turned to my friend. "Did you ever see him at the house, Kane?"

"Maybe two times. Maybe three." He turned back to the doctor. "But, yes, it was clear Cal did not live there."

"Which is why... Oh, Jesus." The doctor's voice trembled, and he turned to Kane, his eyes red-rimmed. "I'm so sorry, boy. I know how much you cared for those two wonderful people. I thought... I thought I was keeping Cal safe. I never thought..."

Fineman broke down, sobbing. He leaned on his desk, and Kane stepped forward, helping him to his chair. My big friend looked at me, a mixture of confusion and anger on his face. At least I think that's what I saw, but I didn't quite understand the anger.

The doctor had his face buried in his hands, unable to hold back the tears.

I felt like I was missing something. "What happened?"

When he didn't answer, Kane pulled the man's hands from his face and stared into his eyes. Had I been the doctor, I think a little bit of pee would have come out of me.

"Doctor Fineman," my friend said, his voice even. "What did you do?"

The old man squeezed his eyes closed and shook his head from side to side. Then he sucked in a deep breath and exhaled.

"It... I thought..."

"Slowly, doctor," I said. "Just tell us what happened."

He opened his bloodshot eyes and looked at Kane, resolved to what might happen next.

"I think I killed your parents."

Chapter Twenty-Three

I'd crawled back onto the exam table to listen to the story. At first, I'd convinced myself I was just uncomfortable in the rolling chair, and I was. But really, I was putting a bit of distance between me and them. I had picked up on Kane's body language and could feel the rage brewing in him.

As the story went on, that only intensified.

"We've got some local thugs," Fineman said, sniffing as he spoke. "They call themselves the Devil's Dawn. I have no idea if there are other chapters around in the world, but they've got a few dozen members in this area."

"Devil's Dawn." Kane said, his eyes never leaving the doctor. "Please continue story."

"They've caused all sorts of havoc. Clever, though. Just out of reach of the law. They'd never bothered me directly," he said, his voice hitching, "until earlier this year. A few months back now."

I saw Kane's body stiffen. Part of me wanted to pull him away from the doctor. He still had his hands gripping the old man's wrists. The hands he held looked whiter than before.

"They—they came here one night," Fineman said, his eyes closed again. "I was sending off Mrs. Halberton, who's been having—"

"Devil's Dawn," Kane interrupted. "What did they want with you?"

The doctor's mouth hung open, his sentence cut off, words caught in his throat. He nodded.

"They'd found out that I had treated Cal, a year ago," he said. "Twice, Cal had come to my office for tests but hadn't stayed long. Didn't matter. I don't know how, but they knew about it."

I hopped off the table and crossed the small room, putting a soothing hand on Kane's shoulder.

"Did they want drugs?" I pointed around the room. "You've got to have some stash around here, right?"

Fineman shook his head. "No, I thought the same thing. It's one of the reasons I don't keep any drugs around here at all, and I let everyone know it."

"Okay, what did they want?" I asked.

He looked at Kane then down to his wrists. I leaned down and grabbed Kane's hands and gently tugged them away. He released the doctor with a surprised look on his face. I didn't think he even realized his grip had grown tighter and tighter.

Kane grumbled and returned to leaning against the counter. He dug into the jar and grabbed another sucker. This time, he didn't even bother to pull the wrapper off.

Chewing, he said, "What did they want from you?"

"It was so strange. I thought they were going to rob me. Instead, they wanted the records I had on Cal," he said, giving me a nod of thanks as I sat back onto the rolling chair. "When I didn't hand them over, they searched the place."

I pointed at the file on his desk. "They didn't find those?"

"No, after that dreadful call, I got paranoid." Fineman smiled for the first time in ten minutes. "So I hid Cal's file away."

"Where?" I asked.

"Well, it wouldn't be a very good hiding place if I went and told people, would it?" he said, and his smile faltered. "They didn't find any records, and I tried to convince them I'd been helping out Linda, not Cal. The young man just happened to be there. They didn't really buy that, and I got a rifle butt to my jaw for it."

"Holy shit. And you didn't tell the police?" I asked, and that got me a slow shake of the head from Fineman. Right, the police would have meant questions he could not answer. "Why were they looking for Cal?"

"I don't really know," the doctor said with a slow shake of the head. "But these office walls are thin, and I could hear their leader, a real piece of work named Crank, talking with his crew. They'd thrown me onto the exam table after I got the bash to the face. I think they thought I was out cold."

I smiled. "You played possum?"

"I was trying not to die, Emelda," he said, his lips pulled back and eyes wide. "But why would a drug gang give a damn about files? I think they'd been hired to find Cal."

Before I could ask my question, Kane interjected. "My human parents. What happened?"

Fineman clasped his hands together, took a deep breath, exhaled, and stared at my big friend with sad eyes.

"I thought I was keeping the boy safe. They said they only wanted Cal," he said, his voice shaking. "When they returned to me, I got the other end of the rifle pointed at my face. So I... I told him where to find John and Linda's farmhouse."

"You what?" I said, louder than I had planned.

"I knew Cal wouldn't be there," the doctor said, speaking quickly, his words all tumbling over one another. "I thought, you know, they would show up and see he wasn't around and just leave. John and Linda are... were... strong people. I knew they could handle them," Fineman said, nodding to the front office. "I tried calling to give them a warning, but they never had a phone. The only way I communicated with them in the past was through email. I sent an email to warn them, but I don't know if they ever got it."

"What. Happened?" Kane said, his face reddening.

"I don't really know," Fineman said. "The next day, word got around their house had burned to the ground. I went out there to look with the sheriff, who thought they might have escaped because they weren't in the home. But their car was still there. Their bodies were not. A short time later, though, the fire investigator found some of their remains. They'd died in their sleep."

Kane raked his fingers through his long brown hair, not looking at either of us.

"Wait," I said. "So they just burned the place down? Cal wasn't even there."

Fineman looked up to my friend. "I expect they'd been watching the property sometime during the day. There are two possibilities. They either burned the home to get Cal to come there, or they *thought* he'd be inside."

I asked, "Why would they try to kill him?"

"Whoever had sent Devil's Dawn to find Cal would have known he was different," Fineman said. "Even if Cal had been injured in the fire, he can heal rather quickly. With blood."

I looked over at Kane, but he turned away from me.

"But Cal wasn't inside!" I said.

"If they had been watching the house, though, they would have seen someone with John and Linda," the doctor said, softly. "They may have thought it *had* to be Cal."

"Why?"

He shrugged. "Because what other young man would be in their home?"

Then, I got it. Slowly, I turned to my friend.

"Kane," I said. "They saw Kane."

Chapter Twenty-Four

My friend closed his eyes, rubbed a big meat hook of a hand across his face, and scratched his beard. Then, quietly, he lifted off the counter and walked to a door I hadn't seen yet. There were posters and small leaflets across its front. I'd initially assumed it was just another part of the wall.

Kane twisted the knob and went inside. I saw the door briefly open and caught sight of a small sink and toilet. I stood and walked to the bathroom, but he closed the door before I could say anything. For the moment, I'd leave him in peace.

I turned to the doctor. I had so many questions. And each second I thought about it, a dozen more popped to mind. But one stood out more than the rest.

"Did Cal tell you anything about the program he was in?"

"Not really, no. I think he felt by keeping it secret, it might keep me and his parents safe. Didn't work out that way."

I sat down again. "But he did tell you something."

"Only that he'd asked me to help find him another medical professional. I think people are under the impression we all know each other."

"Who was Cal looking for?"

Fineman shrugged. "Cal said he'd heard all sorts of different languages when he'd been at the complex. French he understood because of his parents. But he said he'd heard a half dozen other languages spoken. So I can't say for sure if it had been a solely American program. He mentioned the scientist, a geneticist maybe, who ran it. Dr. Pental."

"Jesus," I said. "Pental could have the answers that could help Kane. What did you find out?"

"Nothing." Fineman shook his head. "Pental had apparently favored Cal because the boy had been the only enhanced subject where the treatment responded as he'd hoped."

"'Enhanced'?"

The doctor's face darkened. "Cal said initially, there had been six of them who'd made it to the final stages, and he'd been the star pupil, as it were. Four others did not respond so well. He never saw them again but had heard their screaming. Then one night, gunshots. He didn't hear the screaming anymore."

We both jumped when there was a knock outside on the front door. Fineman stared for a moment then shook his head.

"They may have seen the lights," he said. "They'll go away eventually."

"Wait, wait," I said, my voice shaking. "They killed them? The, um, subjects?"

Fineman nodded. "Cal thought so. That's why he left."

"Left? You mean like checked out?"

"Escaped."

I shook my head. "He *escaped* from some super-secret *military* complex?"

"Cal became everything they'd hoped for. Powerful and strong. And as outrageous as it sounds, able to regenerate tissue when injured."

I nodded and thought of Kane after he'd been hurt. "With blood."

"The blood proteins act as some catalyst to quickly heal. Almost before your eyes. It's rather remarkable," Fineman said and chuckled. "But even being remarkable, he said he would have never escaped without the help of Pental. After they'd killed the others, he helped Cal escape."

"Why?"

The doctor rubbed a thumb and forefinger between his eyes. "The motives matter less than the outcome. Cal has only gotten worse since escaping. He went into hiding and has been searching for this Dr. Pental ever since."

"To find a cure."

"Yes, although no one in that dreadful program would call it that." Fineman sighed. "Poor boy's been hiding in the woods for the better part of a year. Then a month back, I'd made a delivery and saw that the previous one hadn't been collected. That worried me. I didn't know if he'd gone or been captured—"

"He was down in Minnesota," I said. "And I suppose that's where my part in this kicked off."

As I explained the previous few weeks, Fineman listened intently. How I'd discovered Kane. How Cal had terrorized car shows and attacked two people. The virus hadn't made them just stronger. It had turned them into monsters.

"They'd been killing farm animals, but had it not been for Kane and me, they'd have killed people."

Fineman shook his head. "Cal would have never allowed that, Emelda, he—"

"When we found Charlie Boynton, Cal was *helping* him!"

"I suppose, without my blood deliveries satiating him, he must have..." His voice trailed off. "If that is true, I'm not sure how much of Calvin Davis is left in that young man."

"I don't know if there's any humanity left in Cal Davis," I said, a growl in my voice.

"If you've ever been hungry, you know what that can make you do," he said, searching my eyes. I looked away. "Yes. I think you understand."

I hated that, in some way, he saw through me. And, sure, desperation had landed me in the back of a police car more times than I'd wanted to admit. But there was a limit to my own depravity.

Through clenched teeth, I told him, "Hunger never made me want to kill anyone."

He shrugged. "Then you haven't known true hunger. And in Cal's case, there is only one thing that can satiate that hunger."

I was ready to get the subject of "me" off the table. Then I recalled something Fineman had said.

"Wait," I said. "You said six people had been in the program and four were killed. What about the fifth?"

"Cal had been the success, but according to him, another had shown progress. That subject required continuous treatments, his body fighting the viral load maybe. Cal hadn't needed that because his body had accepted the treatment."

"Whatever became of the fifth?"

"Cal never said. He might have faced the same fate as the others."

I nodded. "Did he say who this other was?"

"He'd said the name..." Fineman exhaled, looking at the ceiling. "Garrick. Or Gary?"

"No," Kane said, standing at the open door to the bathroom. "His name is Gregor."

Chapter Twenty-Five

I stared up at Kane, and despite his expressionless face, I could read the turmoil underneath. I wasn't sure if that was me better picking up on his tells or if I was just projecting my own stress onto him.

"What do you know of Gregor?" Kane said, crossing the room to the desk, his eyes hard. He stood over the doctor, who looked up and swallowed hard before answering.

"Only that Cal believes he's been tasked by the Organization to bring him back to the program."

"They've, you know, got the recipe for the eleven herbs and spices," I said. "They could just make others. Why would they need him?"

"Cal thought that when Pental bailed, the scientist took all the research and went into hiding," he said. "So they need Cal to make more like him."

The banging on the front door grew louder, more insistent. I frowned. My little tirade must have given away that someone was inside the doctor's office.

As Fineman cleared his throat and eased out of his chair, I got the impression he'd been looking for a way to get out of Kane's shadow.

I gawked at him. "Where are you going?"

"To see who's knocking on my door," he said, crossing the room. "They keep banging at it that hard, they'll break the bloody glass."

Fineman stepped out of the room, closing the door behind him.

Kane watched the doctor leave with an expression on his face I didn't like. Dude looked like he wanted to eat the man. And trouble is, when referring to a guy who used to be a wolf, that's not hyperbole. I really thought he was considering taking a bite out of Fineman.

I asked, "You don't trust him?"

The big man sighed and looked at the ground, his shoulders rounded. He gave me a grunt and nothing else.

"He seems like he really cares about you, Kane." I stood and took a step closer to him. "And I don't know what it's like in the wolf world, but he may be, in some ways, the only family you've got left."

That earned me a look like he wanted to take a bite out of me.

"I have a family waiting for me in the forest." He rolled his hands into fists. "Each day I am here, they are out there. Hunting, seeking, surviving without me."

Putting a gentle hand on his shoulder, I said, "I know."

"We must find Cal Davis."

"We will." I smiled at him. "Trapper John says Cal has—or had—some hidden-away cabin out here. If anyone can sniff it out, pun intended, it would be you."

The big man furrowed his brow at me. "Who is Trapper John?"

"Doesn't matter," I said, happy to have lifted the needle off his rage record a little. "I just employed an archaic television reference as a distraction."

He nodded his big melon head. "Okay."

"Okay, then."

I smiled again, but it dropped off my face when a man somewhere behind me screamed.

"What the hell?" I said, trailing after Kane, who was bolting for the exam office door. He crossed the room in one stride and pulled the door open, and I heard a low growl bubble out of him.

Looking under his massive arm, I saw the doctor desperately gripping the side of the door, cocked at an angle. Fineman's face turned toward us, red and distended in either fear or pain. Or both.

On the other side of the threshold, a large man was towering over him, clutching the doctor's jacket with his fist. It looked like he was squeezing Fineman's arm hard enough to snap it. When he caught sight of the giant human at the office door, he loosened his grip.

A half dozen others stood behind the guy assaulting the doctor. They all wore wool-lined leather jackets, jeans, and motorcycle boots. All but one had long hair, like the entire getup was some clubhouse uniform.

The bald dude pushed a pair of circular spectacles up the bridge of his nose and stepped up behind the big guy holding Fineman. His face was taut, like a clutched fist.

His frown deepened, and he pointed at Kane.

"I remember you."

Chapter Twenty-Six

Kane

I think I am having a flashback.

This is my first.

How strange.

Like a movie in my mind where I am not only actor but also director. If this is the case, I will be very demanding of myself. And I will also make unreasonable demands from the crew, complaining about my sandwich order.

However, it is only me.

The only actor and creator.

And viewer. Very bad for box office.

Some moments, I see this movie world through my eyes, the small dark room surrounding me. Then I see myself within the space, standing as the wisps of smoke swirl around me.

I find this very frustrating.

Seeing the face of the man at the door of the doctor's office has put me in this replay, and I feel the reason for this will only be revealed to me at the end. This would be the important part.

Sadly, there are no buttons to speed this up. No skipping button. Although, also no "Are You Still Watching?" screens, which had always made me feel shameful when Mère and I would binge-watch her shows.

A strange sound! What was that? Some crackling?

No buttons to reverse, either. While lamenting, I fear I have missed something else. *Merde!*

Flashbacks are frustrating. How do I go back to the—?

Nope, it continues.

I have no control.

I am walking but realize I am closer to the floor. Younger, then? As is my habit when I sense danger, I sniff the air.

Wood smoke. Petrochemicals. Charring flesh.

Yes. I remember this. This is not a time I wish to relive, for it is the night I discovered them. I do not want to see that once more!

Despite these desires, the mind movie continues, and I advance to the door. I grab the knob and notice I am without clothes. Alas, this is how I sleep, because I am still getting used to the feel of clothes.

No, not still.

This is then.

Back then. Months ago, but I am years younger, half of the age I am at present.

Confusing.

I do not like this.

Before turning the knob of my bedroom door, I recall mon père once warning me of fire dangers. I release the knob and put my palm flat upon the door. It is warm but not hot. I proceed.

Once the door is open, there is more smoke now, the hallway filled with it. The particles burn my eyes, and I try to wave the smoke away, but it only swirls in eddies, like a dark storm I am orchestrating with my hands. But it does not lessen.

Floor.

I am on my knees as I crawl to the right, so hard to see, it is dark. My fingers feel for the carpet runner, the metal lip that Mère would often take her tiny hammer to and secure to the floor. All those times I would run through the house, this would frustrate her, and the carpet would lift.

But she never rose her voice. Never angered with me. And when I would retire for the evening, I would often hear her tapping away at the metal lip at the top of the stairs.

Now, as I finger the runner's ragged edges, the undulating waves made from Mère's tiny taps, I know that I am at the top of the stairs. Smoke is twisting in the space, and below, I see the front door and entryway. Both are lit by a wavering orange-yellow light.

Flames snap through the living room beneath me. When I look down between the railings, I see there is also flickering light upon the hallway wall.

There is a fire in the kitchen.

I spin around, and I am fast, for I am a teenage boy, late teens as I have grown since first coming here some six months earlier. I am stronger than I was but not yet a man.

Will I ever be a man? Can a wolf be a man?

I push these distracting thoughts from my mind and spin on the carpet, nicking my finger in the metal runner. I ignore the bite of pain and crawl back in the direction I came.

To my right is their door, and I can see, just in the gap above the wood floor, the room is brightly lit. Are they awake? Do they know of the fire below? Why have they not come out? Why have they not cried out a warning?

I place my hand to this door and snap it back with a howl.

It is very hot.

Within the room of my human parents, there is fire inside.

Chapter Twenty-Seven

I glanced between Kane and the bizarre scene at the door, but my big friend looked dazed. What the hell was he doing?

Fineman let out a yelp as the bald bastard with the glasses yanked him away from the guy who'd been holding him. Gripping the doctor's coat collar, he pushed Fineman to the group of thugs, who all shoved him among themselves. A total playground scene, but these guys didn't look playful.

Menacing assholes.

But I'd had my share of menacing assholes in my past. Weak men, all of them. Emboldened by others around them, but you get them one-on-one and they crumble. But with six of them?

"Hey, pretty boy!" the bald guy in leathers called out, his black-framed glasses fogged by the cool morning air. He took a half step inside then inched back. I guessed he didn't want to be too far from the protection of his shit-for-brains buddies.

Kane snapped out of whatever trance he'd fallen into and growled at Baldylocks. "Let go of the Fineman doctor."

Their leader laughed and leaned up against the doorjamb, stretching his arm up the entryway, so we could both see the pistol jammed into his belt.

I thumbed the strap of my backpack, wondering how fast I could grab my slingdart. But against a gun, I'd have no chance.

"A little birdy told me the doctor had visitors," the fist-faced guy said with a big gap-toothed smile. "You are not what I expected."

"That is a lie." Kane shifted his feet, and I could feel him tense. "Birds cannot talk."

I couldn't help it. I laughed.

"He's got you there!" I said.

Fist-face scowled at me. "Shut up."

From outside, Fineman called out, "Crank, leave my friends alone. They have nothing to do with you."

Crank?

The bald guy shrugged, not even turning around. "I'm always up for meeting new friends, Doc." Crank then half turned back to the door. "Unless you can introduce me to an old friend."

Fineman frowned and slowly shook his head. He yelped as one of the assholes holding him gripped his sleeve harder, pinching the skin beneath.

Taking a step forward, I raised my hands up in a calming motion. "Let's just all be cool, man. Why don't you get your boy band backup singers to stop playing catch with the old man for a second, huh?"

Despite me advancing a little toward him, Crank barely looked my direction.

"You look like that kid..." He squinted at Kane. "You his older brother or something?"

Kane sucked in a quick breath, but his face was placid. Did they know each other?

Taking a chance, I eased forward a little more, and not even looking in my direction, Crank pulled out his pistol and pointed it at me.

Moments earlier, I was thinking about what a puss the guy was, feeling like he was some badass because he had some crew around.

Now, I realized, I'd felt the same thing. The difference between me and Baldylocks, though, was that he had a small group of leather boys backing him up.

I had a six-foot-seven French Canadian man-wolf with an allergic reaction to moonlight.

When I heard the throaty growl growing behind me, I couldn't help it. I smiled at him as I glanced down at the gun barrel, only a few feet away from my chest. "That was probably a mistake."

Out of my peripheral vision, I saw a flash of skin and a large hand swipe through the air like a crashing meteor. The world exploded around me. One moment, the asshole named Crank was standing in front of me, a gun pointed at my chest, and when I blinked, he was launched backward, the gun in his hand now clattering to the sidewalk.

Crank flew through the door, spiderwebbing the pane where his head smacked against the glass. Before he could even land, Kane rocketed forward and threw a punch into the guy's ribs, and he flew at a right angle, landing on the sidewalk in a heap.

The four guys who weren't holding onto Fineman jumped forward. Well, two of them did, while the others stayed in the rear. It seemed, after seeing Dear Leader crumple to the ground, they weren't as emboldened as the other two in front.

My friend, a head taller than all of them, grabbed the throats of the two men advancing toward us. Both of their hands came up to claw at his grip. Kane lifted them off their feet, took a step forward, and launched them into the street.

A woman passing by in her red Chevy truck swerved as one of the thugs rolled in front of her, jerking the wheel at the last minute. She then sped off, happy to have nothing to do with the chaos in the street.

The second wave made the mistake of checking the status of the first. A quick glance away and Thug One got a meaty fist to the side of the head and went down. The second guy cocked back an arm to strike, but Kane blocked the blow before the guy could even swing it forward. With his other arm, my friend smashed the guy's ribs, and I heard a sickening crunch.

The two guys holding Fineman had collectively taken a few steps back, dragging the doctor as they did. One had a 9mm pistol jammed into the old man's gut.

Kane and I had had a lot of time during our drive to the border, and he'd told me about hunting in the woods before he became human. Anticipating what another creature might do often was the difference between success and failure—of living and dying.

In his early years, this took consideration. Then, it became reflex and instinct. The latter—acting instead of wasting precious seconds thinking—had saved his life on numerous occasions.

I didn't have those kinds of instincts, but I could anticipate what might happen next and prepared myself.

"Let him go," Kane said, breathing heavily, which, in the chilly morning air, sent demon-like plumes of mist from his mouth and nostrils. I only saw him from behind, his heaving body seemingly enwrapped in thin smoke.

The guy who'd jammed the gun into Fineman now pointed it at Kane.

Almost as if on cue, the guys who'd been launched into the street scrambled to their feet and headed toward a vehicle parked on the other side of the road. A van that looked like something out of an old Hanna-Barbera cartoon.

Were they going for weapons too?

By this time, Crank had gotten to his feet, wheezing from the blow. He was hunched over, gripping his side.

He barked out, "Shoot the asshole."

A nervous grin crossed over the gunman's face as his finger moved to the trigger. Time slowed, and I could see the weapon hitch slightly, but Kane was faster, leaping to his left and ducking low. The shot rang out and shattered the front glass of Fineman's shop.

"No!" the doctor shouted.

The bullet had whizzed past Kane, who'd rolled to his left. Just as quickly, he was back up on his feet, arms out like a surfer, as if trying to work out what direction he might move next.

For my part, I'd already worked out what direction I was going. Leaving my open backpack on the floor, I'd stepped out the door as the guy's arm swung around to take another shot. With the slingdart's cord pulled back toward my cheek, I let the metal arrow fly.

My aim wasn't good enough to go for the guy's outstretched arm, but at this range, I couldn't miss the meat of the guy's chest area.

The ten-inch dart struck him in the shoulder, and he howled in pain. The gun clattered to the ground, and Kane leaped forward, as if this had been his plan all along.

In the street, the van roared up and did a U-turn.

Kane snatched up the gun but didn't pick it up by its grip. Instead, he held it like he might throw it at Crank or any of his lackeys. Actually, given how strong the bastard was, that might have actually been more deadly than a bullet.

The sliding door to the van opened, and in one final move of defiance, the guy who'd still been holding Fineman shoved the doctor toward us. The old guy fumbled, and I had to drop my weapon to catch him so he didn't fall.

When I'd looked up, they'd all clambered into the van. The engine roared, and they peeled away, leaving a long strip of black on the road and smoke in their wake.

"Are you okay, Doctor?"

Fineman exhaled and nodded. Then he looked at the front of his store.

Door cracked. Front window shattered. And somewhere inside, a bullet lodged in a wall.

Breathing heavily, he wiped his sweating face with his sleeve and motioned us back inside. I pushed the door open, and he patted me softly on the shoulder as he entered the shop. I saw him go to the ancient phone on the desk.

Turning to Kane, I said, "You're lucky you didn't get shot."

"Not so lucky. The man holding the weapon was unsure of himself," Kane said, looking down the street as the van took the corner and disappeared from view. "And I knew you would disable him before he could take a second shot."

"What?" I stood there with my mouth hanging open. "I didn't even know what I was going to do. You were counting on me hitting him?"

"Well, maybe not hitting because your aim is not good."

"Nice."

"But the threat of another weapon, this would be enough of a distraction," Kane said, walking up to me. Standing there, he blocked out the sun. "Then, if necessary, I was close enough where I could rip out his throat."

"Let's avoid the throat ripping if we could, yeah? That just leads to questions, messy cleanup, and potential incarceration."

Chapter Twenty-Eight

Before I could stop him, Kane had dropped both guns into a mailbox next to the curb.

"We could have used those!"

He tilted his head down the street at the fading sounds of screeching tires. "Did not help them."

Okay, he had a point.

We stepped in as the doctor was hanging up the phone. Looking up with a weary expression, he waved us toward the office once again.

I shook my head. "If the police are coming, I don't wanna be around for that. We can—"

Fineman laughed. "No, the police are not coming. Or at least, I didn't call them."

"Who'd you just get off the phone with?"

He nodded just past my shoulder and said, "Need someone to fix my window, don't I?"

"Who were those smelly men?" Kane brushed his boot in the glass at the floor. "The shiny one recognized me," he said then lowered his voice. "And I believe I remember him."

That surprised me. "From where?"

Before the big guy could answer me, the doctor chimed in. "That is part of the crew I told you about. Devil's Dawn. The loudmouthed one, their leader, is Crank. Son of the former police chief, but that's how it always goes, doesn't it?"

"Why did they come here?" Kane was breathing heavily, and I didn't need to look at him to know his anger was rising. I could feel it.

We returned to the office, and Fineman dropped behind his desk again, looking years older than he had just minutes before. He waved a hand toward the outer office. "I expect they had someone watching, or who knows, maybe they've got a camera out there on the street. Damn things are everywhere now. Cheap as chips on the internet."

"At least that tells us they haven't found Cal yet," I said.

Kane crossed the room and laid his hands flat on the map. He scanned it for a moment.

"I cannot read maps," he said. "Emelda. Do you know what all these lines mean?"

"The curvy one is an *S*," I said, straight-faced. "The straight one with a dot on top, that's the letter *I*, and—"

"You know what I mean," he said, a rumble in his voice.

Fineman looked between the two of us. "Are you guys, you know, together?"

"God, no," I said and frowned.

"Just that the way the two of you—"

"Where is the place you take the blood for Cal Davis?" Kane interrupted. He glared at the doctor, and I wondered if the fight had wound him up. Or something else.

Fineman sighed. "Oh, it's been some time now—"

"It has not," Kane said then took a step toward the desk. He placed his fists on top of it and leaned down. "You smell like blood but not your own. But if you lie to me, that will change."

"Jesus, Kane," I said, my anger beginning to match his. "You've got one friend in this town and you threaten him?"

He stood, staring down his nose at the man in the chair. "Friends do not lie."

I was about to chastise him again but noticed Fineman had gone quiet. *And* hadn't contradicted the giant man looming over him. Of course, he wasn't the sort of figure you'd feel easy about contradicting.

Tilting my head at the doctor, I asked, "You have been in contact with Cal, then?"

He looked at his hands, sighed, then stared up at the ceiling, muttering quietly to himself for a moment.

This time, I took a step forward. "Doctor?"

"John and Linda made me promise, swear to them, that I would protect their son." He sheepishly lifted his eyes toward Kane. "Cal. That even if it came to putting *them* in danger, Cal's safety was paramount."

Kane growled. "Where is he now?"

"I don't know. I swear it, but..." Fineman looked between us. "A few days ago, I came to my office because the silent alarm went off. I live on the street just behind the building, so I was here in a matter of minutes."

"That was him."

The doctor nodded. "The lock had been broken when someone had crushed the handle. Took forever to get the door closed again. Maybe he'd been searching for blood, but of course, I didn't have any here." The doctor pointed to the jar across the room. "Found that out of the cupboard and on the counter."

"He stole candy?"

"Not all of it," Fineman smiled sweetly. "Just all the purple ones, which were Cal's favorite. He knew I'd know it was him, so I went to one of the butchers. Got a delivery and dropped it off at the barn."

"Okay," I said, throwing my hands up. "So where is Cal hiding out?"

The doctor lifted his shoulders. "I really don't know. And I don't want to know. That's what's keeping the boy safe at the moment."

"Then you need to show us where you take blood delivery," Kane said, motioning to the map. "Show Emelda so we may go there."

"He's got a supply now, so he won't go anywhere near the old barn for a couple days at least."

Kane said, "Just tell us where you left the blood."

Fineman looked between us, slowly rose to his feet, and crossed to the map. He scanned it for a moment and tapped on a thin line off a main road.

"It's right about here," he said. "Tucked into some trees that have grown around it. But you can't miss it."

I pulled out my phone so we could plot directions, and when I did, I saw I had a message from Denny. Another text, the same as before.

Emelda, Mom wants to speak to you.

I flicked it away and opened the map software, putting a pin in the spot Fineman had noted on the map on the wall.

The doctor dug into his pocket and pulled out a set of keys. He separated two of the rings and handed me one with a pink rabbit's foot and a long key.

"That's to my old Ford F-150 parked in my driveway around back. Blue house," he said. "It may take a moment to fire up since I don't drive it very much."

I took the key and pocketed it. "Does it have gas in it?"

"Always has a full tank. You never know when you might need it," he said. Fineman walked back to his desk and pulled a small white card from a dusty holder.

"That number on the front is this office," he said. "On the back, that's my home number. If I'm not there, I'm at the Tim Hortons every morning. Other than the supermarket and hanging out with my fishing buddy, I don't really go anywhere."

Nodding, I slid the card into my inside jacket pocket. Then I extended a hand. He looked at it a moment, smiled, and then shook it.

"Thank you for the help," I said. "Sorry about all the trouble."

He shrugged. "I don't feel like I've helped much. And to be honest, I'm not sure how much I should help, because finding Cal is the one thing I promised my friends I'd never do."

Chapter Twenty-Nine

I propped my phone up on the dash of Fineman's truck, watching our little red dot traverse the winding roads just outside of town. Like the doctor, the truck had been made last century, but it hummed along, obviously well cared for.

When I dropped the transmission into third, the engine revved slightly. I noticed Kane watching me out of the corner of my eye.

"Have you ever seen a manual transmission before?" I asked him, glancing between the road and the red dot on my phone.

"Père had something similar in his vehicle, but I don't understand it any more now than I did then."

"You can't even drive an automatic."

Kane stared out of the windshield. "There is no reason to mock me for such things."

"Far from it. If you could drive, I would be out of a job."

"This is not true," Kane said, rolling his window down and hanging an arm outside. He tilted his head and let the wind tousle his hair. "You also are good at talking with people to get what we need."

I groaned. "You make me sound manipulative."

"This is the strength of women, yes?"

My jaw dropped, and I pulled my hand from the stick and smacked him on his shoulder. "That's a shitty thing to say. Are you saying women can only get things by manipulating men?"

Kane drew his head back inside. "I am saying that men may be stronger physically. But women are more cunning. It is one thing to be a hammer. It is another to be the hand that can wield it."

I wanted to be angrier at him, but I really didn't know if he'd insulted my gender or elevated it. Or both.

"I suppose the male wolves run the show in the forest, then?"

"No, this is not so. Packs have both an alpha male and an alpha female. They are equal partners."

"Huh," I said. "Wolves got there before we did."

Kane turned to me and lifted an eyebrow. "Naturally."

We drove for another twenty minutes, taking a series of short turns, until we came up to a single-lane road, partially blocked by the trunk of a downed tree. From the driver's seat, I could see where its base had recently split, its white interior looking a little like the fray of a broken bone.

"You think you can move that?" I said, gliding the truck to a stop. "She's pretty big."

He yanked on the door and hopped out. His first efforts to lift it upright didn't move it much, so he went around to the other side, hoisted the tree a few inches, then shuffled his feet to lay it parallel to the road. As he'd moved it, bits of wood splintered and spat from the base.

Once he'd pulled it far enough, he brushed his hands off on his jean jacket and hopped back inside. Slamming the door, he pointed ahead and chuckled.

I made a show of working the pedals and stick, dropping the truck into first and getting us moving again.

Kane wiped his mouth, laughing to himself.

"What?" I said, smiling.

He jammed his hands into the pockets of his denim coat. "You could have simply said, 'Kane, go move tree.'"

"No, because I'm not a cavewoman who speaks in grunts."

"Yes, but instead, you say"—he lifted the tone of his voice into a higher register—"'Do you think you can move such a heavy thing as that?'"

"I don't sound like that." I laughed. "And I did *not* say it like that."

"Similar words." He turned to me, putting a foot up on the hump between the floorboards. "You made it a challenge. As if to say"—his voice went up again—"'Tree is big. I doubt you could move such a thing.'"

"Don't impersonate my voice anymore."

"It sounds exactly like you," he said and laughed. "But the word choice, your word choice, this compels me to prove you wrong."

I tried to recall the words I'd used but hadn't even really thought about it when I'd said them. I'd only wanted the supersized human to move the tree.

Tapping on my phone, I said, "Whatever, man."

Kane looked out the window again, staring into the forest. "Says the hand to the hammer."

* * *

About a mile farther, the single-lane road got skinnier and skinnier until it was a strip of dead grass and rock. The only indication a road lay before us were the two ragged lines of stones and dirt pointing the way.

I put the truck in neutral, yanked on the parking brake, and cut the engine.

Kane stared at the structure to our left.

If I'd just driven past it, I might have initially thought it was an old farmhouse, except it was too tall. There would be no reason for the building to be two stories, peaked at the top, unless there were some purpose to it.

Nestled amidst the tangled embrace of encroaching wilderness, the structure stood as a testament to the passage of time.

A century's weight lay heavily upon the ancient barn, evident in every sun-bleached plank and weathered beam.

The roof had long lost its battle with the elements, now a patchwork of holes and decay. Through these gaps, the sunlight filtered in, casting ethereal shadows upon the remnants of a wooden framework.

The walls, though standing, were no match for the relentless march of time. They leaned and buckled, like muscles weakened after years of hard labor and then decades of stoicism, just trying to remain upright in defiance of the passing years. The dutiful soldier holding their post and awaiting the return of a commander long since dead.

The forest, ever encroaching, sought to take vengeance upon this man-made creation for the land it had sullied. The outstretched branches of ancient trees reached toward the structure, their gnarled fingers snaking into the gaps and cracks, as if nature's intent was to reach in and slowly, clandestinely pull it all apart to erase all traces of this affront by humans.

Glimmers of sunlight danced upon the overgrown grasses and wildflowers, peeking through the cracks and crevices in the floorboards. It was as if the barn itself yearned to be swallowed whole by the untamed beauty of the surrounding wilderness, seeking solace in the embrace of the land it had once lorded over.

I jumped when I heard Kane's door slam, then I saw him walk around the front of the truck. I got out and followed close behind.

"I don't know if we should go..." I started to say, but he just kept trudging through the waist-high grass. "Or we could just go in, totally fine, and it probably won't fall down on top of our heads."

"It will not," he called back as he stomped ahead.

I tilted my face up to take it all in. "You can't know that, wolfman."

He stopped and pointed up at the slouching behemoth, now blocking out the sun above us.

"Barn has stood here more than one hundred years. It would be impossibly bad luck for it to fall in the few minutes we chose to enter."

Kane waited for a response, and when he didn't get one, he turned and went inside.

Dragging my feet through twisting vines, I muttered, "You're obviously not aware of my particular brand of luck."

Within the dilapidated barn, the wind whispered through the gaps in the walls. I felt that if I could just be still and listen, it might reveal its secrets to me. Hopefully, its secrets didn't involve a murderous grudge against humans. Or humans who used to be wolves.

But it said nothing, at least not to me. I heard a rustling in the woods behind us, but when I turned, nothing. I expected we'd become a curiosity to the local wildlife.

I walked through a hole in the barn wall, which had fallen away after being battered by the elements. Or some local teenagers looking for a place to do what bored teens do.

Inside, the temperature felt like it had fallen twenty degrees. The air was heavy with rot and a pungent smell of dead things. Hopefully not dead teenagers.

"This place is spooky as shit, Kane," I said, my voice clubbed short, no echo, as the porous walls absorbed my words.

"I am not fearful of spooky," he said then stopped and looked out of the hole in the exterior wall, which revealed an open field. "However, I am worried about cows."

"*Cows?*"

"I never knew of their treachery before." He squinted, staring hard at the woods beyond the grass. "They seemed so kind and gentle. Until you told me, I did not know how they could be so fierce. What madness must lay behind those sweet, innocent-looking eyes."

I put a hand on my hip. "You still talking about the cows?"

Grinning, Kane stalked down the far wall, got to a corner, then walked to the next. His hands were outstretched, and I wondered if he was trying to divine the location of Cal Davis from the busted-up boards, rusted equipment, and old oil drums.

The ceiling was a patchwork of metal lathing and rotted wood, but at least half of it still remained. Most of the years of rot were centered to my left, where the overhanging trees had dripped and dripped until the wood beneath crumbled away. Maybe the trees knew who those boards had once been. Like a cousin or aunty. Must not have liked them very much.

I could totally relate.

I did notice that where the roof had collapsed, there wasn't a ton of debris below. Either it had also just withered away over time or someone had come to collect firewood.

This left the floor of the barn, at least the middle of it, relatively clear.

Kane was bent over, sniffing at some drums, and I trotted in a circle, looking up at the sun coming in from above. Then I ran toward Kane, stopped, and slid before him, extending my arms.

"Let's daaaance!" I said with a big smile.

The big man slowly turned toward me, his face like that of a stone statue.

"Come on," I said, waving my hands above my head, and sighed dramatically. "Kevin Bacon?"

Ignoring me, he took a step back and pointed at a drum that looked a little different than the rest. I dropped my arms and walked over. The old metal barrel had been lined with a very new trash bag. A big one, like for leaves. It was jet black and, in the darkness, difficult to see.

I reached out, but Kane asked me not to touch it.

"Why?"

"This is where Fineman put his blood packs for Cal Davis."

Turning toward my friend, I asked him, "How do you know that?"

He furrowed his brow.

"Can you not smell it?"

"What? Blood? No," I said then inched forward and sniffed the barrel. I picked up an earthy smell, but hell, the whole place smelled that way. "I take it you can?"

"Yes, but too faint," he said and growled. "I do not understand how humans are dominant species when their senses are so dulled."

I walked over and sat on a stump that lay on its side.

"Don't really need a sniffing superpower to build, you know, airplanes and malls," I said, leaning back against the wall carefully. "Smartphones and sno-cone machines. Hell, I think we've got devices that smell for us."

Kane rubbed his bearded chin. "I do like the sno-cones," he said then raised an eyebrow at me. "We will call it even."

"Gracious of you."

He crouched in front of the barrel, sniffing its sides, and then stretched his legs, leaned over, and stuffed his head all the way inside.

"Don't fall in," I said.

"I am too large," his voice rolled out, muffled. Then he lifted his head and gripped the sides of the drum, shaking it for a few seconds. "Stupid human nose."

"So we wait until Cal comes by? That could be days. Weeks." I sighed. "Is that your plan?"

"It is not."

Standing, I took a few steps until I could stare out the back of the barn. There were several lines of tramped-down grass, but I didn't know if that was natural or had been trodden on by animals. Or some superhuman hiding from the world.

"We could try to follow one of these trails. Maybe it might lead us to wherever he is hiding out."

I heard a shuffling behind me and turned to see Kane sitting in the middle of the floor, legs crossed and eyes closed. His face looked calm. And older than I remembered.

A few more wrinkles around his eyes. A slight softness in the jaw and the hints of a few gray flecks in his beard. After his transition to human, Kane had aged fast. And that aging had only sped up over the past year. It seemed there was only one thing that would slow that down, even revert him back to my age, but I didn't want to think about that right now.

Too gruesome.

"What are you doin'?" I walked over and stood over the man. "Yoga?"

He tilted his head up and cracked an eye open, half of his face lit by a beam of sunlight, the rest in darkness. Dude was menacing-looking even when he didn't try.

"I am waiting."

I laughed. "Waiting? If you're waiting for Cal to stumble out of those woods—"

"No, not for Cal. He will not come." Kane lowered his head and closed his eyes once more. "I am waiting for the night."

Pulling out my phone, I was surprised to see that I had a signal. I swiped a few times to get what I needed then held the phone toward him.

"Kane, sundown is almost eight hours from now," I said then looked at the phone again. Yet another text from Denny. *Mom really wants to talk with you, Em!*

My large friend extended his legs and lay back with a hand behind his head. Taking a deep breath, he exhaled as he relaxed.

With his eyes closed, he said, "In this human body, I will not be able to find Cal Davis. The scent is there but too weak for a human nose. But in seven hours and forty-three minutes, I can... do better."

Ah. Right.

He wasn't waiting for the sun to go down but for the moon to rise in the night sky.

Chapter Thirty

I sat just watching the rise and fall of Kane's chest. Despite the monsters, homicidal gang-bangers, and whatever Tech Sergeant Gregor was, he was able to lie down in the middle of nowhere and drift off to sleep.

How odd must this world be for him? Hell, I was born human, and I'm totally confused by it most of the time. Kane had been human for all of a year, and he seemed more at ease with it than I was.

I tensed at the sound of a snap just outside the barn. Instead of investigating it myself, I watched Kane to see if he might react. Nope. He lay there like he had no care in the world. Maybe he had fallen asleep already. But wouldn't his, I don't know, wolf-sense pick up on dangers even when he was resting?

I'd heard ducks were like that.

They could sleep with one half of their brain while the other kept an eye out for predators. If there were a couple of ducks chilling on some log, the one on the left would keep half his brain on watch, and another on the right would do the same with half their brain. Some lazy duck could drop between them and just snooze comfortably, knowing his duck-bros had it covered. Then, after a while, they'd switch around so everyone got proper rest.

I started to wonder if animals—with their packs and flocks—had worked out shit about this world that us higher-developed species had missed entirely.

My phone buzzed again, and I sighed.

At least animals didn't have to deal with text notifications. That might be worth a bit of de-evolution.

Since Kane was going to sleep for a few hours, I got up and walked outside. When I stepped into the sun, I let it warm my face and radiate that heat through my body.

It left me light-headed, and I had to put my hand out and grab the truck. I hadn't realized how tired I was. When had I last properly slept? If I got too tired, I was going to make stupid mistakes. That is, more of them.

"Like leaving the door open to drain the battery on the truck," I muttered to myself and properly closed it.

I'd need to sleep very soon.

First things first.

I walked down the country road toward a grassy hill I'd spotted when we'd driven in. Up there, the signal would be better. Shuffling through the tall reeds and brambles, I found a flat rock and sat. Then I pulled the phone out and dialed my text stalker.

"I thought you were down in the big city?"

"Emelda?" Denny said, and I heard a shuffling on the other end. "Hold on."

I sighed. "I can call back."

"No, no. Just gimme a sec."

I could hear music in the background, loud at first then its volume dropping as he went into some nearby room. I heard the sound of a door closing, and the music dimmed almost entirely.

I asked, "You at a show or something?"

"Nah, I know a couple bands down here," he said, grunting as he sat. "I'm just checking a few out and seeing if I can help them get some gigs."

"Denny Newman, the star maker. I'm glad," I said. "Got your texts. All of them. What's up?"

"Uh, I texted that Mom wanted to speak to you."

"*Uh*," I said mimicking his tone, "I don't have her number."

"Oh, shit. Right."

"All good. I wanted to see how you're doing anyhow. Unless you're too showbiz now to talk with your friends."

"Hardly," he said and laughed. "Mom went to the funeral for Bridget Mills and wanted to catch up with you."

I stared out at the hills and trees around me, feeling very far away from the events of the previous few days. Monster killing and dodging clandestine military outfits. Basking in the peaceful solace of the British

Columbian countryside, I didn't have a great desire at that moment to get stuck back into all of that.

"I didn't even know Bridget," I said. "I mean, other than a brief encounter where she tried to kill me."

"Aw, she was probably more scared than you were."

"She was two feet taller than me with sharp claws and bits of flesh stuck in her teeth. And there wasn't a whole lot of daily flossing going on, I'm thinking." I lay back on the flat rock and stared up at a cloud that looked like Snoopy. Of course, they all kind of look like Snoopy. "I'm not sure how scared she was."

When Denny spoke again, it was muffled. He likely held the phone to his shirt—probably one of the hockey jerseys he favored—as he chatted to someone near him. A moment later, he was back.

"I gotta go. I'll text you Mom's number. She doesn't have a cell phone; it'll ring at the house."

"All good."

It went quiet on the line for a moment. Denny cleared his throat and said, "You okay?"

"I'm okay." It felt odd. I didn't know what else to say but, weirdly, didn't want to hang up. I'd forgotten what it was like to just have friends. I hadn't worked that muscle in so long, I didn't know how to flex it.

So I didn't.

"Catch ya later, man," I said and clicked off before he could say goodbye. A second later, my phone buzzed with a number. Then it buzzed again.

Call anytime, k?

I smiled and dialed Miss Florida, who picked up on the first ring.

"That was fast," I said.

"I was baking," she said, as if that statement in itself was explanation enough. "Hi, Emelda, you must be very busy. Didn't Denny tell you I've been looking for you?"

"Yes, we've been working on, you know…"

"Monster business, I know,'" she said and chuckled. "I won't take up much of your time."

"No, no! It's not like that. We've just been running around, and this is the first moment I've had to stop and call. What's up?"

"Are you sitting down?"

"Why?" I tensed and put my free hand out onto the flat rock. "What happened?"

"Nothing, dear. I just want to make sure you're comfortable."

I laughed. "I'm fine."

"Okay," she said and took a deep breath. "So I went to Bridget's funeral over the weekend. Her sister put it on, but Bridge had a lot of friends in town, so everyone pitched in. Kane would have loved it."

"Kane? Why?"

"Everyone brought a dish afterward. My neighbor had cooked up enough lasagna to feed an army—I know your boy was a fan."

"He's not my boy," I said, frowning. "And, yeah, he loves his pasta soup."

"Well, it was a lovely affair despite, you know, the circumstance," she said. "But everyone was talking, trading what they'd heard and all."

"I hope my name didn't come up."

"Not much, no," she said. "But I got some intel about Bridget I thought you might want to know."

Intel, ha. I smiled, but it fell when I remembered how the woman had looked the last time I'd seen her. "I really didn't know her, so—"

"Well, do you know who did? Charlie Boynton."

That piqued my interest. Charlie had been the man-turned-monster from the mall in Gisborne. Miss Florida, of course, knew he'd been killed by Kane because I'd told her. I had *left out* the detail that I'd put one of my slingdarts in the guy's neck. Never really came up.

I'd gone quiet, so she filled the silence.

"Seems that the rumors about Bridget's homelife were pretty spot-on. Her husband was an awful sort. Physical with her."

"I'd heard that."

"Well, according to Olivia—you remember her?"

"How could I ever forget her?" I said, my smile back. "The queen of the motor lodge."

"Well, Olivia had been discreet about it at the time, but they're both gone now, and it seems Bridget took up with one Mr. Charlie Boynton at some point," she said. "They'd rented out a room on a few occasions. Paid double, but that was probably hush money."

"Hush money! You're a riot," I said. "So if they were a thing, that explains how Bridget somehow infected Charlie. Still doesn't explain how Bridget got bit by Cal Davis, though."

"I may know something about that too."

Nodding, I closed my eyes to listen. Snoopy wasn't doing much up there in the sky anyhow. "Okay."

"From what one of the ladies at the funeral service told me, Bridget had made a new friend right about the time of all that car show business."

"Who?"

"Just a woman, some out-of-towner, but no one knew anything about her."

Miss Florida explained that since Bridget had been a server at the diner, people came in and out all the time. Mostly locals, but they'd occasionally get visitors. One woman in particular stood out.

"Ian told me—that was Bridget's boss at the diner—well, he says that this lady came by a few times and always ordered the same thing. Waffles. Apparently, her and Bridget struck up a friendship, and she'd even asked for her once, but she'd not been on shift that day. Probably with Charlie at the motel."

I laughed. "You dirty."

"You have no idea." She chuckled. "But according to Ian and Ruth, she's another waitress at the diner, the two of them would sit and chat about *cars* of all things."

"Right, Bridget had been at the show. Get one car nut within a mile of another, and they'll find each other."

Miss Florida hummed down the line. "According to Ian and Ruth, Bridget's *husband* was the car nut, but she never went to those things. He even had a camper he'd bring to the shows and would hit two or three of them a year."

I recalled how one of the organizers of the show, a guy named Dock, had described the condition of their camper after all the chaos.

A bloodbath, he'd said.

A year ago, Bridget's husband had been killed, and she'd gone missing. Bridget's husband had been the owner of the infamous purple car that Cal Davis had stolen and driven back home. Along the way, he'd crossed paths with Kane. Then the world had turned upside down.

"So wait," I said. "If Bridget didn't go to the shows, why did she go to that one?"

"The diner folks felt her new friend had shown up in town solo, so Bridget was going to go keep her company. *That's* why she went to the show!"

"And by 'they felt,' you mean they were eavesdropping."

'Not very nice, but... probably, yes."

I sat up on the rock, and when I looked up, Snoopy had split into a few pieces. Poor Snoop.

Florida continued. "I don't think there was anything particularly odd about it. From what they... understood, the woman liked Bridget and thought it might be fun for the two of them to go to the show together. I guess this lady didn't have many friends. In fact, I believe she said as much."

"Okay," I said and glanced back at the barn, which looked like it was slowly being digested by the forest around it. "Well, with all the big crowds, Bridget may have seen it as a chance to meet up with Charlie without drawing attention. Then Cal Davis goes to steal the purple car, and Bridget, maybe Charlie, tries to stop him."

"I doubt Cal Davis had been after the car," Miss Florida said. "There are far easier ways to steal a vehicle."

"You know that from experience?" I laughed.

"Hush now, I'm *ruminating*," she said, chuckling. "It more sounds like stealing the car was a rash decision. Looking to make a quick escape, but why, I don't—"

"Think I do."

I told her that there'd been a man hunting Cal at the car show Kane and I had gone to.

"His name is Gregor, and I bet he'd been at that same show the previous season. Probably turned up at this most recent one to see if Cal made a repeat appearance."

"Hunting? Why?"

"It's better you don't know," I said. The less she knew about the Organization, the safer she'd be. Not that I really knew anything to tell.

"I'll trust your judgment. Just be careful," she said. "I worry that you're one of those nice people who doesn't know it but subconsciously goes looking for trouble."

"I don't have to go looking. It finds *me*." I chuckled. "Damn, it feels like we've got all the pieces. I just don't know how they all fit together."

"That's because you're missing your anchor piece here."

"Anchor piece?"

"Right, with any puzzle, you need that piece that you can start with and build everything from there."

I shrugged. "Cal Davis is the anchor piece. This all revolves around him."

"I don't think so," she said, her voice dropping in volume as she spoke. "Why did a young man in so much trouble, on the run and with some bizarre disease making him crazy, turn up at that car show? That *why* is your anchor piece."

"Maybe."

"It is," she said, and I heard her grunt as she stood. "Trust me, I'm excellent at puzzles."

I smiled. "Was that one of the talents that helped you win Miss Florida, Miss Florida?"

"No," she said. "It was because I looked amazing in a bikini."

Chapter Thirty-One

I was awoken by a chattering sound and felt instantly on edge. My jaw clenched as I stared out the truck's dirty windshield, seeing nothing down the craggy road. But in tensing my jaw, the chattering had stopped.

Right.

My own teeth had been clicking together. After the sun had rolled itself from the sky out here in the Canadian wilds, it had dragged its warmth with it.

Leaning forward, my body filed complaints with my brain. There hadn't been anywhere to crash for a few hours other than the truck. Kane had claimed his spot in the barn, and even though he hadn't said so, I wondered if it reminded him of those early mornings he'd spent in the barn as a young boy.

Just last year.

I reached into the back of Fineman's truck, and a pain shot up my side. I was too young to hurt myself just waking up. Ignoring the stitch, I grabbed my bag, and my slingdart fell out.

"Dammit!"

Sighing, I hopped out of the vehicle and opened the rear door to stuff it back inside. I'd thought I'd secured it better than that, but I'd have to be more careful. It was a weapon after all.

I just wasn't used to traveling around with a weapon!

Slamming both doors, I slung the sack over my shoulder. I didn't worry about the noise. Hell, we were miles away from anyone. And if Kane were still sleeping, the double bang might have woken him up so I didn't have to.

I really didn't want to be the one standing over him, shaking him awake. I'm not sure what kind of dreams a wolf-turned-man might have, but I didn't need him coming awake ready to fight some oversized rabbits he'd had chasing him through some nightmare hellscape.

I crossed in front of the truck and looked over at the red horizon. Gotta give it to Canada. They do make pretty sunsets.

On the opposite side of the sky, I caught sight of that pale, floating eye that had inspired poets, lovers, and, last century, eager NASA engineers naive enough to pull off the impossible.

Of course, the moon also *affected* my partner.

"Hmm," I mumbled to myself as I crossed into the dark barn. "Affected or infected?"

"Who are you talking to?" Kane said, his voice floating through the chilly night air.

"No one," I said. "Myself."

I heard a shuffling that indicated he'd stood, but my eyes hadn't adjusted well enough yet to see him.

He asked me, "Why do you talk to yourself?"

"It's the only intelligent conversation I'm going to have tonight, so indulge me."

More shuffling, this time from another direction. Where the hell was he?

"I feel you are trying to insult me, Emelda."

Scanning the darkness for him, I said, "There is no try. Only do."

Kane stepped from a corner, hitching to his left to avoid the direct light. "That is a good saying. I like that one."

"Yeah, great," I said. "Totally made that one up."

The shadow of the man glided to the center of the barn where I'd seen him lying down just hours before. He bent down and rubbed his hands in the dirt and dead grass.

I watched him curiously. "Are you hiding your sleeping spot? Is that some wolf thing?"

"No," he said and spat something into the dirt. "Wiping my hands of squirrel."

"Squirrel?" I stuck my tongue out. "You ate a squirrel?"

"No." He took a step closer, his face glowing in the gaze of the setting sun. "I ate three."

"You didn't save any for me? Rude."

He nodded and rubbed his beard, the slight flecks of gray now gone. "I apologize. That was unkind of me. I should have—"

"No, don't worry about it. I'm not eating squirrel," I said. "I'm hungry but not that hungry."

"Not so much for hunger. I needed…"

I put my hand on his arm. "The blood. I know. Better squirrels than purple-haired girls, yeah?"

He blinked and shook his head. "I would never do that."

"I know. Just teasing."

Kane looked back toward the road and Fineman's truck.

"We have a long night ahead of us," he said. "We should go back to town and get you some food. It will be hard to keep up a pace if you haven't eaten."

"I'm fine. I've made all the right choices in recent years that would acclimate myself to missing a meal or five."

His eyes flicked toward me, and I could see a question in them. He took my statement at face value and moved on, which, if I'm honest, kinda bummed me out.

We spent the next few minutes getting ready to leave. I moved the truck, easing it into the long grass closer to the barn so it didn't block the road. I then dialed the office number on the card Fineman gave me, leaving a message.

"We're heading out for a nature walk, so your Ford's just sitting out by the spot you showed us," I said, instantly recalling my dislike of voicemail. Never know how to end it. "We don't know what we'll find so, um, you may want to come by and see if it's still, well, here. Later. Today. Or tomorrow. Whatever suits. I'll leave the keys on the back tire, then. Hope you're—"

Beeeep.

Okay. Canadian voicemail was kinda rude.

Sitting in the vehicle for a moment, I tried to get my head straight. When Kane stepped into the moonlight, we never really knew what we'd get.

Well, we knew what the full moon would bring, but the rest was a crapshoot.

The tiny lapdog I'd met first had been borderline mute—or maybe he'd just been that way because he was worried to reveal himself to me. But also jittery and fierce at the same time.

The Rottweiler was more brooding and contemplative.

The pug had been bold, fearless. Or clueless.

When he'd become the greyhound in the forest the day before, he'd been wired. Borderline playful, which is a word I never thought I'd use to describe Kane.

If he changed into any of those dogs, at least I knew what I'd be in for. A new one, who knows?

I was about to find out.

Chapter Thirty-Two

Kane stood over a collection of detritus in the corner of the barn then dragged the oil drum he'd inspected earlier closer toward the center of the floor. I leaned over and peeked in.

"You gonna turn into a Chihuahua and hop inside?"

He frowned. "I cannot turn into mythical goat-eating beasts," he said. Then he hooked his eyes upward. "At least, I have not in the past year."

"Your experience with Chihuahuas differs from mine." I pointed at the barrel. "What's the plan, then?"

"It smells faintly of animal blood, and given how insufficient this human nose is, there must have been much here. This is where the doctor left his blood deliveries for Cal Davis."

"Got that."

Kane pulled off his jean jacket and held it out. Sighing, I took it.

"Cal's cabin lair will be nearby but not too near," he said, pulling his belt from his jeans. He held it out for me. I rolled my eyes and took it. "I expect, though, it would be no more than a few hours by foot. Of course, Cal is not like other humans. Stronger and faster. In a few hours, he could cover twice the distance you could."

"You'd be surprised." I rolled the belt and stuffed it into the sleeve of his jean jacket. "In my middle school's Presidential Challenge Fitness awards, I was awarded *bronze* in the long-distance run."

He stopped unbuttoning his red-and-black checkered shirt and tilted his head at me. "The US president gave you some metal?"

"No, what would an eight-year-old do with a chunk of metal?" I shrugged. "It means I got third place."

Kane pulled another few buttons free. "That is admirable."

Of course, I didn't tell him there were only five other kids in my group. One of them, Berkley, had run it backward because when you're born with a name like Berkley, I think you're destined to be weird. Another kid had abstained entirely as a protest against the presidential award's "tacit endorsement of imperialistic colonialism," which I think even our teacher had to look up.

I sat on the dirt and dead grass, opened up my backpack, and stuffed his jacket and belt inside. As I did, his shirt flew in my direction, and I snatched it before I got wolf BO all over my head. The boots came off next, but thankfully, he didn't toss those at me. I didn't need to start our long night walk with a concussion.

No socks, as per usual, and he just set the boots aside. When he thumbed the button on his jeans, I spun in a half turn away. I heard him laugh behind me.

"Human distaste for nudity is confusing," he said, and I heard the metallic rip of the zipper coming down. "If there is any commonality between your entire species, it's your physical form. The one thing you all have in common."

"Um, we don't all look the same naked. Depending on whether you stand or sit to pee, you got different bits."

He laughed again, and I heard the jeans slump to the ground.

"But you don't hide your own nakedness from yourself," he said. I knew that if I'd turned in that moment, he'd be standing there, dangling in the breeze, arms akimbo, without a care in the world. "There is some variation, very little actually, yet another's nakedness is considered offensive."

I shrugged, feeling subconscious about the six-foot-seven naked guy hovering behind me.

"Not all of us look like the Super Bowl MVP on the cover of *Sports Illustrated*, Kane."

He grunted. "I do not know what those words mean, but you know that," he said as he held his pants over my shoulder. "I think you say these confusing things to change the subject."

I grabbed the rolled-up jeans, put them in my backpack, and zipped it up.

Standing, I turned, keeping my eyes on his, and said, "Are you ready to rumble?"

He put a hand on my shoulder, sending a slight shiver through my body.

Grinning at me, he said, "Hell yes."

Chapter Thirty-Three

Kane

I instruct Emelda to stay in the barn as I head toward a space created by a rotting break in the barn wall. Beyond that, an open field. After a few paces, just a few meters from the moonlit glade that called to me, I hear her following.

"You should stay inside."

She looks at me and with words and expression, says, "I fear not whatever you might become for we are a pack of two. I know you will not harm me."

Nodding, I try to instill this same confidence within myself.

I cannot.

In the past year, I have transformed only a dozen or so times, for Mère and Père always warned me away from the moonlight. They had seen how I'd changed and did not want that for me. This is some strange trait that Cal Davis cursed me with.

However, he does not change like I do.

I know now the tech sergeant is also one of the Enhanced, but when he stepped into the moonlight at the Minnesota mall, Gregor did not change into a canine like I do.

Of course, for me, it is not always canine. When the moon was full back at that mall, I became the other. What Emelda now calls the wolfwere. Alas, this was not the first time I became that creature.

No time to think of that.

"You going to get going?" Emelda says from behind me, so I cannot read her expressions. "And, listen, if you turn into some big ol' mastiff or something, I ain't picking up your massive turds to keep the neighbors happy."

I twist my upper body to look at her and notice she is regarding my nakedness. However, I am used to this with the humans. Both male and female. It means nothing to me, for my wolf wife awaits me and I her.

However, reading Emelda's face, this does not look like lust. A strange emotion troubles my brain. One I cannot identify.

She points to the field behind me, and I read her face, her voice in my head: "I trust you."

I take a deep breath and stride forward and can feel the pulse in my neck throb. My hands clench and unclench with each step, and there is a slight sheen of moisture there, despite the cold.

My bare feet clutch at the earth, and this warms me within. It is a feeling of familiarity and comfort. I dislike the human clothes and prefer to feel the dirt and sand and grass on my skin.

Stepping from the cover of the barn, the moonlight cast across the field ahead, I take long strides. What might I become? I stop for a moment, hesitating. What if I were to transform and never change back? No, when the daytime comes, I always return to this human form.

And this, of course, is the problem.

But to change into some small, helpless canine and remain that forever? The mutated decedent of a wolf breed that no longer walks this planet. One that nature deemed unworthy.

To forever become the progeny of some cast-out creature?

Yes, that would be hell for a proud wolf such as I.

Emelda calls out from behind me, "Shake your tailfeathers, wolf man. Let's go."

I growl, closing my eyes.

Feathers? I pray not! Yes, that would be far worse.

Two more steps before the moonlight—why am I trembling so?—and I take a deep breath, holding it for a moment. One more step.

I am ready.

(I hope there are no feathers!)

I break out into a run, for I will meet my fate as a warrior, not a coward. Pumping my arms and legs, I burst from the darkness into the pale light of the half-moon above. At first, nothing.

Then my mind begins to swirl, a feeling I now recall from all the times before. At the edges of my vision, the images ripple and bend as still water does when struck by a stone.

Colors mutate and twist, becoming shades I have never seen with my eyes and believe would not even be possible in the world. My heartbeat grows louder, hammering in my ears, and just below that is the rushing sound like that of a river struggling to burst its banks.

I can hear the blood flowing within my body.

The world turns red around me, and when I look down, I am frozen mid-step. Time has slowed for me, for I am no longer running but suspended in air, as I leap from one leg to another in full run, but not moving.

Before my eyes, strange images melt and twist. This has happened each time before, but in this instance, I focus on them and, for the first time, the queer shapes and colors. Not fully formed, they are distortions, but I recognize the creatures whipping around my brain.

First, a small skinny dog. Then another: somewhat larger with a flat nose—this the one Emelda called a pug. And now the large brown-and-black one, which she favors. The skinny gray one from the forest the day before. Then the images bend and twist and melt and bulge, so strange, I do not recognize these.

They all appear canine in some form but mesh together, strange and unsettling, into writhing abominations of flesh and fang.

Breaking from the trance, I grasp for the real world and see my extended leg. I know I am running, but it is barely moving. Ever so slow. Then the real world disappears once more, but instead of the canine images, I see only the eyes. Utter blackness around me and two blood-red eyes.

Those are the eyes of the beast I become when the moon is full.

The wolfwere.

Tonight, though, it is not his turn, and the eyes fade into the darkness. My vision returns to the present, the now, and I see my leg moving slow, upward, but changing as it does.

The human leg, with its long muscle beneath the skin, appears to boil and peel, darkening in color, thinning in shape, elongating and bending.

My back arches, twisting, then bends forward. I feel teeth grow in my mouth, my jaw stretching, shooting ribbons of pain through my neck. My fingers curl, and I call out in agony, but no sound leaves my mouth. I have taken another stride but am closer to the ground now, for I am changing.

Where there were fingers and translucent nails, I now see hair and claws.

Another stride, and my haunches transform; my human thighs are now more powerful, the shape of my new legs better for running, chasing, hunting.

By the next stride, my senses awaken. The night is brighter and more alive. Fewer colors, but my eyes see every movement, every twitch of the night creatures in the forest ahead.

My ears pick up their chattering, their breaths, and their hesitations as they bear witness to my transformation in the light of the moon.

I have changed.

The creatures cowering in the night would be in awe at the sight of this new magnificent creature before them.

I am reborn.

I am a hunter.

I am powerful.

Chapter Thirty-Four

"Oh my god. You're a *golden retriever*?" I said, hands on my hips, as I walked over to him.

"What is golden retriever?" Kane lifted his fuzzy head toward me, and his floppy ears, well, flopped a little. "Is it powerful and fierce?"

I bent down on one knee and put a hand under my chin, regarding him. "Hmm."

Kane lowered his fawny head, his eyebrows folding downward in such a human-like expression, I almost laughed out loud. Then he looked up at me, steadfast.

"You are disappointed," he said. "How may I comfort you?"

The very next moment, he got a look of horror on his face.

"Why did I say such a thing?" Standing there in the moonlight, his body shuddered, as if he were trying to shake off water from a dirty pond. "I-I..."

He seemed distressed, so I put my hands on either side of his doggie head and gave him a warm snuggly scratch.

"It's okay, Goldy. You look cute."

Aghast, Kane took a step back. "Cute? *Cute?* We do not need cute dog for where we are going! What we must do!"

I stood and waved my hands around the darkness all around us. "And what's that? What do we have to do?"

Kane chuffed then blinked, frowning. He looked disgusted by himself.

"I must track the blood scent. How can I—?"

"From what I remember, goldens have a great sense of smell," I said and pulled out my phone. After a quick Google search, I got back results and read them to Kane.

"It says here they're great trackers. They can find trails, people, and food. They sniff the air not the ground. And, this is neat, you can sniff out a peanut a mile away!"

The dog before me dropped to the ground and groaned.

"But it is not peanuts we seek!" He put his paws over his eyes. "If only Cal Davis craved peanuts, this would have been a very good dog to become. Now, this is hopeless. This is—"

"Kane."

"What curse this is? It saddens me so," he said, then his head shot up, his amber eyes wide. "Are *you* sad? Are you okay? Is there anything I can do to comf—no, no! All these alien thoughts, overwhelming concerns for your well-being. When will the madness—?"

"*Kane.*"

"No! Do not look at me! I have become a peanut hunter," he said, whining and whimpering. "I am a hunter of pean—"

"Kane!"

He stopped and bristled, shaking his head. "What?"

I sighed, trying to stifle a laugh.

"When it says you can smell a peanut a mile away, it doesn't mean you can *only* smell peanuts a mile away." I held my hands out to him, shaking them in the air. Basically saying "duh" without saying it. I knew he could read expressions and would pick up on it.

"I am not following you."

"It just means you've got a wicked sense of smell. The peanut thing is more of an analogy."

"Oh," he said and stood once again, back straighter than before. "Okay. Why are they not more clear with what they are saying?"

"I dunno," I said, swiping the screen as I read. "Probably just keyword stuffing to get a better SEO ranking."

He lifted a paw and pointed it at me. And, so weird, the corners of his doggy mouth turned upward.

"You did the confusing word thing again." Then he looked at his own paw and jerked his head back, his eyes slightly out of focus. "Am I smiling? I feel like I am smiling."

Pointing at my phone as I read, I said, "You wanna smile? Here we go."

"Where?" Kane spread his paws, glancing around.

"No-*wah*. Some quick humor training. Just listen," I said, reading from my phone. "Knock, knock."

The dog's smile fell. "I do not understand this knocking thing."

"They're jokes! Come on," I said. "You're supposed to say 'Who's there?' when I say that."

"No."

"It'll be fun. Come on, it's a doggy knock-knock joke," I said then cleared my throat dramatically. "Knock, knock."

"Ugh. Fine, yes. Who is doing the knocking, then?"

Close enough. "Bow."

"Bow?" Kane scrunched his face up. "Bow who?"

"No, no, silly dog. It's not bow who, it's bow wow!" I said and laughed, then I saw his confused face and laughed even harder.

"I have decided I do not like knock-knock jokes," the golden said and headed back toward the barn.

I followed behind him, giggling as I went. He'd tried to stay crabby, but I saw him increasingly trot along merrily, merrily, as he went.

I went around him to the barrel where he'd indicated—before turning into Goldy, the Dog of Love—that the blood had been stored. Kane came up behind me, prancing happily, and came up to my side.

I cleared my throat. "You're going to have to dial that down a notch. I'm used to a brooding Kane. Not a bouncy Kane."

"I..." he said, baring his teeth, "am not bouncy."

Looking down at him, I said, "Yes, you are. Who's a goooood boooy?"

Against every fiber in his being, Kane's tail began to wag, and his tongue lolled out. Then, back in control, he sucked it back in, licked his lips, and cleared his doggy throat.

"Emelda, please do not ever say those words to me again."

"Deal," I said then pointed at the barrel. "Take a good sniff and see if all this was worth it."

Kane instructed me to step back a few feet, then he frowned and looked to my hand.

"The bandage applied by Dr. Fineman. Can you discard it outside?"

"Sure," I said, unwrapping the gauze. "Why?"

"It smells of old blood," he said, looking up at me with his sweet doggie eyes. "And it *staaanks*."

Kane squinted his eyes and chuff-laughed, having a good ol' giggle, which was so weird. I balled up the bandage, walked to the side of the barn near the road, and chucked it into the woods on the opposite side. I turned away and heard it land, which rustled the leaves far more than I thought it would have.

Looking back, though, nothing.

Back in the barn, I saw the golden with two paws up on the rim of the barrel, sniffing around the edges. Then he shifted his feet to the left, going in a tight circle. I did not say—but really wanted to—I had seen TikToks of golden retrievers doing similar moves when dancing with their owners.

Oh, I really, really wanted to tell him that.

But we were there for an important reason. And, I reminded myself, both in very real danger.

After one minute, then two, of Kane sniffing the barrel's edge, I spoke up. "Don't you need to smell inside the barrel? Where the blood might have been?"

He ignored me, pressing his black nose so close to the metal, I wondered if he might get a splinter.

"Kane?"

He didn't answer, so I walked over and gripped his hind legs.

"What are you doing?" he said, spinning his head down toward me. "Control your desirous touch, Emelda!"

"Hold on, doggie dearest," I said and lifted him. "I'm giving you a boost."

He yelped, which gave off a gratifying echo. For a moment, his foreclaws scrabbled at the inside of the barrel, while his rear ones scratched at the outside. After a few moments, he calmed.

Just when my arms were beginning to tremble, his echoed voice lifted from the barrel.

"Okay. Please lift me out."

I did and placed him on the ground. Sweaty now, I pulled my leather jacket off and tied it around my waist. Then I picked up the backpack again.

I pointed in the middle of the barn. "We're leaving your boots here. I ain't carrying those. They're too heavy."

"Of course," he said, trotting next to me. "And your arms are so weak and wobbly right now from all the holding."

"I'm fine."

"Are you sure? Do you want to talk about it?" Kane said then scooted back like he'd seen a snake. "No! No talking. Time for hunting!" He lifted his head, eyes shifting between me and the field outside.

"Well?"

He said, "I smell zero peanuts within a mile of here."

"Har, har," I said then furrowed my brow. "But, you know… did it work?"

Kane turned to me, and this time, the dopey golden smile was gone. He nodded once.

"I have discovered the blood scent, yes."

Chapter Thirty-Five

It felt like each step I took into the dark woods, the temperature dropped by a degree. Still, the brisk pace had my heart racing.

Kane tilted his head toward the darkness ahead of us. "I think you may need to rest. You are perspiring."

"I'm a girl," I said, grunting. "I think they used to call that 'glowing.'"

"Is not glowing. It is blinding."

I kicked a few dead leaves at him. "You're saying I stink?"

"Strong smell. But odor of good labor is never unpleasant."

"Depends on the work, I suppose."

He nodded his dog head. "Also, other... on the air. Many smells."

"That wasn't me," I said, straight-faced. "I haven't eaten all day."

For a moment, he said nothing. The golden lifted his head into the air, pointing the sleek nose to the sky. He chuffed then licked his lips.

"Trying to focus on blood trail. But many animal scents and decay. You're *glowing*, but also other sweating. Hard to place."

"Maybe Bruce the Moose is in here somewhere," I said, referring to our Canadian Uber from the day before. Or maybe the day before that. I was losing track of time.

"I think moose nearby, but it is not him." His lips parted, and he sighed softly. "Such a sadness. Moose are alone in the forest. They do not have packs or run in herds. Solitary creatures. This must be hard."

I forced myself not to laugh. Ever since he'd transformed into the golden, I'd seen a side of him I never knew was there.

Kane was still Kane. But he seemed to pick up on the characteristics of the dog he became.

"We got to get moving," I said. "No time to worry about lonely moose."

He turned his big head toward me, his eyes soft.

"Alone and lonely is not the same."

I sighed. "Tomato, potato."

"One can be alone and content in that existence," Kane said. "Where another may be with many others and yet still feel lonely."

Gulping down the strange feelings fizzing up into my throat, I again pointed at the darkness and the trail ahead.

"How far now?"

"Not far."

For the next hour, we wove through bramble and bush. The canopy of trees above us alternated between a thick blanket of foliage above our heads and, at other times, open sky. The half-moon hung above us, watching us like a sleepy eye.

We'd been quiet as we tracked the scent, and while I'd grown more accustomed to the cold night air, another primal instinct had kicked up in me. Maybe it was the darkness. Maybe it was the spooky forest all around us. Or just my own experience that the world likes to chuck out surprises when you least expect it.

I felt hundreds of eyes upon us as we passed through the bush.

Bugs and birds, squirrels and possums, and bigger animals hidden behind the leaves and branches. But still, I couldn't shake the feeling.

Another half hour went by, and despite a sheen of sweat dampening my skin, I was beginning to shiver. I pulled my leather from where I'd tied it around my waist and slipped the coat back on. It wasn't like we could build a fire to warm up. And slowing down would only make me colder.

I picked up the pace, trotting behind Kane.

He'd heard me and lifted a paw for me to stop.

I whispered, "Do you hear something?"

Kane drew his snout across the air left to right then right to left. He settled on one direction and then pointed forward.

"The odor of blood has grown far stronger," he said, his voice quiet. "And others join it now. The smell of burnt flesh and wood smoke. Some type of oils. Lubricating oils."

"Great," I said, taking in deep breaths. "We've stumbled upon a nudist barbecue."

Kane turned his happy dog face toward me, but he didn't have a hint of joy on his face. Flicking his eyes back then toward me again, he moaned slightly.

"I believe we are here."

"Here? You mean you've found the cabin?"

He bobbed his head once. "Just over the ridge ahead."

"Let's go, then," I said and stepped forward.

"No. If Cal Davis is there, he does not want to be found."

"Sucks for him," I said and moved ahead once more, but he stepped in front of me.

"You forget, Cal Davis is not like other humans. He is one of the Enhanced. Very strong."

As he spoke, another thought hit me. "And ex-military."

Kane motioned to a line of bushes to our left. "It would be far better to wait until morning so that I am human again. This form is good for tracking, but if he were to become violent..."

I dropped my backpack on the ground, digging through its contents. When I found what I needed, I pulled it out and zipped it back up.

Stuffing a few metal arrows into the rear pocket of my jeans, I gripped the handle of my slingdart and hoisted the bag upon my back again.

"It's too frikkin' cold to wait until morning. He's either at the cabin or not. If he's not in the mood for visitors, he'll either attack or bail."

The dog's eyes went wide, regarding my slingshot arrow. "You can't think that will protect you?"

"No one likes pain," I said, striding forward. "If he is here, it'll make him think twice."

From behind me, I heard him say, "That is a terrible plan."

I turned around, walking backward. "I'm tired of plans. Time for action."

"That is... not logical."

"Welcome to being human."

Chapter Thirty-Six

We were a pack of two. A girl with her slingdart and a golden retriever. Against a human altered by science to be some kind of supersoldier with a maddening addiction to blood.

He was right. It was a terrible plan.

But my own instincts were flashing red. I didn't feel like we had until morning. I couldn't exactly define whatever might have set that off. In truth, it could be that waiting would have only made me more anxious, whether there had been any merit to those fears or not.

Kneeling in the cold grass, I stared into the dark foliage over the ridge. Here, the trees were thicker, the leaves making it impossible for light to penetrate from above.

Had Cal chosen this spot on purpose?

I tilted my head up. If I were some kind of animal, I felt that I could get on top and walk the canopy's length. Several hundred feet of the thickest overhang in the entire bush.

I told Kane I felt that confirmed Cal's hideaway would be there.

"Why so? It would make it colder in the day without sun," he whispered back. "And Cal Davis is unaffected by the moon like I am."

I rubbed my eyes, trying to get a better look. But it was near total black ahead of us.

"Remember when we went down to Gregor's encampment by the lake? Well, I went there, and you snuck down after me."

"I remember."

"The place was blacked out. The lights all dimmed and pointed downward. The dark tarps covering everything. They hadn't been worried about locals seeing them."

"Then who?"

"I don't know. But whoever it is," I said and pointed above the tree line, "maybe they've got eyes up there. Satellites, drones, whatever. Gregor's crew at the camp were trying to hide from whatever those eyes in the sky might be. I think Cal is doing the same."

Kane chuffed. "If Cal is hiding from sky cameras, they would belong to whoever has employed Gregor. Why would Gregor have been hiding from his own people back at lake camp?"

"I don't think he was," I said, moving into a crouch. "One of Gregor's crew, a woman named Mon, said something odd before you ripped her throat and sucked out the blood."

He shifted his feet and looked away.

"Sorry, that was a bit harsh," I said, cocking my head to the side. "Mon had asked something like 'are they watching me?' and 'are you with them?' I think there are two groups at play here." I pointed down into the dark void. "Cal's hiding from Gregor's bosses. I think Gregor had been hiding from someone else."

"Who?"

I lifted my shoulders. "How would I know? But they're both after the same thing," I said and nodded down below. "The same thing you are."

Behind us, we heard the snap of a branch and spun our heads to see. Nothing in the darkness, but again, the sound of it only emboldened me. I was done hanging out in the spooky woods.

Crouching low, I moved down the hill, followed by the padding of doggy feet. At the bottom, we crept between massive tree trunks.

Kane trailed behind me, and when I looked back at him, I noticed him looking behind us.

"You see anything?" I whispered.

"I am half your height in this form," he said, frowning. "I only see your backside."

"Count yourself lucky, then."

He growled low, then I felt Kane nudge around me. But before he could pass, I grabbed the fur at his neck and held him steady. He spun his Goldy face toward me.

"I should take lead. I do not want you in dan—"

Shaking my head, I pointed toward the forest floor.

When I'd been a kid, I'd spent those summers with two cousins who didn't want me around. Or if they did, they only wanted me for target practice. My daylight hours, for weeks and months on end, were often spent running, hiding, and getting pelted with paint balls.

All I'd had, after the first summer, was a cheap-ass slingshot to fire back. When I'd gotten better with it, they changed tack, trying to trip me up.

Literately.

I'd gotten so good by the third summer at hiding from them and getting occasional potshots in from my shitty slingshot that they started putting twine between trees.

At first, they'd been about waist height, hoping to knock me from my feet.

When they'd realized those were too easy to spot, the twine got lower. Closer to the ground. And often tied with rusted cans that would bang together when I'd hit them.

A line just like that lay about two feet from Kane's front paw. I pointed at it.

He squinted in the darkness, and when he saw it, he flinched, taking a few steps back. I crouched low, and he came up next to my shoulder. For the next minute, I explained how my cousins used to line the woods with trip wires like these.

"I don't see any cans," I said, staring at the twist of line. "Maybe it's just to trip us up?"

"Like you say, Cal Davis is military man. If that string is attached to anything, it will not be old cans."

He was right. The thought of it made my fingers go numb.

Kane chuffed. "We should wait for the daylight. There will be more string traps than this."

"We know what to look for, Kane," I whispered back, pointing ahead. "I'll keep an eye out for them."

"Those tiny ropes, each of them, could mean death. You understand this?"

"Yeah, but they also mean something else."

He turned his head toward me, and I waited. After a moment, he said, "Pretend I said 'what is this thing you know and I do not, smart Emelda?' to you so you will tell me."

"You're no fun."

"You do the same to me!"

I shushed him, half-laughing at the absurdity of it. "Okay, those trip wires mean we've really found him. Finally, we've found Cal Davis."

He turned his dog snout into the darkness and looked back at me, nodding once. Then he sniffed the air.

"I can smell chemicals. Explosives, yes. I may be able to detect them before either of us gets blown up."

When he turned back to me, I playfully scratched his ears.

"See? Positive thinking. I like this golden retriever version of you."

Chapter Thirty-Seven

It only took about ten more minutes of crawling deeper into the thick forest of trees before we found it.

Right there, plunked down deep in the Canadian forest, was a small cabin.

It had taken three more near-death experiences with the trip wires. Two I'd spotted, and the final one, half buried, Kane had sniffed out.

For a few minutes, we just watched to see if there might be movement inside. No electric, of course, and we didn't see any fire or candlelight, either. If Cal was in there, he might be sleeping.

Unless he'd heard us approach.

Kane lifted his head and sniffed the air, swiping his head left and right. He chuffed.

"Many, many scents here. Hard to tell what is new and what is old," he whispered to me. "And, interesting, I can discern which is Cal Davis."

"Human smell."

He shook his head. "There is much human smell. But also within that smell is chemical. This is what I had smelled when we encountered Bridget Mills. Back when she was naked in the cage inside the truck."

Hearing her name brought back memories of the last time I'd seen her. In a glass box, split open like a high school science experiment. I pushed the images from my mind, trying to focus on the present.

I thought about what he'd said. "You can smell the treatment? Whatever you call it. You can pick up on whatever they'd given him that altered him into, um, the super-Cal?"

Kane nodded. "This is also a scent I carry, but with me, it has been altered by my body," he said. "But yes, I can detect the scent."

"You know, they've got drug-sniffing dogs and even cancer-sniffing dogs." I eyed the dark cabin. "Me? I've got a monster-sniffing dog."

"I am not a dog. I am wolf."

I shrugged. "Not at the moment."

* * *

Kane sniffed around the door, up by the handle, to see if that had been booby-trapped as well. Reluctantly, he told me he didn't detect anything.

"This does not mean there is not something there," he said, looking back into the dark forest. "Too many scents now, a jumble of confusing odors. It would be best—"

"No, no waiting," I said and pushed open the door.

We both stood at the threshold, and the yawning dark ahead of us looked like staring into the soul of a dead man. I blinked then looked down at him.

"Yay. We didn't get blown up."

Once we got inside, I took a chance and fired up my phone, pointing its flashlight at the floor. My dirty boots rested upon dusty wooden planks that had been expertly slotted together. As I traced the beam around, I wasn't surprised to see there weren't any floor coverings.

I didn't know much about Cal, but he didn't seem the throw-rug type.

Ahead of me and to my right, I saw the starburst reflection of my phone's light. Windows. Just the two. But when I cocked my head to the left, I saw one more.

The cabin was about the size of a two-car garage. In one corner was a bed, neatly made with a pillow so flat it almost looked like a blanket folded in half. Razor-sharp creases implied either Cal had never slept on it or he was one of the most fastidious monsters you might ever meet.

"Do you think he's been here recently?" I felt a nervous shiver ripple through me. It almost felt wrong to speak aloud in someone's private space, as if reciting dirty limericks in a church.

The golden next to me padded toward the bed and sniffed at it then went to a nearby table. At first, it looked like a regular kitchen table, but there wasn't any salt-and-pepper setup. No plates or the half-empty cereal boxes you might expect in some bachelor pad.

Then I realized it. Cal didn't need any damn breakfast nook. His meals weren't the sort you served up in a plate or bowl.

At the thought of that, another shiver rippled through me.

As Kane walked the length of the room, he ran his snout up and down a three-drawer dresser. He lifted a paw and placed it on the middle one.

"It is difficult to tell when Cal might have been here, but I can pick up a familiar scent."

"The blood?"

He turned his head toward me. "Yes, that is what led us here," he said and gazed around the room. "And there has been much blood within these walls. But the scent I have picked up must be Cal's."

"Well, sure." I shined the light around the large room. "This is his place."

"Yes, and I can smell the child of my parents. Or it may even be, in part, their scent. Hard to tell. But same bloodline, yes."

Kane's eyes softened and drifted out of focus for a moment. I felt like I was intruding as I pointed the flashlight at his face, as strange emotions danced across his features, so I directed it across the rest of the room. There were no other chairs. Only a single one at the table.

Aside from the bed and the dressers, there was a basin for washing and a simple chemical toilet. Next to that, on the wall that held the door, was a long box with a padlock on it. The padlock, however, hung open. It looked like what soldiers had at the bottom of their beds. Well, at least in the movies.

I recalled the word. *Footlocker.*

That term made my stomach twist a bit. I mean, the dude was a monster. For a guy that craved blood, did he use the footlocker in a more literal way? Like a pantry?

I wasn't ready to open it and find out.

Above that, on the wall, was a wooden rack with three sets of metal hooks. In pairs.

"Gun rack." I pointed at it with my light. "Or, technically, just a rack since the guns are long gone."

Kane padded over and looked up. "Guns make noise. And Cal, of course, does not need a weapon to kill. We much search cabin to find out where he might have gone."

I pulled the chair out to sit down, flinching when it scraped across the wood floor. "It's not like we're going to dig into one of those drawers and find his journal. 'Dear Diary. I ate a little girl today—'"

Kane cocked his head, and I waited for him to shoot an angry word at me... and in truth, I was goading him a bit, sure. But instead of an admonishment, his eyes went to the open door.

"I think—"

The light of the explosion filled the room, turning my entire world white.

Chapter Thirty-Eight

The blast set trees aflame about one hundred feet from the cabin door. In the deep black night surrounding us, the fire looked supernatural. Like someone had performed an ancient ritual that had gone wrong and conjured a demon of flame and fury.

Kane ran across the room and thumped his front paws upon the door, slamming it shut. He turned toward me with wide eyes, his head bobbing left and right.

"Someone is shooting at us? Rockets!" He panted and ran in small circles.

"No, whoever it is, they've tripped one of Cal's defense wires."

I dropped to the dusty floor and crept up to the footlocker. Putting my hands atop it, I fought against the fear of putting my head in the line of fire and peeked out the small window. "They didn't see them."

Kane flicked his eyes up to the window, the reflection of flames dancing across the glass.

"You spotted them, Emelda."

"Right, well, I suppose long summers of teenage torture paid off."

At the edges of the flames, I could see the silhouettes of at least three men, moving quickly. Two were hauling another away from the chaos. The legs of the guy being dragged were on fire.

Kane whispered to me, "What do you see?"

I squinted, trying to separate the ink-black darkness from the sunburst of flame eating away at the forest floor.

Then I saw a bald man in spectacles, with a face like an angry fist, turn toward me. I ducked down.

Shit. Shit, shit, shit.

Kane frowned at me, his eyes dancing in their sockets. "What did you see? Why are you cursing so?"

"What? I didn't say that out—"

Another explosion and more cries from outside. In their confusion, the Devil's Dawn crew had tripped another wire. I crouched back to the floor, leaning back on my heels.

"That asshole Crank that you decked back at the doctor's office. He's here, and he's got friends with him."

Kane took a few steps back. "How is this? How do they find us?"

"I don't know," I said. "They must have followed us."

Shaking his doggy head, my friend wasn't buying it.

"I would have picked up their scent, I am sure of it." Then he blinked. "I am almost sure of it."

I had an idea and scrambled back across the floor, grabbing the backpack. At first, I didn't see anything inside, just Kane's clothes, some water bottles, and what was left of our food. I dug through the countless pockets. There were so many!

Inside a long, zippered pouch, I found it.

"What is that?" Kane said, his nose coming within an inch of the tiny black device. "Why do you have that?"

"I don't *have* it. It's not mine!" I growled, punching the floor. "It's a tracker. And it looks like a smaller version of the one I pulled off the old Audi back in Minnesota."

It was Kane's turn to growl. "Gregor."

I nodded. "I don't see him out there, but you know what that means, right?"

Kane sighed. "Gregor has opened an Etsy shop and is now selling bespoke GPS trackers. The depths of the man's deprav—"

"No, Kane!" I said, standing and fumbling for the latch on the window next to the bed. Once I'd lifted the pane, I chucked the device outside. "Those asshats are working for your buddy the tech sergeant."

The window shattered, spraying glass, and I spun away, covering my face. Instinctively, I dropped to the ground. Or, another way of looking at it, I fell.

Either way, I was on the floor.

Another volley of bullets peppered the side of the cabin, *thut-thut-thut*, and I heard one of the slugs plant itself in the far wall.

Scooting back across the floor on my butt and palms, I pressed my back against the cold wood of the cabin. The place had been well built, and I didn't think their bullets could slip through the walls. I wasn't an expert, but this was far from the first time I'd been shot at.

And not just by paint balls, either.

More gunfire. This time on the opposite side of the cabin. The window there spiderwebbed, and dust burst from the wall, traced in a line. The glass hadn't blown out yet, but it wouldn't last long.

"We are not in a good position," Kane said, his eyes bouncing between the two damaged windows.

"You think?"

A few more shots hit the door. They weren't shooting at anything other than the cabin itself, and I couldn't imagine they'd thought they'd get a lucky shot and hit either of us.

Kane voiced the thought that had begun forming in my head.

"They are trying to pin us down," he said and walked toward the footlocker next to the wall. Strangely, his face was as calm as a morning lake. "How many did you see?"

My head was spinning. All it would take was one of those jerks to rock up to a window, poke a rifle inside, and spray, and we'd be dead. But they hadn't yet.

"How many did you see?" Kane repeated. "You say you saw Crank, yes?"

"What?" I said and scuttled to the wall kitty-corner to where he'd sat. Bits of glass covered the floor next to the bed, and I pushed some of them away with my boot. "Guys. Bunch of guys. One of them on fire, and he didn't look like he'd be winning any hundred-yard dashes anytime soon."

Kane's eyes bore into me. Calmly, slowly, he spoke again.

"Okay. One of them is disabled. And if injured, not likely a threat. They are attacking, so may not tend to his injuries. He may bleed out."

"You wanna take him a goddamn bandage?" I whispered hoarsely at him. Despite being horrified at being shot at, I think I was getting more freaked out that the shooting, at least for now, had stopped.

"They will be assessing. Trying to determine environment and whether we are also armed. But I do not think this will last." He took a furtive glance at the open window, with its jagged glass teeth chewing at the cold night air, and padded over closer to me.

Once again, he sat. Calmly. Serenely.

"How many did you see?"

"I don't..." I tried to calm my breathing and recall what I'd seen outside. Panic muddled my thoughts, but I tried to push through it. "There's fist-face Crank. Two others were close to him and two more dragging away British Columbia's new hopscotch king."

Kane blinked. "This is a time for joking?"

"Joking is how I keep my head clear." I shrugged. "Knock, knock."

He flipped his head toward the door. "Is someone trying to get in?"

I smiled weakly. "You and me gotta work on that."

"Okay, so five people. All men?"

"I don't know. What difference does that make?"

Kane tilted his head, eyes distant. "Human men and women have different capabilities. Men are stronger, more powerful. Women are better capable of considering their surroundings before responding. More clever fighters."

"Nice generalization."

"We have to assess the danger we face then consider the assets at hand."

My mind was bouncing like the googly-eyes of some angry toddler's plush doll. "Fine, whatever. Five guys, I think."

"You think?"

I jammed an outstretched hand toward the door. "There was an explosion, a fireball, and gunfire. I wasn't taking notes."

"Calm."

Frowning, I said, "Never say 'calm' to someone freaking out. It's never worked in the history of language."

"It does for wolf."

We searched the cabin for a weapon, keeping low and out of line-of-sight of anyone who might be aiming through the windows. The one advantage we did have was that the flames outside were bright, and inside, it was dark as a tomb. Unless we were dumb enough to poke a head up, they wouldn't know where to shoot.

The search didn't take long. There was a bed, a washbasin, the toilet, and the small dresser. Sadly, the table and single chair setup wasn't hiding a machine gun. Although that would have been very handy.

We came up with nothing.

Then I remembered the footlocker.

I braced for what I might find inside, but when I opened it, I was both relieved and disappointed. I held up some glossy pamphlets that looked like travel brochures.

"If they get close enough, I could take them down with paper cuts," I said and chucked the pamphlets back into the long box, slamming it shut. "Why haven't they just burst in here?"

"They may be trying to determine if we are also armed. But that will not last."

"No shit."

We retreated to a spot next to the bed. Outside, beneath the crackling of flames and chattering of insects, I could hear the men outside pressing through the bush. Moving closer.

"What are our assets?"

I chuckled. "Bupkis. I've got my slingdart in my pack, but that won't do much against five guys with rifles."

Kane looked around the room. "Emelda, we are trapped in this space. And it is one we cannot hold, yes?"

"Duh."

"Then we must fight these men."

I swallowed hard. Once he'd said it like that, it all became far too real.

"Any way you could switch up and become that beast monster I saw back at the mall?" I rubbed my face, knowing that the wolfwere needed a full moon. *That* was not amongst our assets. "We've got a backpack full of your clothes. My slingdart and a tent. Three bottles of water and some snacks. Armed to the teeth, man."

He nodded toward the bed. "There is also blankets and a flat pillow."

"Great! If they get tired from killing us, they can lie down."

Kane put a paw on my leg, and I looked down at it. "We also have you."

"Me?"

He nodded. "You say you spent many summers running from cruel cousins who hunted you. This is no different." When I gave him a tilt of the head, he amended his statement. "Yes, these Devils have bullets. But it is same. You were trying to avoid getting shot by paint. This is avoiding similar."

I sighed and dropped my face into my hands.

"You also have a secret superpower they do not know of," he said, and I lifted my eyes to meet his.

My voice hitched. "Which is?"

Kane put his dark nose close to mine. "Emelda Thorne has won a bronze-level award for running, given to her by the US president, of course. You are very fast."

I blinked away some dampness in my eyes and laughed. "Yeah, of course. That."

"Good," he said. "Now, tell us of plan."

I slid up the wall, the splinters of the wood ticking at my leather coat. Glancing around, I tried to guess what the Devil's Dawn assholes might do. That's what had kept me safe during those summers. When I got trapped, it wasn't what I could do but what I thought my enemies might.

"They won't go for the door, I don't think."

"They do not know yet if we are armed."

"Right. Right," I said, feeling a rush of confidence. "They need to get a look inside and have a clear shot at the same time." I pointed at the spiderwebbed window across the room. "They would have to bust that one out to do that, burning precious seconds."

"And the window above the floor box?"

"Footlocker," I said, nodding toward it. "When we came in, we had to walk up a slight hill. There's a rise to that wall. If someone were standing out there, the window would be above their head."

"So?"

Both of us turned our heads toward the shattered window next to us. If any of them were to peek in, looking to get an easy shot, it would be through that one.

Kane and I looked at each other and nodded.

Outside, we heard rustling. They were closing in. I looked down at Kane, who was waiting for a plan. From me! How was I supposed to come up with something to save our lives?

He whispered, "Use your instincts."

I dropped to a crouch and scooted over to my backpack that had been in the middle of the floor and began rummaging through it.

"You know, it's creepy when you do that."

"Do what?"

Shooting a look at him, I said, "Like you're reading my mind. Is that part of... what you can do?"

The lips on his doggy mouth turned upward. "Humans put so little merit in what is not said. The true language is not what is spoken. Expressions, hesitations, a hitch of a shoulder. A furrow of brow. These belie one's true thoughts."

I shot him a look. "Can you tell what I'm thinking now?"

He raised an eyebrow, just the one, and despite being seconds away from getting shot full of holes, I smiled back.

Pulling out two more metal darts, I jammed those into my back pocket with the others. They were about as long as my forearm. At some point in the future, I'd need to make something to carry them in.

If we *had* a future beyond the next minute.

I was about to zip up the pack, but then my hands rested on the water bottles. I came up with an idea.

Not a very good one.

But it was something.

Who says you can't learn things at the movies?

Chapter Thirty-Nine

Pressing my back against the wall and trying to slow my breathing, I looked down at Kane next to my thigh. I was about to say "Are you ready?" but didn't have to.

He nodded.

Gripping the end of the blanket, I lifted my hands up to my shoulder and felt the three water bottles inside bang lightly against my back.

Then, I heard movement.

Coming close.

Feet shuffling across the dirt, trying not to make a noise.

I drew long, slow breaths. In and out. In and out. I watched the shadow of a man as it moved across the ceiling, growing larger. The guy had been too dumb to realize he was being outed by light from the fire. The thick canopy of trees above us hid away the only illumination in the sky.

Up there was the moon.

Just a chunk of rock that had fallen in love with the Earth. Always close, as if waiting to be needed. But the Earth did not need the moon.

Or maybe it did?

It affected tides, the weather, and a six-foot-seven French Canadian. Maybe that chunk of rock was more important than anyone had given it credit for?

Crack.

The sound of the snapping branch made me flinch, and I squeezed the end of the blanket tighter, readying my arms, my muscles already beginning to complain from the weight of the bottles banging against my lower back.

The ceiling shadow got a twin, this one passing along the edge of the windowpane.

I lifted my hands off my shoulder.

Breathe in, breathe out.

The tip of the rifle poked through, like the nose of a woodland creature sniffing out what might be a meal. Or an even larger animal.

Everything in me wanted to strike, bring my bottles-and-blanket club down and smash the rifle. Not yet. Not yet.

The barrel poked farther through. Then another inch more.

I knew that in the next few seconds, the man with the gun would quickly switch positions to avoid a strike, sliding to his right. I had to hit him before he did.

I held my breath and launched my hands forward, their momentum carrying the water bottles inside the blanket. I watched as my world slowed down, the dark fabric crossing over my shoulder and toward the rifle stock.

I'd overestimated.

The bottles themselves swung down about a foot on the other side of the rifle. *Shit!*

Still, I pulled the blankets, and when they struck the barrel, it hitched downward. The man gripped his weapon tighter, which created a pivot point, and the part of the blanket with the bottles inside then arched upward in its circuit and smacked the underside of the stock, smashing his fingers.

The Devil's Dawn gang member let out a yelp, releasing his fingers, and the rifle tumbled *out of his hands!* But instead of falling inside, it spun away, falling to the dirt outside.

With the man now disarmed, Kane didn't miss a beat.

He ran to the opposite side of the room, leapt up, and dove right at the spiderwebbed window. The glass shattered, and I saw shards burst into the air and a fuzzy dog ass disappear into the night.

Huh.

I nearly screamed after him for ditching me in the cabin, but at the sound of the shattering glass, the man outside grabbed his rifle and ran.

"They jumped out the other side," the thug shouted as he rounded the corner. "Over here! This side!"

Once he disappeared, I saw my chance. I gripped the slingdart in my hand, threw the backpack over my shoulder, and jumped out the open window.

Then I ran.

As I charged through the darkness, I remembered Cal's traps and lifted my feet higher but didn't stop running.

Until I heard the gunshot.

Chapter Forty

Kane

I am the night.

A creature of the darkness, I am who stalks, who hunts.

The one who will vanquish my prey without hesitation.

I turn my head to look for danger and target my prey. My keen eyes scan...

Something is blocking my vision! Have I been—?

No.

Why do I have a floppy ear covering my eye?

I shake my head to force it back into place. I do not favor this form. It is not built for speed or stealth. And so much fur. I am very furry.

When I had leapt through the open window, the glass teeth drew across my stomach, and now, there is a blood trail as I walk. The pain does not bother me. I have endured far worse.

However, if it were to continue, the blood loss would begin to fog my brain.

I run into the darkness, attempting to keep an eye out for any of Cal Davis's wires and traps. However, the one advantage, and there are very few, to being human is the ability to discern more colors and shades of light.

These canines live in a more muted world.

I snap my head toward the rushing of feet against leaves. Then they stop. The snap of a branch. However, these sounds are also somehow muted. Muddled.

Ah!

Damn these floppy ears!

What higher being would curse these creatures so? My body is too large for these poor excuses for legs. How does such an animal hunt?

Oh. They do not hunt. I expect these "goldies" as Emelda called them are cared for like infants. Coddled. Soft food from cans. Circular padded bed with plushy stuffed animals.

I grimace at the thought.

How far they have fallen from their wolf ancestors! If there is a warm death place, afterward, would they be welcomed into the wolf kingdom above? Or would a creature such as this come bounding up to the gate, tongue lolling, floppy ears, um, flopping, and the gate be slammed in their silly face?

I would expect so.

When I cross into that realm, my everlasting eternity should be spent with wolf kind. Not happy comfort dogs.

There is motion to my right, a shift in the darkness. I am shadow amongst the shadows. The moonlight does not reach here with the trees above.

But I can now see the man as he stalks forward.

Long hair, which looks greasy, its scent betraying his position. He smells oddly like flowers. But not the proper scent. More chemical, artificial. I believe he uses Pert. Bad choice, the combo shampoo and conditioner with fine hair like that. I should inform him that if he were to instead use—

What do I care about this?

Why would I consider consulting this man on hair products? Help him with his poor hygiene choices?

No!

What folly. I must focus. Push down this strange preoccupation.

He creeps forward, and even in the darkness, I can pull his features forth. A dark leather jacket that does not smell like animal. The fibers artificial. Jean pants, like I favor, but these are far too tight. How does one run in these skin-tight jeans?

So many poor choices.

And he has made another.

He has come for me.

I draw in a deep breath and prepare to strike.

What is this hesitation? Why do I feel... *sorry* for this man with greasy hair and skinny jeans? It is not my way! This strange animal form is infecting my brain. I do not like it.

I focus on my need.

I need to pounce.

I need to leap through the air, teeth bared at the man's neck.

I need to lick his face.

No!

No licking of faces!

This strange compassion will kill me. How do such creatures survive?

How can I will myself to take this prey? I have never struggled with this before. What can I do to bring out the wolf within and do what is necessary?

He steps closer, gun barrel pointed downward. His watery eyes searching, reflecting flames from the fire just to the north, where the tiny bomb blew up.

As he moves in my direction, I am still as a stone. He is curious.

I see he is also wearing a ball cap, turned backward.

Good. Good.

My reservations about killing this man instantly vanish.

Chapter Forty-One

At the sound of the man's screams, I crouched low, feeling horribly exposed.

A tree to my left and a clutch of bushes to my right. I crab-walked sideways to take cover behind the trunk.

The voice of the man, his pleas, rose briefly then snapped off like a cupboard being slammed shut.

Five were now four.

Kane was hunting them.

But just how capable would he be as a fluffy comfort dog against four men with rifles? I couldn't leave him out there alone.

I dropped my backpack down off my shoulder and looked for whatever I might have to help. Assets, Kane had called them. I almost laughed.

A collection of the big guy's clothes, my slingdart, and a few granola bars.

I grinned at the foil packages and sighed.

"Hell, maybe one of these guys has a nut allergy?"

Fine, it was all I had. I propped my slingdart under my arm, jammed the two granola bars in my coat pocket, rezipped the bag, and slung it on my back.

I heard two of the guys yelling, maybe three, but couldn't make out their words. But their intent was clear.

They were now hunting Kane.

Chapter Forty-Two

Kane

Pushing aside the bone-deep sorrow, so strange, I drink in the dying man's blood, feeding from the slash in his neck. For such a weak animal, the claws are surprisingly sharp. And teeth do as teeth will.

Deeper I pull the warm liquid into my body, and I feel the rush, the surge of strength.

The pain in my abdomen subsides then is gone. The blood does not only satisfy my hunger but quickly repairs this fluffy body. The scent of blood, both earthy and metallic, is strong.

I pick up the scent of at least two more threats. They are moving closer. I know this because I can hear one of them.

A snap of a twig. The other is also moving closer, having been drawn in by the man's screams.

They are moving from either side, encircling me.

As I draw in the last of the blood I need, I cannot help but smile.

Their plan is to surround and kill. This is the wolf's way, but they enact their plan poorly. When we attack prey, stalk it, we do this in pairs and are mindful to defend one another.

For an individual cannot properly defend against an attack during their own.

This is their folly.

And one they will pay for.

I feel the sadness within rise once again at what I must do. But then I separate it out, like two minds within one. As if it were me, the wolf, and this soft golden creature.

You cannot control me, soft dog.

Over the centuries, you have lost yourself. Forgotten your true nature and fallen to the lure of comfort and compassion.

Let me show you a better way.

Chapter Forty-Three

I stalked back toward the cabin, peeking through the brush and trying not to move into the light from the fire. Each time I did, I felt like I stepped into a spotlight. *Here I am!*

The shouts of the men had grown more panicked. Angry. Crank's voice was discernible. Or, at least, I could tell which was his simply because he'd been the one barking out orders.

For a moment, I just listened.

There had been six Devils from what I'd seen. One burned by the fire. Then another, moments earlier, taken out by Kane.

Listening closely, I could only pick out the voices of three men. Where was the fourth?

Using the trees as cover, I moved from one to the next, heading in the direction of where the man's scream had erupted then stopped.

The voices of Crank's crew grew louder as they closed in on Kane.

But he wasn't the snarling hell beast this time. Not even the Rottweiler, which would at least give him a chance against four armed men.

He was a happy, fluffy dog. And gold in color, so when the light of the flames hit him, the damn dog would glow like some woodland fairy!

I heard a snap.

Shit!

The fourth guy was coming around behind me!

I had to get moving.

Advancing, I stayed clear of the light from the fire. When I finally got to the side of the cabin, I flattened myself against the wall, sucking in deep breaths. Behind me, a rustle of leaves made me go stiff.

Or was it just my nerves?

Could it be the wind?

"No, don't say it's the wind," I muttered to myself. "If you say it's the wind, then it's always something horrible instead."

Peeking around the corner, I saw the fire, which was, thankfully, not spreading but still too bright for me to cross in the open. I'd need to use the trees again.

And I knew what I was getting into. This wasn't any game in the Minnesota backwoods with my cousins. Sure, that hadn't felt much like a game at the time, either. But back then, the biggest threat was welts and bruises.

And getting caught. *Especially* getting caught. Hell, I had been fine with the welts. Getting captured hurt the most. That failure. I would have taken a hundred painful welts just to avoid that. Not so much to win, just not to *lose*. Not to them.

By that second summer, that had been at the core of my being. I wouldn't let them win, no matter the cost. Of course, the stakes were so much higher now.

Didn't matter. Same game. Just with, you know, bullets.

I cinched the bag on my back a little tighter then pulled one of the steel arrows from my back pocket. Loading it into the notch of my slingdart, I drew in a deep breath to put similar steel into my spine.

I took a step forward but flinched back when another man's scream erupted, echoing around me. And as quick as it split the darkness, like the thrush of frightened birds bursting from cover, everything fell silent once again.

And then there were three.

At least, I *thought* there were three.

Voices rose, more insistent this time. I heard running, yelling, then a gunshot. And another.

Fighting against everything in me that screamed *run away*, I instead ran forward. More gunshots.

I briefly crossed into the firelight then burst into the darkness of trees.

"Over here!" a voice called out ahead of me. "Jesus, it's Bart! Holy... He's gone, man. He's gone!"

"Shut up and find them!" Crank yelled back. They sounded like they were at opposite sides of the woods. The first man's voice coming from about my nine o'clock and Crank's from somewhere around two. Or maybe two-fifteen.

Clearly, I needed a better system.

Either way, they were separated. And I knew Kane would be stalking one of the men. Would he go for the lacky or Crank himself?

Then I thought about how wolves hunt. How all animals hunt, and I had my answer. Predators always seek the weakest prey first.

Trying to keep my footfalls soft, I hooked to my left, heading toward the man who'd been calling out. Again, I heard a crackling behind me.

Dammit, I forgot about the third guy.

He had to be behind me somewhere. Had I moved, and he'd lost the shot? Or was it just my nerves firing and fraying, sending panic into my brain?

Didn't matter.

Just needed to keep running forward, quietly as possible.

After a minute of stalking through the bush, my entire body covered in sweat, I heard a low voice. It was Crank's man, the lacky, speaking softly.

I moved forward, listening.

The man asked, "How'd you get way out here?"

Was he comforting one of his fallen crewmembers? No, Kane wouldn't have left any of them alive. Watching my steps, I put my feet only in patches of clear dirt so I wouldn't be heard.

I came over a slight ridge and saw who he was talking to. The long-haired man had his rifle swiping left and right, eyes cutting into the darkness.

He asked, "You live around here?"

There was no answer.

But he wouldn't have expected one. Because he was talking to a golden retriever.

Chapter Forty-Four

Kane

The now-dead man had not heard me before I'd attacked.

And he would not have.

For I am the hunter. I am a stalker in the night.

And he?

He looked like the bass player for a progressive rock band. One of those bands that Père used to favor. He would play their albums on his large cabinet record player and tell me stories of their exploits—many of them fairytales, I knew this, but I do not dislike fairytales.

Père would prop the album cover atop the smoky glass covering of the turntable, sit back, and recount how a singer might meet a guitar player. School friends, often. Then success, fame, fortune would taint and tarnish the love these men once had for each other.

Or maybe it had been the inclusion of a bass player?

Drummers, according to Père, had a "mildly tormented" nature. This was why they had chosen the only musical discipline that offered weapons—two wooden clubs to beat upon their instrument. But they had good souls, said he. The tonal and metaphorical beating heart of a band.

I did not entirely understand the analogy, but it was one that pleased Père.

Bass players, however, were often troublesome, as he explained. I did not follow his logic but often wondered if it had something to do with having been pilfered of two strings from their instruments, left with a meager four.

After I had killed the man who looked like a rock band bass player, something I felt Père would have approved of, I drank from the tear in his neck. Lost in this bliss, the hunger so long denied, I didn't hear this other approach.

Stupid!

So stupid.

"You live around here?" the new man says in a low whisper as his eyes cut right then left. My only saving grace is that he did not see me standing over the bass player, suckling at the man's neck. Had that happened, I would already be dead.

The light from the fire is blocked by a hill, so I am mostly shadow. But he can see my fluffy golden fur. I must accept that it is this silly appearance that has, for now, saved my life.

He steps closer, and I pretend to cower in the dark.

"It's all right," he says. "I ain't gonna hurt ya."

His disposition will change the moment he gets a good look at my face, for I have bass player blood smeared across my mouth. I must fight to not lick the intoxicating remnants from my lips.

There is a *snick!* sound just a few meters to the southeast. There, leaves spit from the ground. This draws my new foe's attention.

He mumbles, "What the hell is...?"

Another *snick!*, slightly closer, which kicks up more leaves and dead branches.

He turns to me.

"Where is your master, boy?"

I fight against the growl rising in my throat. Master? I am my own master! I have no master, and I answer to no one but myself.

When he turns to his left, I catch the look on his face, his fear reflected in the dim light. What a poor soul. The terror in his eyes. I can see him contemplate the years of poor decisions that led to this very moment. How can I slake such fear in this sad man? The pain in his eyes...

No!

I am not here to comfort my enemy!

So troublesome, this canine form. I believe the bald TV doctor that Mère used to watch in the afternoons, the one with the hillbilly voice, he would call this "co-dependent." Then he would say something folksy and bring his wife out to peddle her supplements.

Focus!

I must focus!

Another spit sound from the forest floor. He turns toward it, and it is close. Only a stride away from his right leg. Then he sees what I see.

A steel arrow sticking out of the dirt.

Chapter Forty-Five

I groaned as my third arrow, *third!*, missed its mark like the previous two.

The man was staring down Kane, the barrel of his rifle slicing through the air, back and forth, back and forth. Threatening a dog!

Who threatens a dog?

Sure, the golden retriever was no golden retriever, but this man didn't know that. I reached behind me to grab the last arrow in my pocket, but when my arm went around my back, I felt fingers grip my wrist.

When I spun around, I saw that face. The scrunched, angry expression of the leader of Devil's Dawn.

"Why don't you drop whatever that contraption is," he said, rotting teeth fouling his breath and making my head swim. "You're no damn good with it anyhow."

He lifted an eyebrow, wrinkling his entire forehead. He'd shifted the fogged-up spectacles down to the tip of his nose to look me over.

His grip tightened harder, and it felt like the tiny bones in my arm would snap. I couldn't help but cry out, but I pursed my lips, not willing to give him the satisfaction. He squeezed harder, and I let go of the arrow in my pocket and tossed the slingdart to the ground.

"Chris!" he called out, his eyes never leaving mine. "That you out there?"

"Yeah. You find them?"

He yanked on my arm and pushed me toward the trunk of a tree. I smacked into it, bashing my head, which sent stars up into my brain.

"Found the girl." Crank grinned at me with gray teeth. "You find the big guy?"

I heard rustling to my right, feet shuffling.

"No," the man said as he came out from the bush, "but found their dog. Didn't see it before when I went into their truck."

Crank frowned, pointed at me—a silent warning—and then stared at his man.

The long-haired guy loped up the hill, clearly exhausted. He looked like he wanted to be anywhere but here.

"What dog?" Crank asked.

Kane came up behind the long-haired guy, big soft eyes, head bowed slightly. I was impressed. He was playing the role. When I looked at him, I tried to work out what he was thinking. The wolf would be considering our options, plotting.

He would have a plan.

Chapter Forty-Six

Kane

I have no plan.

Seeing the look on Emelda's face, I know that she is waiting for a sign from me. But she and I would struggle to take these men.

Slowly moving my head from one of our enemies to the other, I assess. Both wear heavy leathers, which reek of oil and petrol. Motorcycle people, I guess. These leathers protect their arms, legs, and body.

Like the two before, the only chance I will have is to take the neck.

But attacking one would leave me vulnerable to the other.

This is what I must do. If for nothing else but to protect Emelda. We are a pack of two. And wolves protect their pack, even at the highest cost.

"What the hell is this?" the man called Crank says as he steps closer. He reaches to his belt and brings up a small cylinder. I brace. Should I make my move now?

Emelda believes this man was hired by Gregor. And I remember the long pole that the tech sergeant had. The one that shot electricity through my body, the terrible pain.

Is the device in this bald man's hand such a weapon?

When he thumbs its side, I take a step away from the beam it casts.

But it is only light.

I have no fear of light.

However, he shines it toward my face, and I hear him gasp.

Yes.

Yes. I should have feared the light, for it has given away my true nature.

"Christ almighty," Crank says, a growl in his voice. "Look at the damn dog's face. It's covered in blood!"

Chapter Forty-Seven

"It's covered in blood!" Crank said, whipping around his rifle and pointing it at Kane.

The man who'd been standing next to him, Chris, shrank back, stepping away, but in the next second, the golden retriever was upon him. Kane leapt up, teeth bared, and I could only watch as—

The crack of the rifle was so loud, I thought I'd been shot.

I turned to see Crank, weapon at his shoulder, already working the bolt to push another bullet into place. I jumped forward to tackle him, and he pivoted, pointing the gun at me.

"Don't!" he shouted, spittle flying from his mouth. "Don't you move from that tree!"

I thought I was brave. I had faced aggression so many times before. But this? Gazing down the gun barrel, down the deep blackness in that small circle, knowing that—with just a twitch of his finger—that dark void would be filled for a fraction of a second and then I would be dead? This was different.

I only stared.

Never had I seen a more horrifying darkness. Just a little circle. And I froze on the spot.

"Back!" Crank shouted, popping the barrel higher in the air. "Back to the tree, or I muss up your stupid purple hair."

Twisting my hands into fists, I held my ground. If I could hold his attention, it would give Kane time—

"Darlin', if I pull this trigger, you'll never even hear the shot," he said, grinning his gap-toothed smile. "You'll be dead before the sound even reaches those pretty ears."

"Emelda," a husky voice said, wheezing from the ground. "Do not."

Crank turned his head, but when I flinched, he raised it again, motioning to the tree. I stepped back and gripped it, pressing my back against the cold, prickly bark.

Helpless, I watched the horrific scene unfold. And I knew how it would end. It didn't matter what we did. We could never leave these woods.

"Did that goddamn dog just..." Crank said, stalking toward Kane, who was struggling to his feet, the blood on his mouth darker than the blood seeping from his flank. The bald guy looked up at his partner. "Did *you* say her name?"

"No, man," Chris said, moaning in pain. "I think it... it was him."

"Him?"

"The dog, man!" he said. "The dog spoke."

Kane stood on wobbly feet, his head hitching, his eyes glassy. "Let the girl go."

Both men tensed and backed away a half step. Then I saw the rifle on the ground.

When the guy named Chris had put his hands up to block Kane's attack—an attack that ended with a bullet in Kane's belly—he dropped his rifle onto the forest floor. He'd not picked it up yet, stunned now by an impossible sight.

A talking dog.

Once they got their wits back, we were done. Hell, we were *dead*.

"I will comply if you let the girl go," Kane said then bared his bloodied teeth. He growled low then coughed.

"What the hell is this, man?" Chris said. "This... this ain't right. What'd you get me into?" He pointed at Kane, who was struggling to keep on his feet. "This ain't natural. Not one bit!"

I could grab the final arrow in my back pocket, maybe, but what would I do with it? Hell, I could throw it—I'd have a better chance of actually hitting someone. But then what?

Even if I did hit Crank with a killing blow—and that would never happen—the other would grab his rifle, and we'd both be dead.

I needed the rifle on the ground.

But how?

When I began reaching around for the arrow, Crank spun to me, pointing his weapon right at my head once again.

"Don't you even try," he said. "Put those tiny hands in your coat. If I see those pink fingers again, I'll shoot them off. Then I'll shoot the dog." Crank looked down at Kane. "Happy to do it too. Jesus, what kind of abomination is this horrifying thing? I'll be putting it out of its misery."

I hesitated, and he took a half step toward me.

Scowling, I jammed my hands into my jacket. The fingers of my right hand rested up against something hard and angular. And crinkly.

Then, I had a stupid thought.

But years earlier, I'd read something that had always stuck with me. Once you've exhausted all the good ideas, all you've got left are the bad ones.

My fingers wrapped around the object in my pocket, and in one quick motion, I threw it toward the dog. It sparkled in the beam of the flashlight.

"Kane!" I shouted as it flew through the air. "Get down! Grenade!"

The silvery packaging of the flying granola bar sparkled in the light, and before it hit the ground, Crank and his man bolted away, running for the trees.

That was my chance!

I bent down and grabbed the rifle, hefting it to my shoulder. The two men dove behind bushes before I could get a shot off.

I fired after them but missed.

A muzzle flash erupted from the bushes, but in the split second before it did, I saw Kane move, lightning fast. He winced as a second slug thudded into his body. Kane had stepped between me and the shot.

Holding his ground, he turned toward the men and howled.

"No!" I shouted, and with my vision blurring, I slid behind the tree and pulled the bolt back to take another shot.

Another crack of the rifle and the dog fell.

"Kane!"

I spun back around the tree and saw Crank standing there. He'd been waiting for me. I shot first, but he didn't even flinch. When my shot whizzed past him, way off, I only saw his gray smile grow larger. He aimed down the sights, lining up the killing blow.

As fast as I could, I ducked back and shifted another bullet into the slot. When I looked back, Crank was gone.

That's when I heard it.

A snarling. Then a strange guttural utterance, throaty, phlegmy.

When I saw Crank again, he was struggling with... something. Using the rifle as a shield, he held the gun between him and his attacker. His feet were moving unevenly as he strode backward, pushed by some odd creature, and the weapon flew from his hands.

Somehow, Kane had transformed but into something different.

More human, but not human.

Long claws came out and slashed at Crank's arm, slicing the leather to ribbons, and exposing flesh beneath it. Before the Devil's Dawn leader could even cry out, another swipe of the claws—the creature moved so fast!—and it bit into the side of the man's neck.

I watched as the long-haired man named Chris popped up from behind the bushes. He grabbed Crank's gun, and its barrel bobbed as he readied to fire.

Crack!

My shoulder ached from the kickback, but I ignored it and watched the side of the man's head cave, blood pouring out as he collapsed.

He was dead before he hit the ground.

That realization hovered over me like an arm cocked back ready to punch, hanging in the air. I had killed someone. My bullet had taken a life. For now, I pushed that thought aside.

When I turned to where the creature and Crank had gone, I saw both stumble into the darkness. Two muzzle flashes lit up the night sky, then there was a scream. A cry of pain then nothing.

In the unnatural quiet, I looked down and saw something that didn't make any sense. The golden retriever lying on the ground.

He looked dead.

"Kane. Kane!" I shouted.

He cracked his one eye open as he lay on his side. "You should get a rifle. You have terrible aim with the shooting dart."

"Slingdart," I said, swallowing a sobbing breath. "How bad are you hurt?"

"Oh," he said and took a deep breath, blood and air bubbling from his side. "A lot."

I heard a shuffling from the forest and raised the rifle. Wiping my eyes, I watched as a massive, strange-looking naked human stumbled from the woods.

Kane hadn't transformed. It had been someone else. Or rather, something else.

"Stay back," I shouted, aiming the rifle at him. But he did not walk in our direction. Not yet.

The creature limped toward the bushes where the guy named Chris had fallen after I'd shot him. I kept my rifle trained on the naked man as best I could. Down my sights, which bobbed all over the place, I saw the crew cut.

The misshapen mouth, elongated jaw.

The long, muscular limbs which made him unnaturally tall.

And then the sleeve tattoo. A snake winding around, its mouth in the palm of the man's hand.

I cried out, my voice shaky, "Don't move!"

Paying me no attention, he bent behind the bushes and then stepped through the brush as he dragged the dead guy. Leaving a bloody trail behind him, he walked toward us. I shook the rifle.

"I mean it, I'll—"

He lifted a dirty long arm, pointing at the golden retriever lying on the ground, breathing heavily, blood oozing from two angry wounds in his chest.

"Is that really Kane?"

Without any idea what I should say, I only nodded.

The Enhanced man grinned and then coughed. Once he was close enough, he threw the dead body next to Kane like he'd just tossed a sack lunch.

"Little brother," he said. "You need his blood or you will die."

Kane lifted his head, eyes out of focus, then they landed on the large, naked man, who stood there as blood dribbled down his chest.

The golden retriever crawled forward toward the dead man, sniffed for a moment, then nodded at the man-creature watching him.

"Thank you, Cal Davis."

Then Kane began to feed.

Chapter Forty-Eight

I stared, transfixed, as this sweet fluffy dog suckled the blood from the dead Devil's Dawn thug. In any other scenario, it would have looked like this man had come home from a long day of work and his beloved golden was nuzzling his neck, happy his master was home.

That, of course, was not the reality of the stomach-churning tableau before me.

Conflicted, I was horrified by this gory reminder that I would never fully understand the person who, for now, was the closest thing I had to a friend.

But I was also feeling pretty good about myself for using the word "tableau." A first for me. Made me feel smart and stuff.

The dead man's expression looked defeated, as if every pull at his lifeless body, every suckle of blood, drew his eyes deeper into his skull. His neck propped up by a rock, it exposed the throat, leaving his final gaze to rest upon me.

I flinched when the large, naked man collapsed and leaned against a nearby tree.

As I sat there, adrenaline from the fight bubbling out of my cells and evaporating off my skin like cold sweat, I listened to Cal Davis wheeze and struggle for air, his shallow breaths rhythmically timed with Kane's suckling of blood.

Just past my feet, a dead guy lay staring up at me with an expression like, "Can you *believe* this day? Crazy, huh?"

Hunched over him, drinking the fluid that used to be his, was a wolf turned man turned dog who only wanted to return to the first.

To my right, some kind of superhuman. Hell, I didn't know what Cal was. Just that this villain had saved our lives.

He sat naked, dirty, and dying.

Forcing myself to turn away from Kane, I looked at him fully for the first time.

Cal looked like just a kid, about mid-twenties like me. At least his body did. Distortions aside, his face told another story. An old man who'd seen too much.

When he'd been standing, he'd been a seven-foot-tall supersoldier.

A killing machine.

Lying against the tree, his chin resting on his chest, which bobbed unevenly with his ragged breaths, he looked like some college kid who was regretting the kegger the night before. As if he were lying in bed, trying to convince himself to get up, get ready, and head to some class.

But he was no college kid. Not that I would know. No one in my family had been the "college type." Not that we weren't smart. We just didn't have the "college type" of money to go to college.

Cal's arms were as long as my legs. Muscular but not like a body builder. Although, when he lifted his hand to wipe blood from his mouth, his bicep bulged to the size of a kids' soccer ball. His fingers were long and thick, capped with sharp nails.

No, not nails. Claws. They were claws.

His head was slightly misshapen in a few places but nothing a jaunty chapeau couldn't cover.

I had seen similar distortion in two others before. Bridget Mills and Charlie Boynton. But they had looked far stranger than he. Like facsimiles of an original. Or a kid's rendering of Cal if the child had too much clay to work with.

His thighs were built similar to his arms—muscular but sleek. Unnaturally long. The feet larger, also terminating with dark claws but shorter than on his hands. These were for gripping as he ran—or climbed—where the finger claws had more murderous purposes.

I pointed to the one part of his body that seemed slightly more normal in my world.

"Nice tat," I said. "You get that after a bender?"

Cal blinked slowly, then a smile crept to his lips, exposing a few teeth that curled into sharp points. It should have scared the shit out of me, but he had just saved us. Still, I was on guard.

I didn't know the man. And, really, he was no longer a man at all.

"The other guys in my squad. Before the program," he said, struggling to get his mouth around the words. "Four of us, we all got one. I should have stayed with them. Sometimes, I wonder what happened to those guys."

He'd given me an opening.

"What happened to *you*?"

Cal drew in a damp breath and exhaled. He looked into the deep, thick woods, as if he wanted to get up and disappear within that darkness. Then he flicked his black eyes toward me. All black in a pool of white.

"When they first approached me," he said with a gravelly, baritone voice that sounded strange coming from someone so young, "I never expected..."

His voice trailed off as he stared down at his body.

"Really?" I smiled at him. "You never thought you'd become a superhuman?"

His face slackened, and his eyes drifted away from me.

"This? I am a monster." He lifted his hands in front of his dark eyes, arms trembling. "You know, I have never even seen this face? I avoided it, but now... I never will."

My heart hurt for the kid. I lifted myself up, slowly and grunting, and put a knee in the dirt. Pulling my grandmother's locket from beneath my shirt, I asked him, "Do you want to?"

Cal stared at the sparkling necklace my fingers for a moment then looked away.

"I only wanted to be the best. To do my best." The deep voice had become a hoarse whisper. "To be useful."

Kane stopped his slurping, and I turned. He'd lifted his head, looking at Cal. "These are the words of Père, yes?"

Slowly, Cal nodded and smiled. When he looked at Kane, his eyes softened.

"'Be useful,' he would say," Cal said. "And I was. When they said I could be *better*? Why would I not?"

Stuffing the necklace beneath my shirt again, I looked between the two of them. After a long silence, Kane went back to his feeding. The sound of it was beginning to really turn my stomach, so I turned back to Cal and repeated my question.

"What happened to you?"

Cal told me that he had been singled out from his unit. He'd always performed well in training and tests and had thought to be deployed overseas. His similarly tattooed friends went to South Korea, to some US military base there.

After that, they would go to whatever war or prewar the US was fighting at that moment.

"Instead, I went to another facility," he said, his eyes glazing and focusing intermittently. "There must have been a hundred of us there. We all bunked together but were forbidden to talk about our pasts. Or what we might have learned of the program."

"Wait," I said, sitting on my heels. "So you just went where they told you? No questions asked?"

Cal chuckled, which rolled into a brief coughing fit. When he spoke again, his lips were speckled with blood. "You've never been in the military. You don't ask a lot of questions. It's.... frowned upon."

"Okay."

"That one hundred then became a few dozen." He closed his eyes, resting his head on the tree. "That few dozen became six. Men and women." He opened his eyes and looked at me. "That was the part that stood out the most at the time. No one was the same. Different skin tones, sure, but not just that. It was like a mini-United Nations."

I shivered and zipped my jacket tighter, waiting for him to continue. After a few shuddering breaths, he did.

"Chinese, Indian, Polynesian... I mean, we ran the gamut."

"So you were the token white guy?" I said with a half grin.

He shook his head. "Half, I suppose. My mother is part First Nations."

"Do you think that's why they chose you?"

Cal shrugged and winced at the pain the slight gesture elicited. "Maybe. I did overhear them, during one of my endurance tests, talking about other 'indicators,' they called it. Something in my blood or genetic makeup, I don't know."

"You were guinea pigs. An experiment."

"Right." He frowned. "The physical stuff ended, at least for a while, and then it got weird. Lots of intravenous drugs. Other drugs, tablets. Hell, we even smoked some stuff." He laughed and fell into another coughing fit.

"I don't think you're okay," I said and realized some of what I'd thought was mud streaming around his chest wasn't. It was all blood. "You're really bleeding, Cal."

"It's okay. I'm okay with it."

I shrugged. "Well, you're the superhuman, so you know best."

Cal told me the tests got more and more strange. In between treatments, there were also sensory deprivation tank sessions that would go on for hours. Then some light therapy, where a unit was strapped to his eyes like some VR video game.

"You couldn't even close your eyes," he said, his voice wavering. "If you did, you'd get this shock. They could tell. So you had to stare right into this crazy light. And sound. It made your head spin. We all got sick on ourselves, but they said that was 'within parameters.' I don't think any of them knew what they were doing, just taking shots in the dark."

"Jesus."

"Except one." He gave me a small smile. "Dr. Pental. It was her research."

"*Her?*" I said and glanced toward Kane, but he was busy with his, uh, meal. Looking away, I told Cal we'd heard the name from Dr. Fineman, but he'd assumed Pental was a man.

"Yeah, I let him believe that. The less he knew, the safer he'd be," he said, and his eyes fell closed. "Me and Dr. Pental became friends. Sort of. When the changes started, it just felt like body aches, headaches at first. But it got so much worse. We'd all been bunking in the same area, and some would wake up screaming in the night. Convulsing in pain."

"Did you?"

Cal shook his head. "No. It hurt, but I didn't have it like they did. After a few days, they separated us. I never saw any of them again. Until I did. Just the one."

"Gregor," Kane said.

He'd finished his feed and now sat, paws in front of him. The wounds that had riddled his body had healed. Dark streaks of blood had begun to dry. His eyes were clear and focused.

Cal looked at him, nodding.

He said, "Gregor was the only other one to come out the other side of the program."

"What does that mean?" I asked.

"The others were executed," he said flatly. "Dr. Pental said they were moving us through the program too fast. She'd designed it to progress over years. Generations even. They were doing this in months. It was too much for some, and they didn't make it."

I frowned. "Didn't you worry what the program was doing to *you*?"

Cal shook his head.

"I could see some changes in my body, sure, but never the whole picture because they'd taken out all the mirrors," he said and flicked his eyes toward me. "Didn't even try to paint over the places they did that. In the bathroom, where I'd seen my face staring back at me for weeks, where the mirror had been had become a big blank square."

His coughing worsened, and he doubled over. He spat out a clot of blood, which splattered like red paint across a rock.

Kane shifted his paws, looking between me and the coughing man.

"You should feed," he said, his words quick and curt. "You have been injured."

Lying back again, Cal steadied his breathing. Then a calm, content look passed over his face.

"I'm tired," he said, closing his eyes. "When I first joined up, I had dreams of having my big Arnie moment."

"Arnie moment?" Kane said, tilting the head of his loving golden form.

"Ha, you know? Like Arnold Schwarzenegger in the movies? Just before I kill some bad guy, I'd drop a cheeseball line and save the world by putting him down. But I'm tired of running. Tired of being chased." He cracked his eyes open and looked at Kane. "I hated you for a long time, Kane. Did you know that?"

The dog stared down and scooted his hindquarters back a few inches.

"Hated?" Kane said. "But what could I have done—?"

"No," Cal said, shaking his head slowly. "I think they loved you. My parents. You know they asked me to leave? Their own son."

Kane's eyes searched the forest floor. "I did not want that."

Cal lifted a hand, blood dripping from his claws, and waved it languidly in the air. "I get that now. My baby brother—the sweet boy you're named after—he died. You know that, right?"

"Yes," Kane said, still not meeting the other's eyes.

"It felt like a betrayal. At least, at first," he said. "But you became... whatever you are... because of me. Because I could not control myself. I think they felt, in some way, responsible. So they tried to protect you."

Kane finally looked up and met the man's gaze. "I believe they perished protecting me."

Cal shook his head. "It was these assholes," he said, tweaking his head toward the dead man on the ground. "Gregor had them watching the house. So I kept away. And went searching for Faria."

I wrinkled my nose. "Faria?"

"Dr. Pental," Cal said with a small smile.

I asked, "Why were you searching for her?"

"Gregor is luckier than I am," he said, fighting back another cough. "He is Enhanced, but it didn't work the same on him as me. He has to keep getting treatments or the effect fades."

"Yours doesn't, then?"

He shook his head. "I was their crowning achievement. I grew taller, stronger, and faster. As long as I feed. If Gregor stopped the treatments, he could be normal again. I'm not so lucky."

Finally, I understood. "You want Dr. Pental to fix you."

Cal turned his head toward me. "I can't live like this. Like some animal. Some monster. They dangle the treatments in front of Gregor as a reward so he'll bring me back. Make more like me. But I wouldn't wish this on anyone. It destroys the soul and leaves rot in its place. You do things you never would have before because of the crushing... *hunger*."

I nodded. "For blood."

"Yes. Faria said there are certain elements, proteins maybe, in blood that sustain"—he motioned down to his battered body—"this. But that had surprised even her. Faria had called it an 'unexpected side effect.' Can you believe that?"

When Cal had said her name again, despite what her work had done to him, I heard a warmth in the tone. "Faria, huh?"

He smiled. "We became close. A friend," he said. "And I wanted my friend to find a way to reverse this. End this torture."

Kane took a step forward. "I want the same! To return to my pack."

Cal reached out and put a hand on the dog's shoulder, gripping the fur. "She helped me escape. We escaped together, and she took all the research with her. Only her assistant, Doc Hammer, knew how any of it worked."

I had heard the name before. When Gregor had held me in a bar in Minnesota, he'd mentioned the name to one of his crew.

"Couldn't Hammer just replicate the program, then?" I asked him.

"Not without Faria's notes, no," he said, and his eyes fluttered. "If anyone knows how to fix this"—he turned to Kane—"fix what I did to *you*, it's Faria Pental."

"Where is she?" I asked.

The man-turned-monster sighed. "I don't know, and I'm tired of searching."

I groaned. "No, Cal. You can't—"

"I nearly *killed* you, Emelda," Cal said, his eyes going moist as he stared at me. "Just back there by the cabin. I had to fight myself to keep from ripping your throat out and taking what I needed. I'm losing who I am every day. I don't know who I might be tomorrow."

Reaching down, I grabbed my grandmother's locket again, exposing the tiny mirror. I held it up to Cal, and he stared, transfixed.

"You're Cal Davis," I said, my voice shaky. "You will always be Cal Davis. And when we find Dr. Pental—"

"No," he said, turning away.

Kane growled. "Yes! I must find her! We have come too far. Malls and farms and car shows, we have searched for you! And now you give up?"

"Wait," I said, stuffing the locket back into my shirt once more. "What was all that insanity at those car shows. Did you attack those people for their blood?"

"No. Not at first," he said and once again was racked with coughing. "I'd almost tracked her down. Faria loved machines—both human and mechanical. She talked a *lot* about cars, so I went to car shows looking for her."

Kane shuffled forward, but I spoke first. "So you *did* find her!"

He shook his head. "No, but I found a woman who carried her scent. I was sure she knew where Faria was, but when she wouldn't tell me. I lost control."

My stomach dropped. I whispered the name. "Bridget Mills."

Cal's ashen face reddened slightly. "I stopped myself from killing her. But in the end, I'd made it so much worse."

"You infected her," I said. "And she became a monster."

"If she'd only told me where Faria was! It would have turned out... better." Tears began to streak the blood on Cal's face. "Dr. Pental told me that the therapy, these changes, were carried by a modified virus. Like a delivery system. When I bit that woman, Bridget, I passed that virus on to her."

"But she was so much more, um, distorted than you," I said, wincing at the memory. "More jumbled."

Cal nodded. "It's enough. Not the actual therapy, but I don't think that matters to whoever Gregor is working for. If they could get one of those things alive, they could make an army."

"They nearly did," I said, remembering the fight at the bar. "They had Bridget Mills caged up, but things got a bit hairy. I think Gregor's crew killed her so she didn't kill them."

"Really?" That drew a coughing laugh from Cal. "That would have royally pissed *someone* off at the Org. Wow, they came too close. I can't let them get it. At least not from me."

I whispered, "What does that mean?"

The man turned his head toward me and smiled weakly. "I don't know how you got mixed up in this, but thank you for helping my little brother. You're very kind."

"Not always, but I'm trying it out," I said, my voice shaky. "The results have been, you know, mixed."

Cal nodded, fighting back a cough. "I like your hair. That's my favorite color."

I wiped away my tears and smiled back at Cal Davis as warmly, as kindly as I could. This would be the last smile he'd ever see.

"They want what's inside me. I won't let them have that," he said and then nodded to the flickering flames behind us. "I'm bleeding out. Once I do, I want you to put me in the fire. End my part in this."

Kane looked down at his paws then to me. I opened my mouth to speak, but he shook his head.

"If this is your wish, we will help," he said. "And you will see your parents once again."

Cal blinked his damp eyes. "Our parents, Kane."

"Yes."

Nodding toward the dog before him, he said, "Don't waste the blood. Take what you can and put my body in the fire. Then go and find Faria. Only she has the answers you need."

Chapter Forty-Nine

I stood at the cabin door and turned back to the hill I'd just come over. Just beyond that, the children of John and Linda Davis shared their first and last real moment together.

One day, I wanted kids myself. I'd long ago been stripped of my rose-tinted glasses about that sort of thing, because I *myself* had not been the easiest child to raise. Of course, that hadn't totally been on me.

Only in hindsight—because these sorts of revelations only come in hindsight—did I realize how hard it must have been for my own parents.

My father had been just a corn-fed white boy from Alabama. My mother, a first-generation American who'd worked to slough off the memories that had brought her parents to the US. It had inspired her to marry Dad, and when she did, I expect that had been a gut punch that had finally killed her mother.

After that, my grumpy old boozehound of a granddad lived at our house until he'd joined his wife. Funnily enough, I actually missed him when he went.

My father had been raised by his mother, a woman who I loved more than anyone else in the world.

Families on television always looked so laughably perfect.

Mom, dad, kids, maybe a weird aunt who favored big hats, and a low-boil racist great-uncle who, really, had a heart of gold beneath the wispy gray hairs of his sunken chest.

The reality was that families were boxes of busted toys. Bits broken and chipped away. Most of that damage likely inflicted by one another.

I suppose we're all just seeking other broken toys but ones that have the pieces we're missing. In that way, when we come together, we're all whole again.

Maybe it works, maybe it doesn't. But it's what we've got.

So what remained of the family of John and Linda Davis?

A headstrong and big-hearted boy who'd become half man, half monster. An adopted son, named after a dead child, who'd been a wolf and now various iterations of dog and human.

As a family, they were a total mess.

But in their own bizarre way, a family none the less.

Soon, Kane would be alone again. The second time he'd lost a family in twelve months.

"I gotta get outta my head," I muttered and went inside the cabin.

After sitting in the chair for a moment, I tried to find something to occupy my mind. Then I remembered the footlocker.

Crossing the room, I opened the long box and grabbed up the glossy brochures I'd seen earlier.

I sifted through at least a dozen pamphlets for car shows. Tucked in one of them were folded, crinkled printouts smudged with long fingerprints. When I opened them up, I saw they were lists of bookings at hotels and motels. In at least a half dozen cases, lodgings matched the dates of car shows across the Midwest.

Wisconsin. South Dakota. Iowa. Minnesota.

Not just Minnesota. *Pine Valley*, Minnesota. The town Bridget Mills, the woman-turned-monster, had terrified. I recognized the name of the motel instantly. It had been where Kane and I had stayed.

"Ah, hell," I said, sighing. "Of course."

After my conversation with Miss Florida about the mystery woman who'd befriended Bridget Mills, I had my suspicions. Now, I had the confirmation in front of me.

The anchor piece Florida had spoken about? It was Dr. Faria Pental.

The hairs on the back of my neck stood, and I spun around. At the door, the sad eyes of a golden retriever. He'd have looked very sweet had it not been for the stain of red across his muzzle.

"Cal Davis is gone," Kane said, his voice hoarse.

I nodded then waved him over. "Take a look."

He padded over and sat next to me as I showed him the stuff I'd pulled from the dresser.

"He'd been trying to track Dr. Pental down for months. Even got his hands on where she'd booked rooms in all these cities."

"How would he have this? Is private, yes?"

Shrugging, I said, "Nothing's private anymore. But maybe he had help." I shook one of the printouts. "But that's not the important bit. Take a look at where she stayed."

I held the wrinkled paper out, but Kane just stared at me.

Ah, right.

"He'd missed her in a bunch of spots and crossed those off," I said. "He finally caught up with her in Pine Valley. Where she booked a few nights at the motor lodge."

He shifted from foot to foot, his snout going to the paper. "This is where you and I stayed, no?"

"It is where we stayed, yes. Olivia's place." I leaned over for my backpack and stuffed the pamphlets and printouts inside. "Maybe Faria left an address. Not likely, but if she *called* someone, there'd be a record of that, right?"

Kane shook his head. "Olivia said to you that phones did not work."

"Wow," I said. "Good memory. You're right, she did. But this was a year ago, right? Maybe they worked back then?"

"We should call Olivia, then, yes?"

I frowned. "No way. This 'Organization' that Gregor works for, we don't know what they're plugged into, what access to public records they might have. If he's US military—"

"My brother did not think this was necessarily so. Only part of the story."

My heart tweaked slightly hearing him call Cal his brother, but I didn't draw attention to it. "If he's not with the military, what's with the 'tech sergeant' then?"

Kane shrugged. "Maybe he uses title to assert dominance over his people."

"That's bizarrely insightful."

"I understand human mind. It is not so hard."

I laughed. "Is that what you learned from the redneck TV shrink?"

He twitched and eyed his paws. "Maybe some. Many afternoons Mère would watch. Much can be learned."

"Either way," I said. "If he's still got any connections—or the Organization does—making a call to Olivia would be a terrible idea. Gregor had cameras in the homes of my mom and grandmother! It wouldn't take much to put a tap on a phone or two."

Kane looked out the window at the fire, its flames flickering in his amber eyes.

"You want to go back to Pine Valley, Minnesota."

"I think it's the best plan."

He nodded slowly then eyed the far wall. "Before he died, Cal told me he has an animal buried on the side of a hill. Carved out, covered in tarp and leaves."

"Animal?"

"From what I know of the creature, they are slow. But better than walking."

"What is it?"

"He says mule is hidden, about a half kilometer from this location. To the north east."

"He buried a mu—" I stopped halfway through my sentence and laughed. "No, a mule is not an animal."

"It is," Kane said, scowling at me. "I see this on one of Mère's nature shows. An unholy mating between horse and donkey. An unfortunate pairing, but who am I to say that those from different species cannot love one another." His eyes got big and he added, "Please ignore last part of that statement. My mind has been softened by this creature I am in."

I put my hand on his furry shoulder. "A mule is a four-wheeler. An ATV."

"Like motorcycle?"

"Right, but with twice the wheels," I said and chuckled. "You couldn't bury a real mule and expect it would be there when you returned."

He tilted his head. "It would if you buried deep enough."

I jammed all our stuff into the backpack. "Let's get that mule running, so we can go find Dr. Fineman. I need him to make a call." I nodded to the open door. "If Cal's right about the Devil's Dawn working for Gregor, he might show up here anytime. I don't want to be within a thousand miles of this place if he does."

Kane hopped onto the bed, turning his sad eyes toward me.

"I need your help, please," he said. "In this form, I cannot do it alone."

"Anything."

"We need to put Cal's body in the tree fire, which is dwindling now. However, it will still suit our needs," he said walking to the door. "These are his final wishes, and I will honor them."

For as grossed out as the idea made me, I still only sighed and tightened the straps on my pack as I stood.

"Okay."

"I am sorry you have to do this."

"It's fine," I said as we walked out of the cabin. "Honestly, dragging a dead monster across the ground to dump it in a fire in the middle of the Canadian hinterlands won't be the weirdest thing I've done all week."

Chapter Fifty

Each second Canadian Border Services Officer Ian Flemming stared at the video feed, he sipped his coffee a little slower. He winced and held the cup up, calling to his partner in the kitchenette.

"How old were these grounds?"

Jack ambled to the threshold of the small room, blinking at the array of monitors, his eyes still squeaky from a long night of staring at the wash of video noise. He took a big, slurping sip from his own steaming cup of brew.

"Just made a new pot. Columbian. Man, those guys are good at coffee."

Ian went to take a final draw from his cup, thought better of it, and put the shit coffee down. He couldn't break himself away from the strange image on his screen. "Yeah, they're known for their stimulants."

Jack stepped forward and sat in a roller chair, spinning as he sipped. Then he noticed what Ian was looking at.

"Is that a *dog?*"

The other man shrugged. "Mmm."

"He's far out, ain't he?" Jack said, setting the coffee down. "There's no properties on the Canadian side for miles and miles."

"Mmmm."

Ian flipped a toggle on the old control board and spun a small black knob. The speakers above them were silent. He twisted the knob far enough to where they began to hiss.

"Maybe some truck was driving by and—"

"*BARK!*"

Ian and Jack froze then looked at each other. Jack grabbed his coffee a bit too quickly. A blurp of black liquid splashed on his blue uniform.

The junior partner looked at his senior. "Did that dog just *say* bark?"

* * *

Jack and Ian, windbreakers zipped up to their necks, pointed their Maglites forward as they walked the southern edge of the slash. The golden retriever sat, panting, staring off into the forest. It hadn't even looked toward them yet.

"He must be lost," Jack said, stepping in the exact footsteps his partner was taking.

Ian flashed the light up toward the animal. It didn't react. For a moment, he considered turning around and grabbing his mace.

He didn't and said, "How'd you know it's a he?"

Jack laughed. "You can't tell the difference yet?"

"I know the difference, goddamn it. But not this far away."

Jack pointed his light at the dog now too. "Saw on the night camera. Definitely male."

"I'll take your word for it."

"I don't know how he even gets around. Ol' boy must be sitting on beach balls."

Ian spun around and shined the light in his partner's face. "Can you be serious?"

As they crept forward, Ian pulled out his radio and paused, thinking better of it. "Shit, who do we call on this?"

"Animal control?"

"You think." He pointed the light in his partner's face again.

Jack lifted his hands, chuckling. "Ow, man!"

The dog looked like it was sniffing the air and let out a queer howl. They stopped moving, frozen in place.

"That's a golden, yeah?" Ian swept his light's beam over the nearby woods.

"They're sweet dogs. My cousin's got one for her kid. Good for therapy."

Ian rolled his eyes. "That damn therapy dog sounds like a goddamn wolf."

"It's not a wolf."

"I know that."

"It's a golden retriever."

"I *see* that," Ian said, gritting his teeth. "It just doesn't sound like a golden retriever."

Jack sighed. "Probably because he's hauling around those monster balls."

Ian spun around, ready to fire off another admonishment, but he thought he'd heard a thud and rustling on the American side, in the bushes.

As he lifted his light to investigate, something glinted straight ahead. Something metallic.

He snapped his gaze toward the slash, took a half step back, put a hand on his holster, and pointed the light over his partner's shoulder.

"Stop!" he shouted.

The young woman in the leather jacket holding a ragged piece of rope stopped and, with the light in her face, held her hands up. Around her neck hung a tiny pendant, reflecting prisms of rainbow light.

"Sorry!"

"Come here, please, ma'am," Ian said as his partner sidled around him. Each had a hand on his hip. "And I would appreciate it if you kept your hands where I could see them."

The purple-haired girl stepped gingerly over rock and twig, crossing into the slash. Ian thought she might have come from the American side but couldn't be sure. As she'd walked closer, he'd wondered if he'd violated some international law by calling her over.

He didn't need any trouble from the US authorities. "They're chill," he'd said many times to Jack and the partner before him, "until they're not chill."

When the young woman got about twenty feet away, he instructed her to stop again. And keep her hands up.

"Are you Canadian?"

The woman widened her big brown eyes and gave him a small smile. "Are you going to shoot if I am?"

Jack laughed. Ian did not.

"Please answer the question, ma'am."

She took a half step forward, her playful expression turning to dread.

"I'm looking for my dog." She pointed to the American side. "We're parked up the road, and I let him out to go pee. Then he ran after a squirrel or something. I've been searching for hours."

"Is it the golden with the giant *cojones*?" Jack said, throwing a thumb over his shoulder.

She tilted her head at him, the tiny smile back. "*Si los tienes, haz alarde de ellos.*"

Ian took a half step forward, running the beam up and down the woman's body. Clearing his throat, he asked, "Did you cross over to the other side, the border, to look?"

"I... uh..." The woman looked around. "I don't know. I saw the clearing..."

"There are warning signs all over," Ian said, sighing. Thoughts of official forms danced through his head, leaving tiny imaginary paper cuts in their wake. "You didn't notice?"

Tears began to well in the woman's eyes. "I was just looking for Bobo. I didn't... I didn't..." She began to sob.

The two border guards heard a crunching behind them and turned. The golden retriever sat on its haunches, just a few feet away. It panted happily.

"Is that dog... smiling?" Jack said, his voice bending around the words. "That dog looks like it's smiling."

"Oh! You found Bobo!" the woman called out. "His name is Bobo."

"Yeah, I picked up on that," Ian said and elbowed his partner. He made a show of looking at Jack's flashlight then nodded to the purple-haired woman. The junior officer took the hint and shone his light at the girl, which sparkled in her damp eyes.

"I can't believe you found him. Thank you! Thank you, thank you!"

Jack laughed. "I think he found us."

"Come here, Bobo," the woman said, dropping to one knee. "Come, boy."

Ian and Jack turned to look at the dog.

"Weird," Jack said. "He don't look like he's smiling anymore."

"What a strange dog. If I didn't know any better, I'd say he looks kinda pissed," Ian said. "That dog safe?"

"Totally!" She smiled wide. "Come on, Bobo! Come here! I've got those marshmallows you like back at the car."

The dog sounded like it groaned then slowly padded toward the girl. When it came close, she wrapped her arms around it and beamed.

"Listen," Ian said, eyes cast down. "If you crossed the border onto our side, we've got to take down your details."

"Aw, really?" She frowned. "I'm just a girl looking for her Bobo."

The dog chuffed, turning away from her. Ian and Jack looked at each other.

"Sorry," Ian said. "Just how it is."

Ian pulled out a brick-style device, slipping a stylus from its side. He asked the woman for her ID, and she dug it out of her pocket.

"Minnesota?" The senior border guard scanned the license. "Long drive to take your dog for a leak, Emelda Thorne."

Emelda nodded slowly, scratching at the dog's neck. "Sometimes, you just gotta get out of the house, you know?" She turned and looked deep into the woods of eastern Idaho and fell quiet.

"You're..." Ian cleared his throat. "Over a thousand miles from home, miss. I mean—"

"Maybe next time, it'll be two thousand," she said, her voice firm but her lip trembling. "And then maybe I won't go back."

The young woman nuzzled the neck of the golden retriever, which, oddly, shifted away from her a step.

"You okay, ma'am?" Jack said, softly. "You need us to, you know, call somebody or something?"

Emelda patted the dog a few times, hard enough to make the animal's head bob. Then she stood and wiped her eyes with her tiny hand.

"No, I'm fine. Just working out my world, sir." She appeared to force a smile to her lips.

Ian busied himself by typing her details into his handset. Jack looked between the woman and the dog and was overcome with the urge to cheer her up.

He chuckled warmly. "Good thing he didn't go too far in those woods on our side."

The woman looked up at him with a wan smile. "Oh?"

"Yeah, there's a big grizzly in there. He'd probably eat ol' Bobo here."

"Well," the girl said, rubbing the golden's head a bit too briskly, "if he runs away again, that bear can have him."

Chapter Fifty-One

The helicopter pilot looked over at the odd-looking man who was running his large palms along either side of his short-cropped silver hair. All during the two-hour trip, he'd wondered—but didn't wonder out loud because he like breathing—if the guy had treated the hair to get it that color. The tech sergeant didn't look old enough to have gray hair.

As the pilot reached up to power down the rotors, he watched his boss unstrap the headset and reach for the door. Then Gregor looked back at him.

"We've only got a half-hour window here," he said. "If you see anything, key the radio and let me know."

The other man had heard the stories and swallowed. "See anything like what?"

Gregor smiled, but his eyes were hard. Maybe because they were devoid of color. All pupil in a pool of white. "Just let me know if you see anything out of the ordinary."

As the tech sergeant stepped out, the pilot called over, "There's a spare coat in back if you want." He then nodded to the other five crew members, already heading toward the thin ribbon of smoke peeling out of a line of thick trees. "The temp will probably drop ten degrees once you're out of the sun."

The tech sergeant frowned at him.

Like I need a coat.

"Half an hour," Gregor said, standing at the open door. "Make sure the box is ready. Just in case."

The pilot looked back and nodded slowly, staring at the steel-and-glass cage. He hadn't been informed what it was for and knew he wouldn't be. The Organization only told its people what it had to and nothing more.

All he had known was they'd supposedly had permission to cross the Canadian border with a max of six hours, top speed there and back. Despite that *alleged* permission, he'd been instructed to fly so low, he was sure treetops had scratched up the bottom of his helicopter's landing skid.

Now the idea that some *thing* might be back there on the return journey?

He didn't want to know any more.

* * *

"Hammer," Gregor called out, taking long strides to catch up to the woman. "Doc, we didn't get a chance to talk in the helicopter. I just want to say, I appreciate you—"

"Are you sure this is the location?" She thumbed her sunglasses higher up on her nose to cover her eyes from the early morning sun. "There's *nothing* out here, Gregor. I don't have time for walking around the bush for an hour."

He smiled with teeth slightly too large for his mouth. Not overly so. Not like the creatures she'd worked on back in Minnesota. Still, the guy looked off, but she needed him. Soon, she wouldn't. However, to get there, she had to finish the research Dr. Pental had begun.

The research she stole! That had been my work too!

"The tracker's ping is still coming from that smoke up ahead. Just above the tree line," Gregor said. "And the last we heard from the crew here yesterday was that they were approaching Cal Davis's cabin."

"Crew?" Dr. Hammer scoffed, trudging over hard-packed grass and rock. "You hired *gangbangers*. Meth heads and morons."

The tech sergeant's smile grew wider, giving her a slight shiver. He said, "Devil's Dawn did find Davis's hidey-hole."

"But not Davis."

"No," Gregor said and blew out a long breath. "Just that big bastard and his little helper."

"And yet there are no signs of them?" Doc Hammer stopped, turned to look up at the man, and caught his expression. "Well?"

He grimaced. "There are reports of a plane, a seaplane, taking off from the Douglas Channel in the middle of the night. Unscheduled."

"So?"

"We don't have the same access to data up here, but it seems the flight plan indicated the plane was supposed to head west." Gregor looked off into the distance. "Our intel says it went south, then they fell off the radar."

Hammer laughed darkly. "Your *intel* is that some local yahoo took a seaplane out for a joyride?" With long, thin fingers, she brushed back a strand of black hair that had escaped the tight bun at the back of her head. "Why is it that this Kane person seems to be one step ahead of you? In every report I read, you're following in his wake."

"It's unclear... why he's searching for Cal."

"Give me a break," Hammer said, barking out a laugh. Then she stared hard into his ink-black eyes. "He's with them, obviously!"

Gregor looked at his feet for a moment then slowly shook his head. "I don't think he's with Covenant."

Hammer stepped closer and lifted her sunglasses to the top of her head. She examined his face. He gritted his teeth, feeling like he'd been laid out on one of her slides. Despite being more than a foot taller than her, he felt as if she were looming over him. Cold. Calculating.

"Forgive me if I don't trust your keen instincts on people," she said, dropping the glasses back down again, her eyes unreadable behind the dark lenses. "You had one of them on your own team for *weeks* and never realized it."

"There'd never been any signs Mon was a part of Covenant," Gregor said, regretting his words. "She'd been loyal and—"

Hammer started walking toward the ribbon of smoke again, laughing darkly.

"Yes, yes! Loyal, just not to you. Despite all the warnings that we had a mole, you let Monique Luper feed your movements, our precious data, back to her Covenant bosses." She turned as Gregor strode up next to her. Hammer jammed a finger at his face. "Right under your nose. I think the Org has too much faith in you. I don't give a whit about your *enhancements*. And keeping you on that treatment is costing us a fortune. I'm not seeing the returns on that investment."

This was not a conversation Gregor wanted to have. The therapy kept him strong and fast—stronger and faster than he'd ever been. More so than anyone he'd ever known.

Well, all but one.

"With all the stuff Covenant appears to know," he said, changing the subject, "I'm not sure Mon was the only one feeding information back to them."

"So you think Kane is with them? That's why he's been hunting Davis?"

Gregor lifted an eyebrow. "Maybe. Although his partner, Emelda Thorne, *did* kill Mon, so I'm not sure if that—"

"Monique's throat was ripped out! You think some little girl did that?"

Gregor shrugged. "Hers were the only fingerprints we found in the camp, and she'd left them everywhere. Had to be her."

Another dark laugh. "Bullshit. She's not enhanced, that much is clear. But the blood under Monique Luper's nails *was* from an Enhanced. Like you."

"Not like me."

"No, you're right about that," Doc Hammer said and spoke slowly. "It was much better. Much, much better."

They stepped into the thick trees, and like the pilot had warned him, the temperature dropped. Gregor shivered but not from the cold.

Chapter Fifty-Two

When they'd arrived at the scene, they'd found the charred remains of Calvin Davis's cabin. Someone had burned it to the ground.

Gregor's pulse throbbed harder, making his ears ring.

The Organization, for all its vast resources—world-spanning resources—had hamstrung him at every turn. He'd gone through their program, excelled where others failed and died. Sure, Cal had been their greatest success, but he had been good too. And unlike Davis, he'd been loyal!

When Gregor had signed on to be an elite soldier, one of the Enhanced, the last things in the world he ever thought he'd have to worry about were budgets!

But he knew the Org had far bigger plans. His role with the Enhanced program was just one part of that. So, cost restraints.

He'd had to get creative. Hiring mercenary teams here and there to work where he could not get a proper team.

Could not afford a proper team!

He'd needed morally ambiguous men and women. Devil's Dawn had fit the bill. Now they lay around him in clumps of flesh in the British Columbian forest.

"No great loss," he muttered to himself as he watched two of his black-clad crew push through the smoldering embers of the cabin with their rifle barrels, searching.

One crewmember, her green armband designating her as lead, strode through the underbrush as if she were walking through some suburban mall.

"We've counted maybe five dead," she said, a slight sheen of sweat making her dark skin glisten. "Hard to tell because not all their body parts are, uh, connected."

Gregor sighed. "Drained?"

"Seems like it, yes."

"No sign of Davis, then?"

She tilted her head, motioning to a secondary smoldering pile. "Actually, we think we've found him in there. What's left of him, but our records show he'd had an arm tattoo, which that body does. It's burnt up to hell, and they'll use DNA to confirm. But yeah, it's Calvin Davis."

Gregor's mouth hung open. He shook his head, trying to get his thoughts straight, his mind a jumble. He knew why that was.

I need another treatment. I can feel my muscles ache. That's doing my head in. But Hammer will want results before I can get it.

"Let me understand what you're telling me," he said, pulling his lips back in a wicked grin. "That Cal Davis killed these men, drained their blood, and threw himself on the fire?"

The woman grimaced. "I didn't say that at all. Just that we've got Davis's remains over there. And dead bodies all around us."

"Ma'am!" The excited voice split the cool morning air. From behind a hedgerow, a head popped up. "Ma'am, over here!"

"What is it?"

"I think this one's alive."

Gregor and the lead woman ran over to where the crew member was standing. He pointed, obviously not interested in stepping any closer.

The tech sergeant had hired the local outfit of thugs after a short meeting a year earlier. But he recognized the man with the squished features and dark-framed glasses. He'd been the only bald member of Devil's Dawn.

The man was wheezing, his eyes dancing in their sockets, the tongue in his mouth darting in and out as if he were trying to drink the air.

Gregor knelt down. "Crank, isn't it?"

The Devil's Dawn leader nodded as he stared bug-eyed at the blood that had coagulated on his chest. He was torn up to hell.

"You don't look well, Cranky," Gregor said. "No. Not at all."

"Need... hospital," the man said and coughed up blood.

"In time." Gregor leaned closer. His expression changed when he saw the man's eyes. Wide pupils, no color, in a pool of white. "Oh, my. My, my! You were bitten?"

Crank groaned. "Pain."

"More of that to come, I expect."

"Hospital."

Gregor chuckled. "I have a much better plan." He pressed his finger into the blood on the other's chest and examined it. Then he licked it clean, eliciting a groan from the woman standing behind him. "But first, I want you to tell me what happened here. I want you to tell me everything."

Chapter Fifty-Three

Pulling up to the Pine Valley motor lodge, I got a grin so big my face felt like it had split in half. I elbowed Kane awake, but without even looking, he swatted at my hand and pressed his face deeper into his balled-up jean jacket.

"We're here," I said, the jeep bouncing over the curb. And the tiny thud his head made against the glass? Rewarding. "Wow. Hopefully, she's got room for us."

When we'd gotten back into Kitimat after leaving Cal's place—or what was left of it—we went to the house behind the old doctor's office. He'd initially been hesitant to call his fishing buddy when I'd ask him to. However, he'd relented when the golden retriever next to me made the same request and he heard Kane's voice come out of it.

Inside, Fineman went to his fridge, pulled out a Tupperware bowl, and gave it a two-minute ride in his microwave. When it came out, I got a steaming bowl of stew that tasted better than anything I'd eaten in years. Didn't even care I couldn't identify the meat.

So good!

He looked down at Kane, lifting an eyebrow, and got an "I'm good" from the dog.

"I don't want to know," he said and left the room to make his call.

Within half an hour, we were standing on a dark pier next to an ancient white-and-yellow seaplane. I couldn't help but get a crooked grin when I saw Fineman's pilot-friend was a woman in her sixties named Christine.

"Fishing buddy, huh?" I said to him as she fired the plane up.

Fineman shrugged. "Mostly fishing."

Christine didn't even blink when I'd come aboard with a dog in tow. I don't know what story Fineman told her, but she'd accepted that this was literally a below-the-radar run and didn't ask me a single question during the five-hour flight to Kootenay Lake.

A truck driver heading to the US had been kind enough to let us tag along, dropping off me and my doggy just before the border. He even let me have one of the sandwiches from his Coleman's cooler.

I decided I liked Canadians a lot.

After our brief run-in with the border guys, it had taken two days of driving to get back to the tiny Minnesota town, but seeing it again felt like returning to my childhood. Not just time elapsed but from innocence to awakening.

I now saw the world so differently from the first time we'd visited Olivia's motel. Part of me wished I had some of that naiveté back. But only a small part.

Back then—only a week ago, really—we had our pick of the rooms.

As I drove the jeep under the overhang, I had to slip between two cars. One sedan belonged to a family, all bustling out of the front doors, eyes scanning around like they were about to head out to Disneyland.

"Why so many white people are here?" Kane said, hunching lower in his seat.

I laughed. "Like you?"

"There is no other like me."

"True that."

We watched as the family wrenched open their doors, all four near simultaneously, fired up and ready to head out for the big day.

In Pine Valley.

"Huh," I said as I hopped out of the jeep.

As the big doors automatically split in front of us, enthusiastically welcoming us inside, a kid in an ice cream-stained T-shirt bounded out and smacked into Kane. He fell back onto his butt, staring up at the big man. For a second, the look on my friend's face? I didn't know if he was considering whether to help the kid up or what sort of garnish might go best with human toddler.

Thankfully, he went with the former, dropping to a knee and extending a hand.

The kid looked wild-eyed at Kane's arm. With his sleeves rolled up, his muscles twisted like rope beneath his forearm.

"You're big," the kid said.

"And you are small," Kane said, a warm smile bending his bearded face. "But one day, you will be big."

"As big as you?"

"Not likely, for I was born wolf," he said as he helped the kid to his feet. "You were born a tiny, pink, helpless thing, and had I seen you in the forest, I may have eaten you."

The boy stared at him for a moment, and I held my breath. The kid then got a big grin on his face.

"Cool!"

"Yes," Kane said, walking past and patting the kid's head. "I am cool."

The mother rushing toward us, calling the boy's name, threw a cursory smile at Kane and then, when she got a better look at him, slowed her pace.

"Thank you," she said, tucking a stray lock of hair behind her ear. "Sorry about that. He's a handful."

"Is okay." When he tried to walk around her, she put a hand on his arm. Then looked down at the muscles beneath her fingers and drew in a tiny breath.

She looked up into his amber eyes and asked, "You're staying here?"

"Yes," I said, grabbing his other arm. "We are."

We walked toward the reception desk, the top of a head bobbing at the counter level as the person there looked to be organizing something below.

I squeezed Kane's arm. Yeah, sure, it was a nice arm. "Don't encourage the locals."

"I do not seek to encourage. I cannot help when others find me desirable."

"*Puh*-leeze."

At the sound of my voice, the head snapped up, and the woman behind the counter beamed at us. Without a word, she rounded the counter and embraced me.

"You're back!" she said into my hair.

"Just a quick stop in."

She then let go of me and looked at Kane, spreading her arms. He stared down at her upturned palms and slapped each with his own hands, earning a quirky smile from Olivia.

"He's still weird," she said. "Beautiful but weird."

Waving us up to the counter, she hustled behind and then leaned forward, crossing her arms.

"I've got *so* much to tell you," she said, unable to dim her smile.

And I never wanted her to. The last time we'd seen her, she'd been a bright, wonderful woman, but a year of chaos had darkened her. Now, it was like all of that had been a bad dream which she'd finally awoken from.

I glanced to my left and saw teenagers—both looked like high schoolers—cleaning the once-dormant buffet area.

"Those are Val's kids," she said and cocked an eyebrow at me. "You remember her—she runs the garage. They're the ones who towed away your Audi?"

"Right. We never met. I don't—"

"Well, her kids, they have no interest in getting into the family business. It's very greasy, and you come home smelling like a NASCAR season-ticket holder, but they needed a few extra bucks for summer, so she let me borrow them."

"I see that."

"The girl is pretty good, but her brother? I've got to smack the phone out of his hand every few minutes. He's getting a bit of a following on TikTok or whatever the latest *me-me-me* app is today."

"Right," I said, smiling. "So, you're a bit busier."

Olivia laughed. "Girl, two weeks ago, if a hobo came up and whizzed on my doorstep, it would have been busier than the previous six months! Now…" She drew her hand around as if showing off her prize rose garden.

"What happened?"

She took a step back and did the finger guns at us. "You guys happened!"

Kane frowned. "I am still happening."

"Yes, you are," Olivia said, the smile obviously permanent now. "Actually, I guess I shouldn't feel too bad about Hunter—that's the boy over there—and some of the others in town posting their stories. Word got around fast."

Then it clicked. "Ah, right. No more monster?"

"More than that, hon, *more* than that," she said and leaned on the counter again. "Pine Valley is now a tourist destination."

"It wasn't before?" I said, giving her a sly grin.

"Well, we don't got the world's largest ball of twine or nothing," she said and put a hand to the side of her mouth. "That's Darwin, Minnesota."

"Of course."

"But we are now the monster capital of Minnesota," she said, screwing her face up in a playful way. "Who thought that would be a thing?"

"It is?"

"Uh-huh. In fact, when Stu Clarrat got wind of all the hubbub, he walked right out of the hospital, ass hanging out of his gown and everything," Olivia said and giggled. "Had his stuff under one arm, dressed in the taxi. Got on the first plane back from the Cities."

I thought for a moment then recalled the name. Clarrat had owned the farm where pug-dog Kane and I had fought Bridget Mills in the milk shed. Stu had gotten hurt by Bridget but, thankfully, not bitten from what I'd heard.

I wondered about that for a moment. Maybe Bridget had been clear in the head enough, knowing how she'd turned her boyfriend, Charlie, and made sure she hadn't done the same to Stu? Maybe.

I decided that's how it had gone. It made Bridget a little less of a monster. At least in my eyes.

Olivia explained that within a few days of our monster eradication, people started arriving in town. Showing up at one storied location then crossing the street and searching there too. As if they were looking for bloodstains and errant claws left behind.

Of course, these were just *rumors* of monsters. But rumors turned places like Loch Ness and Transylvania into tourist meccas.

The maintenance crew who'd been trapped in the mall all got interviewed by WCCO, the CBS affiliate out of the Twin Cities. The man who'd been injured got a bedside interview at the Pine Valley Night Clinic. Olivia typed on her computer as she told us all about it then spun the screen so we could see.

The thumbnail on the online article showed the man pointing at injuries. Three gashes down his calf, freshly stitched up. I laughed when I saw, just over his shoulder, the intense look of the health-care worker on duty.

Nurse Taylor stood there, fist on chin, as if he were posing for *Esquire Magazine*. He must have been loving the attention. And now, finally, had what he'd always wanted. Stories of his own that people wanted to hear.

"The day Stu Clarrat got back, he had a dozen people standing at his property line taking pictures," Olivia said, her voice lowering as a couple came through the door, looking around, wide-eyed. "Since then, he's been taking people in groups. His wife, Joanne, she even had to put up a board with *tour times*."

This thought sent Olivia into a fit of laughter. I drank in the joy of it.

"How much is he charging?"

"Originally five. Now seven a head, but you get a discount if you've got a group of ten or more," she said, tapping on her computer again. "He shows them the field where the 'creature' came through, where he's set up this board and a big, blowed-up photo from one of his security cameras. I've heard it's pretty grainy as *monster* photos go, but that just adds to the mystique, right?"

"Of course," I said, letting her glee wash over me.

"Then the tour moves on to the burned-out barn. The tire marks where it got hauled away. And, finally, the grave where Stu had to bury his dog, an innocent victim of the Pine Valley Monster."

I winced. "Dog?"

"Stu didn't *have* no dog. It just kinda looks like there's one in the big blurry CCTV photo," Olivia said, stage-whispering again. "Still, ol' Stu got him a big mound of dirt and a picture of some pooch he downloaded off the internet. Says 'Beau' across the top, but he never had no dog named Beau."

Olivia giggled to herself as she pressed a white card into a black box. It hummed for a moment, and then she handed the card to me.

"You're staying here, by the way," she said. "Miss Florida said you might be coming, so I saved you the best room. Right around the corner."

I went to reach into my backpack, and she placed her fingers on the top of my hand.

"Don't even bother with any of that," she said warmly. "You will find, anywhere you go here, your money won't work. Just point out what you want, and it's yours."

That thought warmed me far more than it should have. Then a cold bolt shot down the middle of it.

"They're not telling people about, you know, us, are they? Because—"

Olivia held up a hand. "People know to keep a lid on it," she said. "The best they can."

"The best they can?"

"Don't worry about it," she said and let out a breath. All business. "So what brought you back?"

* * *

Ten minutes later, we were in the room. Olivia had said she had to attend to guests but, being nearly at capacity, that she'd have to start turning people away.

Then she could dig around for what I'd asked for.

I'd pulled out the paperwork we'd gotten from Cal's cabin prior to burning it down. A final request from Kane's brother. Everything the Davis family once owned had now been turned to ash.

When I'd showed Olivia the dates of Dr. Pental's stay at the motel, she'd nodded and put the heel of her palm to her head. Of course she'd remembered the woman.

"Indian, I think," she'd said. "Or Pakistani. One of those places. She didn't check in under *that* name, but it's gotta be the same woman if those are the dates."

When I'd asked about Pental's phone records, she'd told me the same as the first time we'd come. The phones in the rooms had stopped working shortly after some guy had come to fix the lines. After that, the monster troubles had scared people away. Money got tight, and she hadn't had them fixed. Now the place was hopping again, she'd booked someone to come out, but they wouldn't arrive until the following week.

Dr. Faria Pental had paid cash, so no handy credit card numbers to dig into. Not that I had any idea how to do that.

I'd asked if the scientist happened to leave behind anything in the room. Given what went down at the car show, she would have left in a big hurry.

"No, and if she had left a suitcase or something, I probably would have just chucked it out," Olivia had said, tapping away at her computer. When she brought up the date of Dr. Pental's booking, she spun the screen toward me. I didn't recognize the false name she'd checked in under.

Kane did.

"Priyanka Chopra is big star," he said, smiling. "Mère liked her movies very much."

I pointed to the line below, my finger hitting the screen hard enough to make it tilt. "What about that address she gave you? Do you think that's where she lives?"

Olivia copied and pasted the address on Taylor Street in Springfield, Massachusetts, into a search bar and hit enter.

I frowned.

Some place called the Stacy Building. Mr. Google explained this was where the very first American-built, gasoline-powered car had been built.

Miss Chopra—or, rather, Dr. Pental—sure loved her cars.

But another dead end.

"I remember her checking out now, because it was a big rush. I hadn't heard about all the hubbub down at the car show yet, of course. She told me home was a long way away and she didn't like to drive at night. It was afternoon then, so I asked how far she had to go, and she held up her hand with all her tiny fingers poking out—five hours. I remember that clearly because her fingers were *shaking*."

I'd asked Olivia if she had any other ideas. Anything that might help. She got a strange look on her face, staring down at her fingertips.

"I-I'll look. I can check some other records and stuff."

After that, she'd handed me the key to the room, pointed out where we were staying on the paper map, and said she'd come by in a few minutes with whatever she might have.

Inside the room, I threw my backpack on the bed farthest from the door and dropped into the single chair. I leaned forward onto a small circular table and put my head down.

"I'm tired. I've never driven so much in my life."

"Is your job," Kane said, scanning the room. "You are driver."

"I should get a raise," I said, talking to the chipped wood of the table. "I think my job duties expanded since our initial arrangement."

Kane pulled the passport wallet out of his jean jacket and dropped it on the dresser. I'd been happy no one had stolen it from the jeep. I'd stuffed the money that had been inside into my pocket, but if anyone had broken in and robbed us, getting him a new ID would have been a nightmare.

Yeah, I suppose I was brave enough to battle monsters, tweaked-out homicidal gangbangers, and Enhanced supersoldiers, but the idea of having to deal with the DMV terrified me.

Kane pulled off his jacket and threw it on the other bed. His T-shirt came off next.

I laughed. "You're going to just do a strip show right here in front of me."

"It has been some time since my last bathing," he said, unbuckling his belt. "My scent could give me away to enemies."

"Yeah, it hasn't been doing too much for your friends either," I said. Then I grinned at him, squinting my eyes. "Friend."

When he unsnapped his jeans, I turned away.

Not that Kane was awful to look at—far from it. I just didn't need those complications in my life. The last guy I'd been with had temporarily cured me of any thirst for romantic entanglements. But, at the time, I'd felt I needed a strong guy like Roy in my life.

He'd been confident, charming, and a career felon.

My favorite qualities in a man, it seemed. Or, at least, the guys I felt myself drawn to. I supposed him getting thrown in prison was the only reason I wasn't incarcerated at that moment. Or dead.

Roy had gotten in a bit deep with his criminal underworld buddies. He'd paid the price, and I got free of him. He had spared me from an extended stay in the Graybar Hotel after I lost it on some assholes and done the sort of damage someone's got to answer for.

That had been Roy.

Even so, he'd gotten me into all sorts of shady shit, and I didn't owe my ex anything. Not sure if Roy felt the same way, but that part of my life was over now.

Still averting my eyes as Kane undressed, I glanced up at the picture above the bed near the window. Flowers in a vase. How sweet. Then, I noticed the reflection on the glass. A six-foot-seven naked French Canadian. I felt a bit skeezy sneaking a glance, but hell, Kane didn't care about nudity at all.

I tracked the ghostly image of Reflected Kane as he strode into the bathroom, wondering how he kept in perfect shape but never worked out. Whatever that virus-therapy was, hell, they could sell it and make a mint.

I got up and looked down at the pile of clothes on the floor and sighed. Kane was a wolf who became a dude, and with that came dude tendencies. Guys just drop their clothes where they stand and, *boop*, the memory of them deletes out of their minds.

They were piled like he'd suddenly vanished and his clothes dropped right to the floor.

Something about that thought drove a panging sensation into my chest, so I stood and scooped up his stuff and chucked it onto the bed near the window, next to his jacket.

I jumped at the knock on the door then shot a quick glance at the bathroom. From behind the door, I could hear the hiss of the shower.

Opening the door, I saw Olivia standing there with a sheet of paper in her hand.

"Everybody decent in there?" she said with a wide grin, trying to peek around me.

"Are you asking on a moral level?"

"Ha, no." She giggled, and a slight flush rose to her cheeks.

"Good, because that answer would be complicated," I said and sat in the chair again. Olivia stood at the door, like a vampire waiting to be invited in.

Tracing her gaze, I said, "He's in the shower."

"Oh, right." She stepped inside then put a foot back out the door. "He may need some fresh towels. I can get some—"

"No, he's fine. He'll probably just stand there and shake off the excess water." I smiled at her but then remembered she didn't know about his four-legged past. I pointed to the sheet of paper in her hand. "What's that?"

"Huh?" She was still a bit transfixed on the bathroom door. Then, as if waking from a daze, she finally came in and sat across from me on the edge of the bed. "Right. First, how are you?"

"I'm fine. We're fine," I said. "Glad to hear things are picking up around here."

She laughed, putting a hand to her mouth. "It's all happening so fast, but it's nice to see our town come back to life. And everyone knows who to thank for that."

"Everyone?" I frowned.

"Don't worry." She held a finger to her lips. "We're all keeping it on the down-low. I know you guys prefer it that way."

"We've got people after us, Olivia. It's not preference, it's trying not to be dead."

Her smile faded a bit, and she nodded at me. I could see a question forming on her face but didn't want to get into it. She knew about Gregor—or at least, that he'd come looking for us the last time we were here—but nothing more.

"You got something?" I motioned to the crisp sheet of paper in her hand.

"Yes, but... I mean, I don't want you to think badly of me."

"I'd never." That got me smiling. "What'd you do, you nasty thing?"

"Don't say that!" She laughed again. "Well, I've got to, you know, keep tabs on our guests here. Just cursory stuff. I don't want to house international terrorists or pedophiles or anything like that."

Nodding, I thought, *What about a guy who turns into a hell beast at the full moon?*

"Fine, fine. You're protecting the dignity of Pine Valley. Got it," I said, reaching for the paper, but she playfully swatted my hand away.

"Just let me *explain* first. Two seconds."

"One..."

She frowned, handing it over. "Okay, okay." As I traced my finger down the page, she made her case. "So, we haven't had phones for a while, but everyone's got a cell phone so no biggie. But we do have Wi-Fi all over the motel. One of my upgrades, actually. I put it in after I took the place over from my parents."

I squinted at the page, which was a horror-show jumble of words and symbols and numbers. "How am I supposed to read this?"

"I'm getting to that, Emmy," she said and cleared her throat. "I've got a few Wi-Fi extenders through here, but all of it goes through the router. And... you can turn on a feature that, um, logs some stuff."

At the top of the page, a date range from the previous year. Below that, just a mess of words and numbers mashed together.

"Some stuff," I said, looking up. "Like what stuff?"

"Just, you know, to make sure people aren't using my internet for weird things. So it logs websites and some search terms that people on the network are, well, searching for."

Then I recognized the dates. "This is what Dr. Pental was searching for. When she stayed here."

"It should be. She was the only guest at the time. Although I think some locals use my internet every now and then. I catch people pulling up next to the rooms, and if nobody is staying, I just switch it off until they drive away."

The readout was something an engineer would love. Or another computer. It didn't go line by line with easily read web addresses or terms. But in the info dump of text I could pick out words I recognized. A search for local restaurants. Bridget Mills's name stuck out.

"Looks like she googled her friend."

Olivia shrugged. "People do that."

"Did you google me?"

Another shrug.

"Olivia?"

"I check out all my guests. And it was back before we were friends," she said, and I couldn't help but smile. I liked that she thought of me as a friend. "You got yourself into a bit of trouble a while back."

"Yeah, old story. Girl meets boy. Boy turns out to be involved in some minor organized crime work and major felonies. Girl nearly beats a few assholes to death with a shovel. Boy goes to prison. I'm done with all that," I muttered as I tried to read the confusing page. "There are quite a few searches for 'firemen' here. Fireman with dog. Fireman no shirt. Fireman—"

"Don't mind those!" Olivia said, waving her hand over the page. "That's, um, my stuff. I was researching a calendar idea to help with, you know, a fundraiser. Help out our local guys."

I pointed at one search term and grinned at her. "Fireman, big hose?"

"Forget the fireman stuff, 'kay?" she said, covering her face with her hands. Then she peeked through her fingers and laughed. "Don't look at me like that!"

"Right." Scanning lower down the sheet, another group of words stood out. "Is there a coin-op laundry in town?"

"Sure. We ain't a town full of fancy people, so yeah, got a couple around. Why?"

"There's a washing machine name that pops up again and again. Maytag. If this is all Pental's stuff, she searched for that more than anything."

"Maybe she dirty." Olivia leaned forward and snatched it from my hand.

"Hey. I was reading that."

She traced her finger down the ever-crumpling page. "Yeah, there's a bunch of searches for Maytag. Could have had some time to kill and did a bit of shopping."

"Maybe." With a flourish, I snatched the paper back. "She searched out the car show too. They sell a lot of junk at those shows. Maybe they sell washing machines?"

"I don't know," Olivia said, snapping her head to the bathroom door at the squeak of a spigot. The hiss of the shower had silenced. "Never been to one."

I leaned forward, gently grabbed her chin, and turned her back toward me. I shook the page. "Is this all you have?"

"Yep, sorry." She turned back to the bathroom door. "But if you want to find out about what they were selling at the show, you can talk with the organizer. Dale Brubaker lives here in town."

"I remember him. People call him Dock." I smiled at the memory. "Dude has a wooden motorcycle."

The bathroom door rattled. Then it shook again, harder.

"Why am I trapped in this tiny, steamy room?" Kane said, his voice muffled behind the door.

I laughed. "The world is safer that way."

Another rattle. "Emelda. Have you locked this door?"

"No-wah," I said and put my feet up on the bed. "Doors don't lock on the outside, Kane. Unless they're jail cells."

A big sigh from him. "I will have to defer to your expertise in that matter."

I leaned forward, banging my feet on the ground. "Sarcasm? Look at you! Every day, you get more huma—" I hesitated, trying to recover from nearly blowing his secret. "Humorous."

Smooth. What a save, I thought to myself, hiding my frown from the woman next to me.

Not that I had to. She wasn't looking in my direction.

The door shook, and Olivia put a hand to her chest.

"He won't break it down, will he? He's quite, um..." Her eyes drifted downward as she searched for the word. "Powerful."

"Nah, he's a pussycat," I whispered. "But don't tell him I told you that. He doesn't like cats very much." *Unless they're slathered with mustard*.

She called out, "Um, did you try turning the knob the other way? These doors, sometimes—"

The door burst open, and Kane stepped out and, yep, not a stitch of clothes on the guy.

Olivia squeaked—yeah, she *squeaked* for crissake!—half turned away, then spun back and jumped up.

"Are there no towels?" She tried to walk around the bed, but I put my leg up to stop her. She frowned at me. "I don't want the man to catch a cold. N-Not like the cold seems to have any effect on his... him."

Kane ran his hands through his long hair, trying to shake the water out of it. When he looked my way, I gave him a wide-eyed expression and nodded toward Olivia. He furrowed his brow.

I said, "Can you at least put on a robe or something?"

"You do whatever's comfortable for you, Kane," Olivia said, bubbling with weird laughter. "You're the guest, but I always want guests to treat their suites like their own home. If you're used to walking around—"

"Kane," I said, pointing at the horizontal metal bar across from the bathroom. Six hangers, looped at the top so they couldn't be removed. Two of them held flimsy white robes.

He grabbed one and put it on, his muscular arms barely fitting through. Then he cinched it up. It looked comical on him. Well, at least to me it did. I think Olivia groaned a little.

"We're heading out," I said. "You remember the dude with the wooden motorcycle?"

Staring in the mirror, Kane nodded slowly. The expression on his face shot a twist through my guts. For all my playfulness, sometimes, I forgot he was a guy who just didn't belong in our world. It seemed the weight of that rounded his shoulders as he stared at the strange human looking back.

Olivia told us Dock lived in a town house just up the road. Across the street from a Hardee's.

"Can't miss it," she said. "His trailer takes up the entire driveway. Looks like a big silver suppository."

"I remember." I stood and grabbed my coat. "Let's go, man."

Slowly, he turned from the big guy staring at him through the glass. He looked over at his ball of clothes I'd chucked on the bed.

He asked, "Can I wear this?"

Chapter Fifty-Four

I grew up in the Minneapolis area. Not a big city when you compare it to a place like New York or Los Angeles, sure. It's just the perfect size.

They've got all the major sports. Football, baseball, hockey. Probably even have a soccer team, but no one I knew actually watched soccer. Oh, there were the pretentious guys you meet who natter on about British teams like Man United or Arsenal. But Americans who talk about teams like that just wanna seem sophisticated or cosmopolitan.

Doesn't make 'em fancy. It makes 'em wankers, as the Brits might say. At least they do on those PBS shows.

But when you get to smaller towns, that's when you realize just how big the Twin Cities actually are.

If you want to go to a game or a mall or a movie, you bring snacks in the car, because it might take a little while to get there.

Not so in smaller Minnesota towns. You get in the car, and by the time you've closed the door, you're already there.

Why do they even bother with cars?

Pine Valley was like that. You could drive from one edge of the town to the other before the song on the radio ended.

"There is the silver trailer," Kane said, as if I couldn't see the massive bullet-shaped monstrosity parked in Dock's driveway. It took up the entire space, glimmering in the afternoon sun.

I stared at it. "You think that's the right one?"

He looked up and down the street. "Do many humans have such things?"

"It's what retired people buy," I said, pulling up to the house. "They spend decades paying off their mortgage and then spend their twilight years in a tiny home on wheels."

Kane frowned at me. "Is that true?"

"Far as you know," I said, clicked off my seat belt, and stepped out. Kane did the same.

Thankfully, he'd left the robe behind. For the most part, he was still wearing the same clothes he'd had from day one. Boots, jeans, belt, and T-shirt. The only changes had been the jean jacket after his motorcycle leather had gotten torn up. When we'd prepped for Canada, he'd picked up a thick, wool checkered shirt. Very lumberjacky.

He'd had a flirtation with hockey jerseys and sweatpants back at Miss Florida's farm, but he preferred the jeans and jacket.

He didn't seem to mind the dirt, mud, and bloodstains. I did.

I'd have to do a bit of shopping for him at some point. He didn't strike me as the shopping type.

"We'll have to hit up a Walmart or something soon." I nodded at his clothes. "Despite the shower, you're starting to get rank."

Kane lifted an arm and smelled himself.

"I have a powerful musk. For this, I am not ashamed."

"*For this*, Gregor won't need a GPS tracker. He can just follow the smell."

I guessed that Dock's home in the short block of town houses was the one closest to the driveway where his big silver pill sat. We walked up the path, and just as I was about to knock on the door, Kane put a hand on my shoulder.

"Word sounds," he whispered to me.

Looking around, I said, "Yeah. We're in a neighborhood. There's word sounds all over, buddy."

He then motioned to the driveway. "It is the man we met. His voice. Inside."

I looked at the door one more time, shrugged, and then crossed the grass toward the silver camper. As we got closer, sure enough, I heard the guy talking too. He had a house ten feet away and was hanging out in his camper.

Dudes, right?

Chilling in his mobile man cave.

Kane went to the window to peer in, and I punched him on the arm, shaking my head. Wolf Boy didn't give a whit about privacy and didn't seem to realize everyone else did.

"Don't peek in windows, weirdo," I whispered. "There are laws against that."

"I do not concern myself with the laws of men."

"You will when you get locked in a cell with some big ol' corn-fed boy looking for a date."

He squinted at me. "This is another of those times where you say something confusing to distract me."

"Did it work?"

Kane tilted his head and shrugged. I smiled at him and knocked on the door. The moment I did, the chattering inside stopped.

Hopefully, I hadn't disturbed ol' Dock while he was wooing some lady friend. Then I remembered he was married. The wife who'd forbidden him to buy a motorcycle, so he'd built one himself. Out of wood.

The trailer tilted, and the suspension creaked. A moment later, the door cracked open. When he saw us, he got a big smile.

"Emelda! I never thought I'd see you again."

"I am also here," Kane said, stepping forward.

Dock laughed. "I can see that. Hellfire, boy, no one can miss a fella as big as you. I think you might affect the tides."

When I stepped inside, I felt a mild sense of dread and realized it was because being in a camper reminded me of those summer days with my uncle and his asshole kids. Dock's trailer was much nicer than the beat-up Rambler my Uncle David had.

No crampy fold-down upper bunks here.

There was a table setup next to a kitchen area. Two bench seats facing each other. At the front, a U-shaped couch with foam seats I knew by looking at them would be terribly uncomfortable.

Just beyond the kitchen, two faux-wood doors on opposite sides. One would be the bathroom, the other some utility closet. After that, a big spread of a master bedroom. It was actually kinda great.

Dock returned from the fridge and handed us two brown bottles.

I smiled. "Leinies?"

"You betcha," he said and laughed. He sat on the bench seat, sliding his gut up against the table. A practiced move, and I wondered if he had a dent in his belly from how many times he had done that. I sat on the opposite side, stretching my legs out across the thin cushion.

Kane looked down, and I pointed to the U-shaped couch.

"You ain't going to fit back here, Kane. That looks comfy, though."

For a moment, he stared at the space. I glanced beyond Dock, back at the bedroom, then back to our host.

"I hope we're not disturbing you."

He laughed. "I'm retired. I don't even have a clock in here no more, so no disturbing done."

"It's just that when we walked up, we heard, you know—" I shifted in my seat, feeling like I was prying. "Maybe you were on the phone or something. Never mind."

He looked at me with glassy eyes, nodded, and pursed his lips. "Probably heard me talking to myself. Since my girl died, my wife, I do that a fair bit."

"You talk to her?"

Dock smiled and looked at his stubby fingers, lost in thought.

The trailer jostled as Kane dropped onto the couch, and we both looked over, happy for the distraction. He stretched out, his boots up on one end of the sofa and his head at the other.

"Don't put your boots on people's stuff, man," I said, waggling a finger at him. "What? Were you raised by wolves?"

He frowned at me. "Yes."

Dock laughed and waved off the violation.

"Don't worry about it. Those slipcovers are designed for travel. Damn near like Teflon and don't stain at all. Mud resistant. Grease resistant. Even monster blood washes right off, I reckon."

He looked at me with a wide grin.

"So, you heard, huh?" I said.

"Girl, *everyone* heard. You two were the talk of the town last week!"

So much for keeping it all on the down-low. That said... I didn't entirely mind the notoriety. At least this kind.

Still, I didn't need my name in the paper. If this town had a paper anymore.

"Actually, we'd prefer if we weren't the talk of the town."

"Why?" He laughed and sipped his beer. "You got people looking for you?"

I shrugged. "That same asshat as before. You remember that guy with the gray crewcut who ran Kane over with the bike?"

"How could I forget?"

"Yeah, well, we'd like it if he forgot us," I said, tapping the plastic tabletop with a chipped fingernail.

"Ah, don't worry. The older folks in town know how to keep out of other people's business," he said then shrugged. "Well, that's not true. But they do know to keep it 'in-house,' as it were. Just between us good folks."

Kane growled. He wasn't one for small talk. "We are looking for a little brown lady."

"Who isn't?" Dock said with a wide grin.

I playfully tapped his hand and leaned in. "I can always introduce you to my aunt. On my mother's side."

"Really? Is she nice?"

Shrugging, I said, "No."

That got a big smile out of him. "Good. I prefer the nasty ones."

Blech.

Time to get down to business. I took a sip from the beer Dock had given me. Kane had left his on the table. "I know you had hundreds of people at your car show."

"Thousands, hon. Tens of thousands."

"Right," I said and felt a bit deflated. "There was a woman, probably of Indian or Pakistani descent, who might have been around Bridget Mills a bit."

The mention of Bridget's name wiped the smile from his face. Dock surprised me when he made the sign of the cross and put a thumb to his lip.

"She was a good woman with a bad man," he said. "But he's gone. And now, so is she, as I understand it. Tragic all around."

I'd wondered how much he knew about Bridget. Did the town *know* she'd been their monster? Right now, that wasn't my problem.

"Well, this woman we're trying to find, it seems like she'd befriended Bridget. So maybe you saw them together?"

Dock leaned back and ran a hand down his mouth, scratching his gray goatee. Staring up into space, he took a swig of his beer then shook his head.

"I didn't see much of Bridge at the show. She was in a bit of a battle with the asshole. I *had* heard… she had a fella on the side."

I smiled. "Is that some of that 'keeping out of other people's business' you mentioned a moment ago?"

He shrugged.

"Don't fault her for it. Whatever makes you happy," he said then switched the subject to my original query. "But no, I don't remember Bridget with any brown woman."

Letting out a long breath, I nodded. "Okay. Worth a try."

"Hold on now. There was a lady walking around the vendor sheds who might fit that description. I chatted to her a bit about Dombivli."

"Uh," I said. "Is that a car?"

"No, darlin', it's near Dubai. I did a month-long stint at their hospital."

Ah, right. I'd nearly forgotten Dock had been an actual doctor at one point.

"Years ago, now," he said, staring at the ceiling of the camper. "She had family in the area. Brought back some very nice memories. The loveliest people you ever will meet."

"Great," I said. "So you talked to her for a while, then?"

"Well, she had money to spend, which is always my favorite type of patron."

The trailer shifted as Kane spun and put his feet on the floor.

"Where is she now?"

Dock laughed. "Son, I didn't get her digits or nothing like that."

Kane frowned. "Why would you take her fingers?"

"Right," our host said, taking a small sip from his bottle. "I remember you say weird stuff."

"He's French Canadian," I offered.

"That would explain it," Dock said, smiling at me. "Only talked with her a few minutes. Why you looking for her?"

I nodded. "Nothing serious. She knows some people we know. Trying to, you know..."

"Doesn't matter to me why. That's your business. But I don't know much about the woman. I introduced myself, but now I think about it, she never did give me a name," he said, peeling the label on his beer bottle. "But she was asking about some very specific parts. Old, old ones. I doubt she found any. That's how I got called over. She poked around a few stalls and didn't find what she was looking for. One of the vendors thought I might know where to get the stuff."

"Why you?" I asked.

"Because I know what everyone's selling," he said and beamed. "Part of the job when you organize a show."

I sighed. "I don't suppose she left an address or anything."

"I can ask around. I know all the folks there, so I send out an email to all my people."

"Maybe," I said, trying to think if this would cause more trouble than helping. I had no idea how plugged in Gregor might be. Would the Organization be monitoring email traffic? "If it comes to that—"

"Hold on, now." Dock snapped his fingers. "Right, I remember. She was looking for... something to do with her grandaddy, as I recall."

"Oh?" I said, looking back at Kane. He was lying flat—or mostly flat—again on the trailer's couch. It looked like he was sleeping.

"Right. Right." Dock stared up at the ceiling, like he was checking his files. "She... Her grandfather or great-grandfather had worked in an old factory. Musta been like a century ago. One of the early places."

This wasn't helping. "Back, um, in the old country?"

"No, no. India didn't have any automakers back then. They got some now, but they make bullshit cars. Death traps. I wouldn't hop into one of those even if I was running from one of your monsters."

"Says the guy who rides a wooden motorcycle."

"One I *built*," he said, smiling. "The gas mileage is for shit, but I don't take it for long trips or nothing."

I nodded. "So her granddad worked in the US, then?"

"Had to be if it was that long ago." His eyes got wide. "Right, hold on. It does ring a bell, now."

"What?"

"She'd been looking for parts for a 1910 touring coupe. I told her she needed to have them machined because, hell, she ain't gonna find those lying around anywhere. Even if they were in some landfill, they'd be rusted to dust."

"So she didn't find them?"

"No. But I told her that if she ever did and got the ol' girl up and running again, I'd be happy to feature it at one of my shows." Dock whistled. "I've never seen a real Maytag-Mason model C. Seen pictures in books, but—"

"*Maytag?*" I said and looked at Kane again. His eyes were closed, head back. Whatever. "Maytag, like the washing machine?"

Dock nodded. "The same. They dabbled in cars for a few years, only made about fifteen hundred of them before the factory went belly-up. In fact... damn... I suppose that's where your lady's ol' pappy had worked."

"So she had one of those Maytag-Masons. Are those rare?"

"Very. I can't imagine where she got it." He shrugged. "Unless, of course, it had been her grandfather's from back in the day."

"And he'd worked at the plant?"

"Yeah, but don't take that as gospel. My memory isn't what it was. There was a time…"

Dock prattled on, but I wasn't hearing him. I thought that if she had gotten the car from her grandfather, handed down, maybe she'd inherited more of his stuff. Or all of his stuff.

And if he'd worked at the old plant…

"Where is the old Maytag factory? Near here?"

"Closed down ages and ages ago." Dock shook his head. "From what I recall, it had been down in Waterloo."

"Iowa?"

"Well, yeah, not the one in Belgium where Napoleon got his ass handed to him," Dock said and laughed. "Did you know he wasn't really short? Total myth. Likely propaganda put out by his enemies. In fact—"

"Right, tall guy," I said, speaking quickly. "How far is Waterloo, Iowa, from here?"

"That factory would be long gone, hon. Probably an Amazon warehouse now."

"Yeah, but if granddad worked at the factory, he would have lived nearby, right?"

"Sure, he'd have walked to work. They didn't hand out cars to employees or nothing."

I nodded. "Well, if she got a car from him… maybe she got his old place?"

"Maybe."

Kane's eyes popped open, and he stood, shifting the weight of the trailer.

He asked, "How far from here?"

Dock exhaled and drew chubby pink fingers through his thinning hair. "You could make it to Waterloo in a day. Probably about three hundred fifty miles or so. But it'd be dark by the time you got to town. And like I said, the factory's gotta be long, long gone."

"Three hundred fifty miles," I said, slipping out of the bench seat. "That would take about…"

"If you're driving straight through?" Dock shrugged. "About five hours."

Chapter Fifty-Five

I'd plotted the trip from Pine Valley to Waterloo, Iowa, on my phone. Sure enough, it was just over five hours.

How had we even gotten around before we had GPS in our pocket? I didn't really remember a time when I didn't have a disembodied voice acting as my highway Sherpa. Sure, there were fold-out maps. At least there used to be.

I looked at the display on my phone.

And along the way, there were notifications, each with bespoke icons and colors, about congestion, roadworks, a fender-bender three hours down the road, which my map software estimated would likely be cleared up before we got there. There were even some user entries about speed traps. It laid out the entire drive ahead of us, showing us troubles long before we encountered them.

When someone finally worked out a *life* GPS, the human race would have it made. It could tell you which job would be better suited for you. Which route to take to avoid bad roads. Or bad boyfriends.

Although, when I thought back to those times Uncle David would pull out one of the old paper maps during those long summer drives, we'd begin a circuitous route toward our destination. And often get lost along the way.

That sounds like a bad thing, sure, when the goal was to get from point A to point B. But had it not been for the shitty, non–real-time map, we'd never have stumbled upon so many cool things along the way.

Once, a restaurant in the shape of a spaceship with—*why?*—a donkey petting zoo.

A farm that, for five bucks, gave you a bucket and let you go out and pick as many strawberries as you could carry.

An old store, some hobby for a retiree, that sold old soda bottles. You'd think that sounds awful, but with all the colors and shapes and sizes? Once you got past the musty smell, you had one hundred years of history captured in thick, chipped glass. Clear, green, blue, yellow, every color you could think of. And you could imagine some teenage boy getting the courage up to ask some girl if she'd like a grape Nehi—and how that bottle might have helped bring two people together. Started a family. And their kids starting families of their own.

All because of a glass bottle that now sat, battered and nicked, tucked up on a shelf in a store on the side of a road in rural Minnesota.

If my uncle had had a stern GPS lady back then, we'd have never seen any of those weird little moments. The things that, these days, have a fond place in my memory. Like my own little bottle store in my head.

Technology made life easier, no question. But it just might rob us of some accidental magic we might have discovered along the way as well.

Still, rolling down I-35 toward Iowa, I was happy to have it. I had enough weird magic in my life at the moment. Monsters, superviruses, a maniacal tech sergeant pursuing us. All the while caught in the middle of some shadow battle between the secret warring factions of... whatever the hell they were.

None of that mattered to me. My job now was to help Kane find Dr. Faria Pental. If anyone knew how to change him back to a wolf, it would be her.

Kane shifted in his seat, leg kicking out in little shivers. That made me smile. For a big dude like he was, he did have some doggy traits. Like little twitches as he slept.

What was the expression? Chasing rabbits?

Of course, I'd seen him change into something else entirely. The wolfwere. I preferred to think that in his dream, he was chasing rabbits rather than whatever *that* creature might be chasing.

Chapter Fifty-Six

Kane

My eyes burn from the smoke, which is also making it hard to breathe.

I can feel cool trickles on my cheeks, especially noticeable because of the heat all around me. Beyond the bedroom door, Mère and Père. I bang my fist, so tiny compared to now, and call out to them.

They do not answer.

The fire is stalking up the stairs toward me. I could race back to my room and leap from the window. It will be safe beyond the home, away from the fire.

But I cannot leave these two kind people to die in the flames. I would have never survived without them. For this, I have a debt, and while it can never be fully repaid, I must honor that debt.

But it is more than this.

More than this.

I want to help them. Within me, I have a compulsion to ensure they are safe. It is a queer feeling for me, this human pull. When I was wolf—

I am still wolf!

—before, when in the forest, I cared for my wolf wife and our pack. But this feeling now is different from that.

Before, it was simply the way to survive. Affection, although, before, I did not know such a term.

For these two wonderful people, there is more. That may be because I am now more; I do not know. But I know what the humans call it.

Love.

I have love for these two people. And from the little I understand of it, I do accept I am reflecting the love shown me. That they took in a young boy they did not know—one they were not responsible for despite their reasoning—can only be explained by a love that defies reason. Or explanation.

When one is filled with that kind of love, I think it is impossible not to give some of your own in return.

This is the true currency of humans. Not their tiny pieces of paper with queens and presidents on them. Of course, you cannot buy Coffee Crisp candy bars with love. These require the paper money.

But the most important aspects of human life, these require love. The choice to receive and the temerity to give it. At its purest, this is a brave, selfless act.

However, from what I have seen on television, you can purchase love with the tiny paper for short periods of time. This confuses me, so I think no more of it.

I pound once again on the door, calling out to Mère and Père. Again, they do not respond.

A quick glance over my shoulder, and the smoke is so thick I can no longer see my room, which is just a few strides away. I reach up and grip the knob of their door.

My fingers snap away, stinging. The metal feels like it is close to melting.

I ignore the pain and reach up again, turning the knob.

When the door opens, I feel the heat blast against my face. I push forward, keeping low to the floor. There is more water in my eyes. Lifting a hand to my face, I wipe it away.

Before me is flame.

The bed where they lie is burning. The furniture in the room is all on fire.

My wolf sense knows to run. Turn away. Fire is a threat, one of the greatest threats, but the human side of me ignores this. Lifting myself up, I walk forward, hunched low, as the ceiling is roiling like the dark sky of a terrible storm.

When I step to the bed, I see my human parents in an embrace.

They are gone.

They are here but gone.

Their skin blackened, lips pulled back to show brilliant white teeth. In their last moments, they held one another. This is how they died, and if there is a place after this, I know this is how they forever will be.

I hear shouting now. Strange sounds.

When I step to the window and look down, the flames reveal the faces of men. There, I see a man who I will later know. Bald with tiny glasses and a face like a fist. I know his name is Crank, but at this time, I do not know this. He is with many others.

All are dressed similarly. Black leathers and chains. Two are holding small red canisters.

They do not help. Why do they not help?

Crank is smiling as he looks at the burning home. For a brief moment, he seems to lock onto my face, but then he turns.

The flames that have taken my human parents. They are not helping because they are the ones who have done this. They have burned this home and killed two lovely people.

I feel an anger rise within me as I watch Crank walk away. Some of the others follow, but there are a few who remain. To watch my parents burn!

My heart begins to race, my mind spins. My anger has become fury but more than that.

In the short time I had with them, Mère and Père knew things I did not understand. One of their rules—I was never to see the light of the moon. This, they had not explained, but it was their rule and one I obeyed.

When I feel my pulse throb, my limbs ache, and my mind splinter, I get an idea of why this was the rule in our home.

Something is happening to me.

Standing at the window, looking down at these men, for the first time that I can recall, I have stepped into the moonlight.

Chapter Fifty-Seven

They always say you shouldn't wake up people who are dreaming.

Or is that sleepwalking?

Kane kind of looked like he was walking, his legs twitching as he slept. Was that the same thing as sleepwalking? But he was also whimpering. That was a sound I'd never thought I'd hear from one of the largest men I'd ever met. And it sounded less animallike, which I might expect, and more... childlike.

"Kane," I said, one eye on him and the other on the road.

He didn't respond.

My big friend had fully recovered from the battle in the British Columbian woods. That recovery had come from *feeding*, of course. And I'd noticed, like before, it had taken years off him. The wrinkles around his eyes had smoothed. His skin had become tauter and his lips fuller.

How old might he get if he didn't feed for weeks? Months? Would he even *live* months without taking in blood?

Despite being back to perfect health, he hadn't stirred from the moment we'd gotten in the car, heading toward Waterloo, Iowa. He hadn't missed anything other than a dull ride—35 to 218 to Highway 1. By the time we got to Highway 63, we were basically there.

As we drove, there'd been a constant stream of vehicles headed north.

Many of those held people driving up for a late shift up in the Cities. People who don't live in the Midwest or in a country as big as the US probably would be aghast at the commutes some Americans endure just to live somewhere nice.

Even if that nice is Iowa.

As the cars and pickups formed like a battalion on its northern assault, I imagined many of the drivers heading to work at chemical plants, furniture factories, and massive warehouses where people put little things in big boxes.

Before my father joined the military, he'd worked in a popcorn factory. And from what my mother told me, he would have been satisfied to make that a career. Thirty years of stuffing tri-fold vacuum-sealed packets into cardboard boxes.

Then he'd met my mother and gotten her pregnant. And with that had inherited a father-in-law who wanted better for his daughter. My grandfather had been a hard man who believed in harder labor. Mainly for others.

Just out of high school with few options ahead of him, dad joined the military. His plan had been to get the money and grants to go to college. A rucksack by the side of the road in Kandahar had changed all that.

My mother hadn't spoken to her father much after that despite sharing our house with him. I think she blamed Grandad in some way. And maybe blamed herself more. That's when her drinking had started.

Why am I thinking about my mother?

I needed to get out of my head and focus on finding Pental.

"Time to get up, wolfman," I said, giving his thigh a smack. "We've got the Waterloo turnoff in less than a mile."

With a groan, he sat up, dragging the seat belt strap across his face. He rubbed his neck. "It is uncomfortable to sleep in car."

"It is more uncomfortable to drive five hours while someone else gets to sleep in car."

Kane flicked his eyes toward the steering wheel. "Maybe I should drive."

"No," I said, shaking my head. "It would be even more uncomfortable to end up upside down in a ditch in the middle of Iowa."

Before we left, Dock had searched through his dogeared magazines to find old-timey pictures of the Maytag-Mason automobile factory. It had been a large facility. The bottom floor, which I assumed was the factory itself, looked as long as two or three football fields.

The second floor was half the size.

It seemed that's where management had been—maybe so they could look down on the laborers below. Bark out orders, drink coffee, and eat things made out of corn. I mean, this was Iowa.

We weren't interested in the factory itself.

If Dr. Pental had inherited her grandfather's old home and was using it as her hideaway, I guessed it might be a mile or two from where the factory had been. That could easily have been a gross underestimation. Old people loved to talk about the great lengths they had to take just to do simple stuff. Like walk to work.

But this would have been rural Iowa a century earlier. How far from the factory would he really have been?

"Maybe farther than others," Kane said as I shared my thoughts with him. "Old man Pental was from India, yes?"

I shrugged. "I suppose. Yeah."

"Humans seek out differences and do not like those who do not look same."

I smirked at him. "You mean like pack animals?"

"Hmm." Kane stared out the windshield. "That is fair."

Kane swept his hand toward the countryside as I took the exit. "So he may have been farther out. Local corn people may not have wanted people like him too close to their land."

Cocking my head toward Kane, I wondered how a guy who was an animal a year before knew so much about human psychology.

As if in answer, he said, "As you say, it is similar with wolves. Markings and scents. Those who are not like you pose danger."

I laughed. "The guy had been an auto factory worker. I don't think the Pentals posed much danger to locals."

"Change can feel like danger."

While I didn't agree with that sentiment despite some of my own encounters along those lines, he had given me an idea.

We rode in silence for a few more minutes, looking for some greasy spoon to stop at. I'd remembered something Miss Florida had said about Dr. Pental. One of the only things I really knew about the woman.

The town had not one but three Waffle Houses.

At the first, an older heavy-set woman told us, no, she hadn't seen anyone fitting Faria's description.

"She'd probably stick out a bit, even these days," I said. "Brown woman."

"We got lotsa brown folks."

"Indian," I clarified. "Not, you know, Native American."

She'd shrugged. "Can't say I know anyone like that, but people love their local spot. I got folks who come in here every day. Every day for years.

I know how they like their eggs, what they want with them, their coffee orders, and whether they like their hash smothered, covered, scattered, or chunked."

"You are an impressive Waffle House person," Kane said, nodding at the woman. "A credit to your species."

She eyed him. "Uh-huh." Then she looked toward me. "You might wanna try the House on the other side of town."

I didn't have high hopes for location two. And if that hadn't worked out, location three was even father out.

"Positive thinking," Kane said. "The Phil doctor says this is important."

"Well, if any shrink can guide us on our Waffle House search, it would be him."

At the second restaurant—or cafe, I'm not even sure what you'd call them—we hit pay dirt. Smothered and covered and chunked pay dirt.

"Sure, I know her, of course," said a white-haired man who was so rail thin, I wondered whether, if he ate any of his own product, you might see it stick out of his T-shirt. His crooked name tag said Dave. "Always waffles, never flapjacks. Butter in a ramekin because she don't like it to make her breakfast soupy. And our girl drowns them waffles in maple syrup. Hell, I don't even know how Pri can taste anything but syrup."

"Pri?"

Dave nodded. "She got one of them, you know, longish names. I tried a few times but only embarrassed myself."

Damn.

"Priyanka Chopra Jones," Kane said. Right. His useless TV knowledge was not so useless after all.

The Waffle House guy had gone a bit stiff when the big guy had spoken, so I said, "She's a friend of the family."

"Whose? Yours or the giant's?" Dave said with a half smile, keeping his eyes on me.

I entwined my arm into my friend's. "Kane here is my uncle, and we're headed down to Texas so he can try out proper barbecue."

Dave whistled. "Hell of a long way to go for barbeque. Don't they got restaurants up in the Cities?"

"How'd you know we were from the Cities?"

He laughed. "You got a Minneapolis look about you." Dave stared and did not clarify the designation, whatever that was supposed to mean. Then he added, "And he don't look old enough to be your uncle. You both look darn near the same age."

I sighed. "It's complicated. My mother's sister, my aunt, her husband died in a lawn jart incident."

Dave's face darkened. "I am truly sorry to hear that."

"Anyway, to deal with her grief, she got her a boy toy. And since she's laid up for a few days with gastro-surgery, drinking her meals, she's pretty picky about what she likes to eat. She wanted proper barbecue, so we're going to get her some."

The old white-haired man whistled again. He was a whistler, so, obviously, we could never be friends.

"But Mama also said to look in on, um, Pri, right? They were in high school cheerleading together."

Dave looked between the two of us, blinking rapidly, like his brain had gotten caught up on a bad sector.

"Right. Well, she comes in a few times a week."

"We're just driving through," I said with a big, dopey smile. Then I remembered she was trying to keep off the radar and took a punt. "And she doesn't have a home phone or anything. All we've got to go on is Waterloo. So here we are."

"Right."

"Mom wanted me to give Pri her old pom-poms, right? She's had them for ages. Borrowed them for a Knights–Warriors game and just never—"

Dave perked up. "You got them with you?"

"Yeah, in the trunk."

"Can I see them?"

I fought to keep my smile. "They're, you know, packed away." I realized I might have pushed it too far. "Trust me, they're in there, but the way Mama packs—"

"I'll give you ten dollars just to rub them on my face," he said then jerked his head up, realizing what he'd just said was out loud. "Just, I mean, the feeling of the..."

I shrugged. "Packed up. Sorry."

Embarrassed, Dave was happy to get us out of his restaurant quickly. He told us "Pri" rode up the road but couldn't be too far away because she often came in, and her hair was still damp from a shower. We thanked him and headed back to the jeep.

Climbing back, I fired it up.

"You are a complicated woman," Kane said with a quirky smile. "All the cheerleading story made up on the spot? You are a very good liar."

"It wasn't all lies. Just wasn't talking about her."

Kane pointed at me. "You were one of these cheerleaders!"

"What does it matter?" I dropped the vehicle into drive and spun the tires a little, not wanting to get into it. The past is behind you for a reason. If you want to keep moving forward, sometimes it needs to stay there.

For the next half hour, we drove the side streets and came across dozens of homes with huge properties. We could have started knocking on doors, but that would have only raised suspicions. And if we had come across a friend of Faria Pental's—aka Priyanka Choplin something-or-other—they might have then given her a heads-up someone was looking for her.

It was Kane who spotted it. He told me to stop the car.

Shaking his head, he laughed. "Yes, Alanis Morrisette confused me, but I understand now."

"Wut?"

"Irony, yes?" he said and popped his eyes wide. "I get it now."

"You wanted me to stop because you worked out song lyrics?"

He shrugged. "Irony, yes? Very good."

I gritted my teeth. "What are you talking about, Kane?"

"A person who is trying not to be found but in enacting such a desire, this leads to their discovery," he said, beaming. "This is irony, yes?"

"Sure," I said and then saw him point upward.

Next to us was a lone light pole next to a property set deep back from the road. Trees and long rows of bushes prevented anyone from seeing in the home. In fact, you couldn't see the house at all. However, just below the solitary streetlight was a box with a lens on it. A black wire snaked from the back of it and bit into the coupling at the base of the light.

"A camera," I said, finally seeing it.

"Yes. And someone not wanting to be found would be looking for those trying to find," Kane said, clasping his hands together. "In doing so, they reveal by mistake. Irony, yes?"

I looked down the long, dark road.

"You think she's down there, then?"

"Yes," Kane said, putting a fist over his mouth. "I really do think."

I frowned at him. "Too easy."

Turning down the dirt road, I considered flipping my lights off. But with a storm rolling in, it was so dark and windy, that would have only put us in the ditch.

The property went on and on. The bushes I'd seen hadn't concealed a house. They'd only been the first line of defense on what was damn near a mini forest. I'd glanced at the odometer before we'd turned down the road.

As we drove at least a quarter mile, Kane pointed out two more cameras. These were more obvious, both above signs that read "Private Property." Nothing about violators facing big dogs or a Smith & Wesson. Just those two words, but they were enough of a threat.

When we finally got to the big house, there was a metal gate blocking our way. Kane hopped out and looked at the latch. He flipped it aside and was about to roll it away when a woman slipped out of the bushes, dressed entirely in black.

Staring down the sights of a shotgun leveled at Kane, she spoke calmly.

"Private property," she said with the slightest hint of an accent. "Did you not see the sign?"

Kane lifted his hands in the air, but I saw him eying the weapon. Before he did something stupid, I rolled my window down and called out.

"Cal Davis sent us," I said, and she bristled at the name. "That big man there is his brother."

Dr. Faria Pental stepped forward, raising the shotgun higher. "Cal didn't have a brother."

"Cal Davis made me his brother," Kane said. "When he bit me."

She lowered her weapon.

Chapter Fifty-Eight

Dale Brubaker flipped through the album of photographs, ticket stubs, and the menus his late wife had coyly slipped into her purse over the years. He'd been looking at all this old stuff more and more. Increasingly, when friends came around, they'd find him here. In the trailer.

The trailer she'd picked out.

She'd also picked the curtains, the color of the fabrics, and the light fixture above the tiny kitchen table.

He'd earned the nickname Dock simply because he'd been the only one amongst his friends who owned a boat. The boat had been his pride and joy. The trailer was hers.

From the sheets on the bed to the tiny pictures on the walls. All Iris's toiletries where right where she'd last used them.

"If you'd only had chronic dryness, I'm sure one of those bottles woulda had what you needed. And you'd still be here, doll," he said, running his fingers over a smudged photo. They'd both been so young when it had been taken. Standing in front of the car his father had given to them for the wedding, her arm wrapped around his trim waist, his arm draped over her lovely bare shoulder. Joy on both their faces so powerful it nearly warped the picture. They beamed at life's promises of the grand adventure ahead.

Some had been kept. Most, actually.

The others? Abandoned after their two-lane highway dropped to just the one.

Dock didn't harbor any bitterness in that thought but, sure, a hint of sadness there. What he wouldn't have given for one more year with Iris. One more day. One more hour.

He laughed. "It's not the same if you're not here." Dock took a tiny sip of his beer, grinned, and took a big slug, feeling the slosh of bubbles fill his round belly. "Maybe I'll have another? Who's gonna stop me?"

The visit with Emelda and her big, brooding friend had put him in a nostalgic mood. The two of them didn't appear to be a couple, but they were, well, a team. Battling the world together. And not just against the monsters.

Life's biggest threats don't look like monsters. If they did, it certainly would be much easier.

Dock lifted his head, glancing at the bedroom window. In the gap between the wrinkled curtains, the ones Iris would iron every spring, he saw two dark figures pass by.

"Who now?"

The rhythmic footfalls on the pavement sounded like clockwork, growing louder and louder. He could grab one of his rifles, but in the confines of the trailer, too cumbersome. He had the pistol. That would be better protection. Less unwieldy.

Then a calm settled over him.

He fluttered the toes of his bare feet and, in his mind, could feel bits of sand drift away. Pensacola? That *had* been a great trip. Where was the photo for that day? Maybe they hadn't taken one. Didn't matter. He remembered every moment. So hot that day. So sunny. Yep, so sunny.

Dock shook his head and squeezed his eyes shut. Then exhaled and smiled.

"It's okay," he said, standing and running his hands down his overalls. "It's all okay."

When the knock came to the door of his trailer, Dock was up and his hand already hovering over its handle. He took a deep breath and exhaled shakily. He pulled the door open.

A man and a woman stood there, dressed in black suits. He was taller by a head with a haircut that looked like he'd used a coupon. Her dark hair had been pulled back into a ponytail so tight, it probably hurt to blink.

Neither wore sunglasses, but with eyes as empty as theirs, why bother?

Dock nodded and smiled pleasantly. No use in making it too easy for them.

"Can I help you?" he said.

The woman looked at the man, who was peering into the trailer. He craned his neck around then poked it inside.

"Who were you talking to?"

"Noneya," Dock said, grinning. Then he beer belched. "As in Noneya Business."

Dock had a fleeting thought of calling out. These two may be reticent to harm him if he made a scene. Surely, someone in one of the neighboring houses would hear them. Of course, that could only get someone else hurt.

No, he'd seen enough pain in his life.

He didn't want any more pain.

Chapter Fifty-Nine

Crank stared at his employer across the small square table. His stomach churned, and he could feel rivulets of sweat trickle down his aching legs. The constant hum from the jet's engines filling his brain wasn't helping calm his thumping heart.

His vision had turned blurry, and his eyes hurt. When he stripped off his glasses, he found he could see more clearly without them.

What is happening to me?

He didn't think all the chaos churning inside his body was about flying. He'd been on planes before, and they'd all been small like this one. When he'd been younger, his pilot brother had often shuttled hunters up to Alaska for weekend trips, and he'd tagged along as crew.

And, of course, to go through the wealthy tourists' stuff. When the fat cats would head out for hours on end, it gave him ample time to copy down credit card numbers and sneak a few big bills out of their wallets. That had been a solid racket until he'd gotten fired.

By his own brother!

But Crank had gotten a taste of easy money and never lost that craving.

He'd only met the guy across from him once before. Gregor had always paid on time and in full. Easy money. A retainer for keeping an eye out for that kid, Calvin Davis. They'd nearly found him, too, a few months earlier.

Burnt down his parent's house after Wally had sworn up and down he'd seen the kid inside. Whoops, they'd gotten *that* wrong! Crank had watched the place burn, but nope, no Cal Davis, just some *other* stupid kid, much younger, standing at the window, surrounded by fire.

After they'd gone back to HQ, which was just a run-down shithole someone had abandoned, a few of the Devils hadn't returned. They'd stayed behind to watch the flames, and those morons ended up getting goddamn mauled to death by some animal!

Then, yesterday, that stupid little kid's dad or uncle showed up back in Kitimat with some purple-haired chick, and now, a bunch of his Devils were dead! The big bastard had to be related—Crank never forgot a face.

And he'd certainly never forget the strange one sitting across from him now. Especially the eyes on Gregor.

"It would seem our business relationship has changed," the tech sergeant said, his smile best suited for a sticker chemical companies could put on bottles to scare off children. "We hired you to find Cal Davis. He's dead now, so..."

Crank rolled a dry tongue around his mouth as he looked around the jet's interior.

Sure, he'd been on small planes before, but none like this. The ones his brother had flown were little six-seaters, and he'd often been relegated to a fold-down jump seat so the wealthy assholes could sit comfortably.

This was like some Fortune 500 CEO's personal plaything.

The jet was twice the size of those prop jobs he'd been on before, but with only four seats. Not seats—these were loungers! You could even lean back and kick up a footrest.

If this was the world that the tech sergeant lived in, Crank wanted it.

He'd have enjoyed the fantasy more—and he wanted to—if only he could get his stomach to settle. To get his pulse rate to drop low enough where it didn't constantly feel like his heart would crack his rips open and leap out.

Crank could hear himself wheeze as he breathed. His entire body was drenched in sweat.

Yeah, he was nervous... but not *that* nervous.

He reached for the bandage wrapped around his chest but got a shake of the head from Gregor. God, how it itched! Crank let his hand fall back into his lap.

For the first time since he'd been loaded up onto the aircraft, the Devil's Dawn leader spoke.

"What ith it—" he started then stopped. His eyes grew wide. What the hell was wrong with his mouth? "What d-d-did you do... me?"

Gregor laughed and clapped his hands together. The tech sergeant sipped from his drink, the lime wedge bumping against the man's thin lips.

"You did this to yourself, Alan."

Crank frowned at the use of his real name. No one called him Alan anymore. He felt like he was back in school again.

"H-How?"

Gregor shrugged. "That's not important. However, given these new developments, I think we can come to an *amended* arrangement. In the woods, you said you overheard Cal and the girl talking about a doctor, yes?"

Crank tried to work his mouth and answer, but the words got lost somewhere in his throat, unwilling to escape his lips. Instead, he nodded.

"Do you remember the name?"

The leader of the Devil's Dawn looked between the man across from him and the woman seated nearby. She had her legs tucked beneath her, leaning back. A few wispy black strands of hair had escaped the tight bun and draped across her smooth forehead. Crank guessed she had to be in her forties. With the skin of a twenty-year-old.

Money. These people oozed money.

He wanted that.

"Do you recall the name, Alan?"

Crank shook his head just the once since any movement made the roiling nausea worse.

"What about Pental? Dr. Faria Pental?"

"Y-Yuss. I think," Crank mumbled. "Wh-Who is that?"

Gregor sighed. "A geneticist with a brilliant mind. And not a bad little body for an older lady."

"She's a traitor," the dark-haired woman said, the venom of her words twisting Crank's stomach further. "A thief and a traitor."

The tech sergeant nodded once. "Yes, Doc Hammer. She is indeed."

Crank heard a rumbling in his chest and realized, oddly, that he was laughing. Such a queer feeling, like he was two people in one body.

He said, "I-I-Is everybody a doctor in this outfit? St-St-Starting to feel outclassed." His laughing grew, and he coughed, which sent stabs of pain through the bandaged wounds across his chest.

"Oh, you are *definitely* outclassed. No question," Gregor said with his big, horrifying smile. "But you're still of use. Once we find—"

The door to the cockpit opened, and the copilot stepped out, lifting a handheld device in the air, nodding toward Gregor. A moment later, he handed it to the tech sergeant, who stared at the screen. Then he looked up to the copilot.

"You are sure?"

The man nodded. "They're heading to Waterloo, just south of the Minnesota border. Got the location from some car nut they spoke to," he said. When he saw the frown on Gregor's face, he shook his head. "No worries there. He won't be warning them. Or anyone else." The copilot then leaned down and traced his finger across the screen. He tapped at the image. "This is them."

"Where was this shot taken?" Gregor said, scanning the photo, his voice pitching higher.

"I-35 south. About four hours ago, as they passed through St. Paul," the other said. "We'd flagged the plate and got this hit."

The tech sergeant stared at the image, thumbing his lip. He swiped back to the previous screen, reading.

"No address? Just Waterloo?"

The copilot tilted his head and shrugged.

"Get someone on the cameras there. We won't have all of them, but the Org can get into some of the fed stuff." Gregor looked up at the ceiling. "If Faria's there, they may have already found her. Find that jeep."

"You got it," the other said, taking back the device.

"Ironic that this is the town she chose to hide in, don't you think?" Gregor said, humming to himself. "Napoleon's last stand. Fitting."

The copilot returned to the cockpit, closing the door behind him.

Gregor spun back to the wreck of a man across from him.

"You do *not* look so hot, Alan," he said in a singsong voice. "Here's what I need from you. When we land, we want something from Dr. Pental. It's beyond valuable. Worth more than you, me, and even Doc Hammer over there."

"Shut up," the woman said, not looking over.

"Well, I'm not the *near*-genius who couldn't replicate her research, so—"

"Wha' do you n-n-need?" Crank said, his lower jaw trembling.

The tech sergeant sucked in a breath and blew it out slowly.

"Something doesn't add up. Not entirely," he said. "We know about Emelda Thorne, and you said something about an animal with her."

"A d-d-d-dog. Yusss."

"What about Kane? The big guy."

Crank shook his head. "Saw... in town. At b-barn. But n-not at c-c-cabin."

Gregor rubbed his jaw. He felt the ache coming on, and he'd need one of Hammer's injections. That could wait. Not long, but it could wait.

"Still don't understand how he..." His voice trailed off. Then he snapped his head up at Crank. "Doesn't matter. If he's Enhanced or not, doesn't matter. Not if I've got a small army of them with me."

Crank's eyes danced in his skull, and he stared, trying to focus. *Did he say army?*

Gregor leaned forward and squeezed the sweating man's shoulder. "I know what you need. This will come as a shock," he said, lowering his eyes then fluttering them. "But all this pain and heat and jittery business? That will calm once you've had a bit of blood."

"B-Blood?"

"Yes. A side effect that even the vaunted Dr. Pental hadn't predicted. Made *such* a mess of everything, frankly. At least, for now."

"Wh-Wh-Wh..."

"Wh-Wh-What I'm saying," Gregor said, mimicking the man's words, "is that we rounded up your crew from that place you'd called home sweet home. Well, what's left of them, but the five plus you should be plenty. Your friends are waiting for you in the back in the master suite."

Crank turned his shaking head to look at the rear of the jet. Gregor gripped his jaw roughly and spun his face back toward him.

"You'll need to get a bit of blood from each of them," he said. "That will make you right as rain, Alan! But no killing, okay? We'll need them for when we land."

"It... wh...wh...wh—"

Gregor stood and nodded to a large man in black standing behind Crank. The muscular thug lifted him by the shoulders to his feet and held him steady.

The tech sergeant waved a lazy hand toward the woman.

"Doc Hammer isn't totally useless. She's got a bit of a cocktail to speed up the process," he said then lowered his voice to a whisper. "It'll be very painful, but you're a big boy."

"It—what? I don't—"

"You will," Gregor said. "Or I can show you to the door! You can leave at any time!" The tech sergeant pointed to the exit, the darkening sky just outside the portal window.

"N-N-No."

"Good!" the tech sergeant said, almost growling in excitement. "Now go back there and get me my Enhanced army."

The man in black led him away toward a reinforced door.

At that moment, for the first time in as long as he could remember, Alan didn't care about easy money anymore.

Chapter Sixty

Dr. Faria Pental had instructed me to pull the jeep around the back of her home.

Kane stood a few feet away from her, the angry end of the shotgun pointed at his stomach. She motioned for him to walk forward, behind my vehicle.

It was getting dark, and I looked up to see if the moon was peeking out. Of course, the moon and the sun don't hang out on opposite sides of the Earth, like two lovers forbidden to see the other.

In fact, I'd seen the moon in the sky plenty of times when the sun was shining. A faded orb up in the sky, like a ghost standing at the door, looking in. I'd never paid too much attention to it, but I took some consolation in the fact that the daytime ghost moon had never effected a change in Kane.

At least not in the weeks that I'd known him.

I drove down a short gravel drive and saw a carport with four vehicles in various states of disrepair.

On the far left, a cherry-red Chevy truck that looked like it had just rolled off the showroom floor. *If* this were the 1950s. The others looked more like junkyard scrap—wheels, axles, and engine parts laid up on risers behind them. I suspected one of those heaps was the old Maytag-Mason.

"The bay on the far right, please," she called out. When I looked in the mirror, I saw her scanning the sky. Had *she* been looking for the moon?

Couldn't have.

Sure, she was, according to Cal, chiefly responsible for the program that had shifted the world on its axis, but I didn't think she had any clue about that large man standing next to her.

After I slid into the carport, I got out then opened the back door to grab my backpack. Just a lady getting her big purse. Inside was my slingdart. I still wasn't very good with the damn thing, but it was all I had.

"You won't need that," she said. She had the shotgun lowered but still pointed in the general direction of Kane. I slipped the bag onto my shoulder, spun around, and put a hand on my hip.

"I don't expect you've got much use for feminine products at your age," I said. "Some of us still do."

Pental eyed me for a moment, nodded once, then waved the shotgun toward the rear door.

I went first, followed by Kane. As we climbed the stairs, she looked up to face a camera just under the eaves. A moment later, the door clicked. We went inside.

"Please take your footwear off at the door," she said, took a long look at the two of us, and then put her weapon on a rack just inside. It fit snugly into a slot. Above it were two handguns. Below that, what looked like a hunting rifle.

"You some kind of prepper?" I said, nodding to the four weapons on the wall.

She ignored my question. "Do you drink tea?"

"No," I said. "I mean, not really."

Dr. Pental looked up to Kane. "What about you? What is your preference?"

"Answers," he said, his face unreadable.

The little woman chuckled at that then wiggled her fingers in the air next to her head.

"Always in a rush, young people," she said and walked down the short hall with bedrooms on either side and into the kitchen. "Unfortunately, I only have lemon and sugar. I don't do milk in tea." Flicking the lever at the base of a kettle, she turned and leaned against the counter. "Foul idea."

She motioned to a small circular table in the dining room and dug into the cupboards for cups.

"Sit over there."

I looked up at Kane as he stepped forward. Even without the shotgun in her hands, she commanded the room. This was someone who was used to telling other people what to do and having them comply.

When I sat, I looked around the quaint farmhouse. It looked like something out of time. Neat. Tidy. A bureau that looked handmade. The centerpiece in the corner was a large, beautiful wooden desk with a rollaway top. A secretary, I believed they'd been called.

"This is where your grandfather lived, Dr. Pental?"

The kettle began to rumble and roil as she prepared the cups. Looking down as she dropped the bags into each, she smiled to herself.

"It seems you know far more about me than I do you," she said then lifted her smile to me. "Let's start with names, yes? Please call me Faria."

My big friend was scanning the room, his eyes taking everything in. I decided to play nice. He was darkening the mood enough for both of us.

"I'm Emelda Thorne, and the little guy here is Kane. Like I said outside, he's Calvin's brother."

She raised her eyebrows and looked at him. "Kane Davis, then?"

He nodded once then resumed scanning the room.

"Calvin's *brother*," Faria added and lifted a shoulder. "But his brother is dead, of course. Died as a young boy."

That got Kane's attention. "You know of this?"

"I know everything about Calvin Davis. Well, everything up until about a year ago." She looked up at us, and her plastered-on smile faded by a measure. "How is he?"

Kane said, "He is dead."

She nodded slowly and dropped her eyes to the cups. For a moment, she moved each, just slightly, adjusting the tea-bag strings at their edges.

"I thought as much. I know he'd been looking for me." She sighed. "I would have liked to have seen Cal one last time."

I cleared my throat. "He made it sound like the two of you were friends. Not sure why you'd hide from a friend."

"It was safer," she said, a faraway look stealing into her eyes. "More for me than Cal. I'm not as brave as I seem. But then, who is?"

The kettle clicked, and she grabbed it at its base, pouring water into each cup. I watched as she dropped equal amounts of sugar into all three cups and then a squeeze of lemon for each. She lifted the tray and brought it to the table.

Standing next to Kane, she put a hand on his chin and lifted his face up toward the light.

After a moment, she patted him on the shoulder and sat down.

"You have beautiful eyes, Kane. Lovely color."

"I am sorry," he said, "but I am betrothed to another."

That got a hearty laugh out of her, and she clasped her hands together as she sat across from us. Faria then leaned forward and splayed her hands out across the long wooden table.

"You are the first guests I have ever had in my home," she said. "It is good to talk to people again. I've been keeping to myself of late."

I pointed at Kane. "You were checking his eyes."

Faria casually lifted one shoulder. "You can read a lot in a man by looking at his eyes."

"Like whether he's one of your Enhanced."

She reached for her tea bag, methodically lifting and dropping it back into the water. I watched as the dark-brown stain began to spread through the liquid in her cup.

"My, my, you have me at such a disadvantage," she said in a pleasant voice. "You know of my work. You know about my grandfather and this house. But all you have given me is a lie."

This got a frown from my friend. "I do not lie. Lying is a human compulsion."

"Oh?" She grinned, taking a tiny sip and looking over the rim of her cup. "So what are you, Kane Davis?"

I interrupted before Kane could say anymore. "What lie?"

"You said Cal bit your friend here," she said and replaced her cup on the saucer. "If that were the case, he would be different than he is now."

"The black eyes?" I said.

She nodded. "That, of course. And far more dangerous traits."

"I am very dangerous," Kane said, stiffening.

Faria reached over the table and patted his hand in a grandmotherly way. "Of course you are, dear. We are low on time, so why don't you tell me why you have invaded my home."

"You got a date or something?" I said, scowling.

"No. But if you're here, they will soon be too. I would prefer to hear your story before that happens," she said, the false smile returning. "I don't expect there'll be much time for stories after that."

"Who?" I said, leaning forward. "Who will be here?"

"Covenant, of course," she said.

"What? I thought Gregor worked for something called the Organization."

She sighed. "You have no idea what you've gotten yourselves into, do you?"

Chapter Sixty-One

Before we went further, Faria insisted we tell her Kane's story since, ultimately, his story was also a part of hers. How her work had progressed when it had gotten out into the wild, as it were.

For the next ten minutes, I explained what I knew. What Kane had told me and what I'd seen over the past few weeks. She never nodded. She never shook her head in disbelief. Just listened.

As if the idea of a wolf becoming a man was just what she might expect to hear?

I found her calm unnerving.

When I felt like we'd told her enough, I waited for a response. She merely sipped the remainder of her tea.

"You," I said, "don't seem surprised by any of this."

Faria laughed. "Oh, very little would surprise me. But no, the thought that this beautiful man was once a creature of the forest? That is hard to comprehend. I believe you, of course, but it is a fantastical story."

"But you do believe it?"

She nodded and motioned to the four monitors on the rear of her kitchen cupboards. Each showed a grayscale view of her property with a slight stain of color. I'd seen similar tech before. Gregor had had it on his phone when he'd shown me how he'd been keeping tabs on my mother and grandmother.

The memory of that angered me, but I tamped it down.

"I have sensors around my property," the doctor said.

"We saw the cameras when we came in," I said, flicking my fingers toward the monitors.

"Not those. You likely wouldn't have noticed my various devices unless you were looking for them." She stood and walked beneath the monitors. She pointed to a small panel, about the size of a palm, that read 2.017.

"That's how I knew one of you was different."

"Oh?"

She nodded and smiled at me. "It's an atmospheric measure. That reading was caused by your friend. And, I suppose, it's why I believe what you've told me. At least about Kane."

"What is it?"

"The people involved in my program slough a chemical from their skin. Like a pheromone. Do you know what that is?"

I frowned at her. "I'm not an idiot."

"No, I suppose you're not. You would have been dead some time ago if you were." She motioned to the panel and sat down again. "The cameras warn me of intruders. The sensors tell me if any of the Enhanced are among them."

"You're worried that your own monsters will come and attack you?"

"I am worried those who *control* them might. And they're not monsters, Emelda. They're warriors. The best the world has ever seen."

"Bullshit!" I said, leaning back against the chair and crossing my arms. "Your Enhanced are killers! I don't know if that had been your plan, but they terrorized people in two different towns. You had to have known about that."

"They weren't *my* Enhanced." She shrugged. "And there was little I could do about any of that."

I shook my head. "Not true. They were yours. Cal infected two good people. Turned them into things who lost their humanity. And then there's Kane. What you did ripped him from his family."

"I am sorry," Pental said.

"If there's a monster here"—I pointed at her—"it's you."

Faria lowered her head and nodded. When she looked up at me, her eyes were distant.

"It wasn't supposed to happen like this. Not any of it." She sighed. "I was chosen by the Organization to help make soldiers better. It was so enticing. As a geneticist, there are so many restrictions and rules in place. The Organization gave me a laboratory and took all of those restrictions away."

I huffed. "All for a government program. A government that secretly ignores its own rules."

She looked at me, her mouth hanging open. Then blinked, her eyes wide.

"You think this has to do with the US government?" Slowly, she shook her head. "In a tangential way, sure. They could benefit from my work." She shrugged. "If that suited the goals of the Organization. It's far more complic—"

"*Not* complicated," I said and dropped back into my chair. "You create something that makes supersoldiers and sell it to whoever will pay the most."

Faria sighed. "You're not entirely wrong." She then stood up and went to the window, staring out at the night. That was when I realized how dark it was.

"Can you please close the curtains?" I hadn't yet told her about Kane's moon allergy.

She sighed. "It won't matter in the end. They won't—"

Kane spoke up. "Please do as Emelda asks."

Faria looked back at him, a question on her face, but then slid the drapes closed. She turned and leaned against them, ruffling the fabric.

"I am playing such a small part in…" The scientist started then got a small smile. "'We are just ants. Ants rolling a grain of sand across the bottom of a boot at the back of a closet in a cruise ship.'"

I finished the verse. "'Rolling on the waves of a hurricane sea.'"

She raised her eyebrows. "You have heard this?"

"Gregor," I said. "The asshole said that in a shitty little bar. A bar the tech sergeant was planning on *killing* me in, by the way."

"He's still calling himself that?" Faria smiled. "He hasn't been a tech sergeant since he joined the program. Men and their ranks."

"What does this strange saying mean?" Kane asked.

"That would take all night to explain. It comes from… Well, the person heading the Org is rumored to be…" Instead of finishing the sentence, she let out a low chuckle.

"What aren't you telling us?"

She sighed and sat at the table once again. "I'm not hiding anything, but we're running out of time." She turned to Kane. "What that silly little saying means is that my program and Gregor's work since, these are just very small machinations in a massive, well, organization."

I huffed. "You sound like a conspiracy nut."

"I was *in* the conspiracy, Emelda," she said, her voice shaking. "In the middle of these two forces fighting for control. It's like a chess board on a global scale. But instead of sixty-four squares, there are 64,000."

Putting my hands to the sides of my head, I growled. "*What does any of that mean?*"

Her eyes flicked up toward the monitors. When I followed them, thankfully, I saw nothing on the cameras.

However, I wondered if she did because she began to speak quickly.

"These are two groups that are beyond corporations. Beyond governments. They are fighting for control. Not in big moves but thousands, maybe millions, of small moves. Our program was just one chess piece in all that."

I put my hand up, trying to comprehend what she was saying.

"You said there are two groups. The Organization and who?"

She frowned and shook her head. "Covenant. But even those names are said to be some sort of ruse. Conspiracies within conspiracies. The two have been fighting for control for years. Decades. Maybe much, much longer."

"Control of what?" Kane said, his hands rolling into fists.

"Us, of course." Faria threw her hands up. "Everything. The ultimate fight for dominion over humans on this planet."

"So Covenant has been trying to stop you?" I said, my head spinning.

She nodded. "They had spies in the Organization, leaking details about my work. I couldn't let them get it."

Then it all became clear to me. At least, Dr. Pental's part of it.

"Cal thought you'd left the program, took all the research, because you'd realized you'd created blood-sucking monsters. The good doctor doing what's right for humanity. But that's all bullshit." I jammed a finger in her face. "You left because someone was leaking your work to this Covenant group!"

Faria gritted her teeth as she spoke. "It was mine! My work! And the Organization had lost control of it."

I jumped up from the table, staring at the monitors again. Pental kept glancing at them. I still didn't see anyone approaching.

"I joined up with Kane with one goal. To help him get back to his family. His pack. How can we do that?"

She shrugged. "I don't know."

"But you know how this infection works! You created it!"

When she spoke, her voice was just above a whisper. "I had designed it so that the effect would be temporary. That way, we would always hold the yoke. The Enhanced would need to return to us, get continual treatments, or the effect would fade."

"You missed something," I said, remembering what Cal had told us. "Blood."

She winced at the word. Then nodded. "Yes. Inexcusable, really, but I'd been so rushed. Cal had been the first to discover it, naturally. The treatments have a similar effect to illicit drugs. Those cravings were supposed to allow us to control the Enhanced."

"Your supersoldiers would be the drug addicts, and you'd be the dealers."

Faria nodded. "Yes. That was by design. A way to keep them in line. But the human body is so clever. We think we know everything, but we've barely scratched the surface. When our Enhanced got low, the cravings kicked in. We'd tested that. Withheld doses to see what might happen. And then there was an incident."

"Oh?"

"Cal wasn't himself. He'd been our greatest success and felt all that strength, that power, ebbing away. We just wanted to test what would happen if it left him entirely."

I winced. "Jesus."

"We found one of the lab workers. Half of her blood had been drained before Cal could stop himself. We were able to save the woman, but she'd been bitten."

"That hadn't been a worry before?"

"The virus can't be spread through coughing or a scratch or anything like that. Bodily fluids only, and we *never* imagined..." Pental said, her eyes losing focus. "Within hours, right in our clinic, the lab worker turned. I wanted it all shut down, to reassess, but the Organization saw it as a cost-cutting opportunity. The treatments are very expensive." She looked at me, her face placid. "And they realized they could make more Enhanced, cheaply, with a simple transference."

"But it's not the same," I said, pointing at her. "The people Cal infected were disfigured. *Monsters.*"

She nodded. "A mutation of the virus container."

"The what?" I asked.

"It's not important."

I slammed my hand on the table. "Make it important."

She sighed. "The treatment uses an inert virus to deliver the treatment. The core cells multiply, and the virus delivers it through the body. But Cal's immune system changed it. The T-cells—"

"Get to the point!"

"The blood proteins and virus were working in ways we hadn't planned," she said. "It mutated the virus carrying the treatment."

"Why would that matter?"

"The method of delivery is everything," she said and almost laughed. "If I threw a bullet at you, it would bounce off your skull. If I put it in a Glock and fired it, it would put a hole in your head."

I sat back, shaking my head. "Are you saying that Cal's body weaponized the treatment?"

"When a virus rolls through a population, it makes people sick. In very rare cases, a person can sort of make the virus sick. They change it. It happened with Covid."

"How?"

"Someone with HIV in South Africa got sick with the coronavirus. Their immune system was haywire, and their body changed the virus. They gave us the Omicron variant. One person's body created the most dominant version of Covid on the planet at the time. And... oh my." Faria stopped speaking and rubbed her hand on her mouth, lost in thought. "I wonder. I wonder, I wonder."

I slapped my palm on the table to bring her back to the present.

"So the Organization's 'cost-effective' Enhancement program could make monsters, but they were flawed." I took a quick look up at the monitors then stared at her again. "They couldn't find you to get back on track, so they were chasing down Cal to get the original recipe or something. Is that about right?"

Faria nodded slowly.

"Fine, great. Don't care," I said. "What I want to know is can you reverse it? Can you help Kane?"

"Maybe," she said and began to nod quickly. "I still have all my notes on a drive here in my study. If there is any way to help Kane, it will be in there. But it would take weeks—"

"Then let's get started," I said, jumping from the table.

Slowly, she shook her head. "We can't."

"Why not?"

Faria pointed to the monitors. "Our time is up."

When I looked, I saw she wasn't pointing at the camera monitors but the readout next to them. The ones that had detected the chemicals Kane was emitting.

Before, it had read 2.017.

It now read 11.14.

Chapter Sixty-Two

"You want us to go *out* there?" I stared at Kane, wanting to say more but unable to find the words. He looked at me with gentle eyes and placed his hand on my shoulder.

"Not us," he said, his voice even. "You stay inside with evil scientist."

"Hey!" shouted Pental from the table as she whip-scanned through her computer tablet.

Kane smiled. "All good stories have evil scientist, yes?"

I wrung my hands, avoiding his gaze. "Your human parents sounded like they were great, but I think they let you watch far too much television."

He shrugged. "Is for learning."

"No, is not for learning," I said and looked out the window. All I saw was pitch black. No stars or moon to light the yard on the other side of the glass.

I pulled him away from the window.

"What about our pack of two? If you're going to go out there to face off against those things, we should do this together, Kane!"

He looked over at the kitchen and walked away from me. I took a few steps toward the door and contemplated blocking him from leaving.

Next to the double fridge, he opened a long, skinny cabinet. Kane pulled out a mop and held it up, a goofy smile bending his bearded face.

Before he could say whatever he was thinking, I held up a hand.

"No." I shook my head. "No weird Schwarzenegger lines right now. This is not the time."

"*Que?*"

"Never mind," I said, and he strode up to the front door, the mop under one of his arms. "I've got my slingdart. I can help you—"

"You can help by staying in with evil scientist."

This time, the moniker only elicited a low groan from the woman behind me.

"You can't take on those things alone," I said, my vision blurring a little. "We should do it together."

"I can heal, yes?"

I rolled my eyes. "Yeah, but to do it, you've got to kill one of them first."

"No, not one. I will kill all."

"Then let me help you!"

He reached for the door handle. "You can help." He nodded to the little woman at the table, engrossed in her tablet, tapping the screen. "She has more than just cameras."

"What?"

Kane shrugged and nodded outside. "There is a, ah, hum around this place. Wires. Whatever this is, it is something you should use."

Before I could say another word, he glanced up at the cameras on the back of the kitchen cupboards. Two just showed bushes, trees, a small garden, and a long box next to it, which likely held tools to work the soil and plants.

He gripped the door handle, and I held his shoulders. Leaning up on my tiptoes, I gave him a peck on the cheek. "For luck."

Grinning at me, he leaned down and kissed my cheek in return.

"Now you have luck too."

He unlatched the door, held the mop like a warrior-janitor heading into battle, and ran. For a moment, I could only watch my brave friend disappear into the darkness. Then I closed the door and spun back to the table, my anger rising like a river after a storm.

"Is he right? Do you have other shit out there you haven't told us about?"

The woman continued to thump away on her tablet, giving no acknowledgment I'd even spoken. I sat down next to her and put my hand across the screen. She looked up as if only realizing in the moment someone else was there.

She blinked once. "How could he have possibly known about the devices I have out in the yard? Is that part of his enhancement?" Pental looked away, eyes out of focus. "Couldn't be. I can't imagine—"

"Kane isn't like the others. He's not like anyone else on the planet," I said but left it at that for now. "So what do you have? Spring-loaded nets? Bombs? Laser cannons?"

Pental frowned at me, and I pointed a hooked finger at her lips. "Keep it up and I'll smack that expression right off your face. My friend is out there, and every second he is, he's in danger. Because of you! They're not after us."

She nodded and lowered the tablet to the table then looked to the back of the house.

"I should have destroyed it all. Everything," she said, her voice distant. "But it's my life's work. And it could do so much. It could make us so much... more."

I laughed and shook my head. "Kane was right. That sentiment, making people *more*, has probably caused more pain and suffering than any other in human history. You are an evil scientist."

"You know nothing." She waved my words away like a bad smell. "You know less than nothing. There is a war raging all around us, Emelda. Fought by powers beyond world governments. They've got their enhancements, and we have ours."

"You think that's Covenant out there? It's *your* people. The Organization. Gregor and whatever monster he brought with him."

"They are not my people," she said. "Not anymore."

"I don't care."

The woman blinked and drew her head back, wincing. She said, "You should care. They affect everyone you care about. Everywhere you go, everywhere you work, all of it."

I shrugged. "What the hell can I do about it?"

"We can start by making sure neither side gets their hands on my research," she said, grabbing her tablet again. "It would tip the balance. Covenant has been working on their own enhancements. A sort of fear suppressor. My program was to counter that, but my work on the Enhanced program succeeded far beyond expectations. It's far too much power."

"Which is exactly what the Organization wants!"

"Of course they do!" the woman shouted, the first time I'd seen her lose her cool. "But the best outcome is a balance, a perpetual stalemate."

"Best for whom?"

She looked at me, and I could see real fear in her eyes. "The human race, of course."

"Fine," I said, throwing my hands up. "What can we do to keep them off your precious research? What voodoo have you got out there?"

For the first time, she gave me a genuine smile. "My grandfather was a tinkerer. One of the first auto mechanics."

"I know that."

"Right. Right, yes, you do. My father also. And his daughter, better than the two of them," she said, lifting a shoulder. "I went into the mechanics of the mind and body, but I never gave up my love of practical engineering."

"The cars. You were looking for that part."

She nodded. "That doesn't matter anymore. But your big friend is right. I do have some additions to my property most homeowners do not."

Standing, she walked toward the screens lining the ceiling next to the kitchen, cradling her tablet like an infant.

"Finally, I will see what they can do."

Chapter Sixty-Three

Kane

I can hear them as they breathe.

In the darkness, their claws clatter against the stones embedded in the earth.

When I look to the sky, it is pitch-black. My eyes slowly adjust, and I can see a swirl of angry, dark clouds. Tonight, the moon will not help me. If it ever has.

However, the changes it brings about in me linger, even after I recover from whatever creature it transforms me into. Each time I become human again, I am different than before.

There is an odd sensation flowing through me. One that confounds me, but I recognize it from when I was a smaller creature. When I encountered Emelda that first time. While I am no longer such a useless creature, being in that body has stained my mind. My soul.

If I have a soul.

For I am a wolf. Always wolf, even beneath this human flesh.

People say animals do not have souls.

However, being inside that small, shaking creature has altered something. A soul? A mind? What does it matter?

I feel fear.

And I do not like it.

To my right, I hear a rustling. I dart forward and press my body against a tree, trying to block myself from being seen. I can smell it now. The chemical odor. Can it also sense me?

Mixed with my unwelcome hesitations, I have a joy for life I do not remember from before.

Was this imbued into me when I was the sleek, skinny dog in the Canadian forest? The one Emelda called a greyhound? I had never felt such unbridled joy to just be alive.

And when I became human once again, some of that remained. Again, a stain upon me.

However, it is a joy I do not wish to lose, and now, this makes me fear dying!

This conflict, confusion, it clouds my judgment. I need to leap out but worry that—

More movement, and I crouch low.

The scent stronger now. Not one creature but two of them are creeping toward me. As my eyes adjust, I can see one just passing to my south. If I ran for him—it is a male, for I can smell that too—I believe I could kill him before he could get a swipe at me with those terrible claws.

I hesitate as more sensations flood my brain.

No, no!

The golden. It has also changed me. *Stained* me and made me a weaker hunter!

I am poisoned with—what is this?—concern? No. Empathy? Maybe.

Something deep within does not want to cause pain. Does not want to hurt.

But hurt I must.

For my empathy extends further to my pack. My new one. Our pack of two. I must take down this creature to protect Emelda.

A snap of a branch beneath a foot is my cue.

The long wooden handle of the mop gripped in my hand, I launch forward, silent as the night, swinging the end of it toward the creature. I see the white of its black eyes turn, and I jam the fibers of the mop into its mouth.

The creature falls to the ground, unable to call out, gagged by the tendrils of the mop.

Its muffled scream is lost in the material. I press down harder, with all my weight, and it buckles forward, clawing at the air. Shifting my body to avoid the razor-sharp nails, I push further and hear a crack. Its hands fly upward, exposing the neck.

Yes, the neck. Always the best choice.

But this time, I am not in a form to chew and tear. Instead, I lift the boot of my foot and ram it down, lifting myself with my arms upon the mop handle. Another crack as my boot smashes the creature's windpipe.

The dark eyes flutter.

When I pull the mop head away, blood gurgles from the creature's mouth. Its breathing has stopped.

I do not wait for the secondary attack. Holding the mop several palm lengths from its top end, I swipe my hand toward the tip and snap off its end.

When the second creature leaps for me, I duck low and hold the base of the mop. It had thought to catch me when I was not looking. Foolish creature.

I stare up at its eyes as it holds, suspended in the air, the mop end poking out its back. It looks at me so strangely. Confused. Sad. I have taken the most precious thing it held.

As blood dribbles out from a silent scream, the eyes find me. Judge me and find me wanting.

I feel a stab of pain in my chest and look down. The creature has lashed out at me in my moment of confusion, weakness!

No.

No.

Its arms flop low as its life flits away.

The pain was not from claws. From something else within me. Sadness floods my body, and I feel a constriction in my throat.

I do not like any of these sensations. They are not warrior. Not hunter.

Frowning, I strip the dead creature from the broom with my foot, pushing his body to the ground. It lands with a soft thump, having fallen across its dead brother. I stare down at these two hideous creatures. The shape they make troubles me, but I do not understand why.

No matter.

I have more to kill.

As wolf, I will use the darkness to my advantage. I can—

But in an instant, the night turns to day.

And I am blind.

Chapter Sixty-Four

"What are you doing?" I shouted at Pental as the four screens flashed white. Floodlights around her property illuminated every corner. Every shadow was exposed.

When the screens righted themselves, I saw creatures stopped midstep, throwing hands and arms across their eyes.

"They are sensitive to light, as I expected."

"Was that another of your controls?"

She shrugged. "Not planned. But the dilated pupils, a side effect of the treatment. It would make bright light very painful and temporarily short out the brain."

"Will it stop them?"

Thumbing her screen, she flipped through texts and notes. Again, it was as if I hadn't even been there.

I repeated louder, "Will it stop them?"

"What? No, not for more than a few seconds," she said. "I was just interested if I could predict the outcome. And I did." She beamed at me with that smug face, and I just couldn't help it.

When I hit her, she fell to a knee, and the tablet bounced from her hands and clattered to the floor. Pental looked up at me, a hand cradling the side of her face, her smug look replaced by fear.

I pointed up at the third screen.

"Your little experiment just exposed Kane!" I looked back and saw him run, crossing from the edge of one screen then across the top of another.

Behind him, he'd left two dead bodies, which gave me hope. But across the rest of the screens, I counted at least six more monsters. Six! Where had they come from? Gregor, of course. But where did he get a small army of them? Then I saw one I recognized.

Crank.

The Devil's Dawn leader with his bald head and face like a fist. But that face was distorted. His body larger, limbs that didn't look quite right. And at some point, he'd lost his glasses.

"Shit," I muttered. "He survived the attack from Cal. Dammit."

For now, Crank and the other five were frozen. Two had dropped to their knees, crossing their arms over their eyes.

Pental was back on her feet but had stepped a bit farther from me. She eyeballed the tablet, and I scowled at her. For now, she left it on the floor.

"How is your friend not affected? You said he was bitten by Calvin. But he's *sprinting* through..." Her voice trailed off.

I stepped forward, searching for him. Did he know where the cameras were? Know how to avoid them? Or was he just hiding from the six deadly monsters spread out around the property?

"Kane is different," I muttered, searching for him. Where did he go?

"How?"

I ignored her. When I stepped toward her, she flinched. Motioning to the screens, I said, "How long will they stay like that?"

"Not much longer," she said, ducking around me to grab her tablet again. "With the change in physiology, it rewires the neural pathways."

"Fucks their brain up. Yeah, that was pretty clear when they started *eating* people!"

She flinched, squinting her eyes.

"Yes, but it's like a river. The old neural pathways, those thoughts pass back and forth for years. Like water across land. Eventually, it creates a route. Thoughts move more consistently." She thumped the tablet again. "The bright light is one way to disrupt the new connections, which are akin to a, well, a new river. Water moving across flat land. There aren't really the grooves there, the riverbed, so when you rattle it, the brain goes haywire. But it won't last."

Finally, I saw Kane.

He flew across the top of screen two and drove his broken mop into the skull of one of the kneeling creatures. He extended his arm backward, and the handle came free, blood spurting from the monster's head as it fell to the ground.

Then, screen one. Kane was running full tilt and tackled the cowering monster to the ground. When it was beneath him, he raised the sharp end of the stick and drove it home. I covered my mouth, watching. Without the full moon, he couldn't become the hell beast.

But he didn't need it.

Even as a mere human, Kane was a hunter. A killer.

However, after the new kill, he didn't jump up like before. Didn't run. He arched over the body of the man. Then he did the strangest thing.

I inched closer.

Kane laid his hand on the side of the man's head. I could see the eyes of the creature fluttering as it died. It stared up at him, nodded once, then went limp. Kane rounded his shoulders and began... shaking?

I whispered, "What the hell?"

When I looked over at screen three, my stomach lurched. Crank had gone. No longer in the picture.

"Where did their leader go?" I pointed, finger shaking. "The one that was right there?" Then I saw another creature on another screen move off, running now. Then the third and fourth were up.

All of them, briefly, out of frame.

I knew where they were headed.

I shouted at the screen, "Get up, Kane! What are you doing? Get up!"

Behind me, furious thumping on the tablet caught my attention. When I spun around, I saw Faria's face, all grim determination. Her eyes ping-ponged from the tablet to the screens above.

Then I heard a *thunk-clank!* outside, followed by the sounds of grinding gears.

When I looked up at the screens, at the edges, silver spheres were splitting the ground, lifting in the air as dirt and grass tumbled from them. On each of the screens, they were dotted along the fence line. One at the end of a pole extended down from a tree.

Another slid down from a telephone pole at the end of a telescopic arm.

"The light can confuse them," Faria said, finger hovering above the screen. "But that's just a finger tap."

I squinted at the screen. "What are those?"

"Carbon-fiber rods. The sphere is brushed steel. Simple enough design, and I charged the capacitors the moment you came on my property."

I spun around to her. "Charged the—"

My attention shifted when I heard the wails above me. I hadn't even realized the screens had audio before then. On screen three, all four of the creatures were converging on Kane. Slowly at first.

Kane was doubled over, his face buried in the chest of the dead man.

What the hell is he doing?

"I can stop them," Faria said, her voice shaky. I realized she was asking for my permission this time. "Your call. Do you want that?"

"Yes," I said, my eyes watering. "They'll tear him apart!"

"Your call, Emelda Thorne."

She hit the screen with her thumb, and all four screens exploded with thick, ropey tendrils of arc light, a lightning storm engulfing the property.

Chapter Sixty-Five

Kane

My body seizes, and I can hear the tears on my cheek sizzle, and the world around me turns to light. Pain and light.

I remember this sensation.

It is similar to when I'd been struck by Gregor in the mall restaurant. When was that now? Days ago? Weeks? Years?

I have lost track of time.

And my vision is no longer of Dr. Faria Pental's property.

I am standing in a burning home.

When I look to my left, I see my parents. Dead. Their bodies on fire. I feel heat burning my own flesh, but I do not care.

Below, there are men.

Dressed in black. Long hair. Laughing through scowls.

My head swims. When I look up, I see the moon. So big, so bright. It calls to me like a lover, and I feel a warm rush through my body.

My arms stab with pain. My legs and torso too. My neck twists, and my fingers feel like they might rip right off my body.

I open my mouth to scream, but my throat has seized.

The window lowers.

Lowers.

Lowers.

Is the house falling?

No. I am growing.

The heat I felt before, this I no longer feel. Below, I only see the men, three of them, laughing. It is they who set the fire. They who took my human parents away. People who loved me. Those who I loved.

I leap from the window.

These are memories but new to me. It is as if I am a passenger, watching as my hand strikes. My teeth gnash.

There is blood. So much blood.

I feel a frenzy. For the first time, I taste blood in my mouth, and it is intoxicating. I drink it from their bodies. And I only want more.

When I look up, I see the lower floor of my parents' home collapse and a part of the roof slide off.

Racing back, I leap to the second floor with barely a thought. Our home is no longer a home. It is hell now.

I will not let this be where these two beautiful people rest forever.

Gathering their remains in my arms, parts of their bodies falling away like ash, I take as much as I can and charge back through the flames to the window. Landing below, I cradle my human parents in my arms as I run and run and run. If only I could get far enough from the flames to save them.

Then I collapse to my knees.

I lower what remains of these two lovely people to the ground. With my claws, beneath the moonlight, I dig into the earth.

When, before, one of my pack fell, we did not waste the flesh. We honored them by consuming. It was a way to forever carry them with us.

However, there is no flesh left of my parents. Only ash and bone.

But I will carry them with me. I place a hand on both of them then press the ash to my mouth.

"You will always be a part of me," I whisper. "Forever a part of me."

This is the first time I feel true rage. Rage at the fist-faced man. Rage at those who took them from me. But with that, also, the deepest sorrow I have ever felt. Wolf does not feel sorrow. Loss, yes, but not sorrow.

It overcomes me, and I weep.

I weep for them.

Then the world is electrified once more, white fissures across a gray-black sky. I have awoken from the dream and been returned to terrible pain.

My body is burning from within as electricity dances across the cells of my human body. I try to turn my head left. It is hard, but I force this motion. Then, I look right.

Around me, I see four of the creatures. They are also trembling, shaking. However, each of their black eyes is fixed upon me. I am their prey.

When I try to stand, my body will not obey. I am surrounded by predators and cannot move. One on one, there would be little contest. Against a pack of four?

The world turns black again. I try to throw my arms out to cover my face, but I cannot move them. However, I have not drifted into unconsciousness.

The lightning above us has stopped, leaving only the darkness behind.

It is colder. So much colder.

When I look to the monsters around me, twitching and shifting, gurgling as they growl, all their foul eyes once again turn to me.

Chapter Sixty-Six

I watched as all four screens went black.

I screamed at Pental, "Why did you turn them off?"

She furiously banged away at her tablet as she spoke.

"It's not... They're not off. Someone's cut the power out there," she said, the lines in her face growing darker. Deep lines looked like valleys cut through stone. She sighed. "A weakness of these defenses. No generator."

The screen rolled, and then the images turned green. Night vision.

Kane lay on his back, staring up at the sky. Around him, four of the monsters lay twitching and shifting.

"How... how long does that jolt—?" I blinked away tears, unable to complete the thought.

Faria held the tablet out, staring at it. Like the answers would magically roll up upon the screen. For now, it offered none of that.

"Under a number of testing scenarios, we were able to incapacitate the subjects but never for more than a few minutes," she said, and the corner of her mouth twitched. "Calvin was always the first to recover. A splendid specimen."

I swung my head toward the small woman. "Kane was right. You are evil."

She scoffed. "Grow up. This is science. There's no evil or good in it. Just the work."

"Right," I said and stepped closer to the screens. "Tell that to Oppenheimer."

I willed Kane to get up. His face grew on the screen as Faria pushed in. She then redirected another camera, and the screen on the far right showed the other four trying to regain control of their bodies.

The first to get up would survive.

Kane lifted a trembling hand toward the screen. I pushed my fingers toward him, as if he were reaching for me. My heart shattered. I could do nothing.

Then, I realized he couldn't see me. Of course he couldn't. He was reaching for the sky.

No, not the sky.

In the green tint of screen one, I could see the swirling clouds of a storm. The vast power roiling in the clouds.

The moon.

Behind that thick blanket of clouds, of course, was the power to change him. But what would he become? Could a Shih Tzu fight monsters?

No, of course not.

The previous day, he'd been the golden. Had it only been one day? But if the moon were to come out, not full yet, he *could* become the Rottweiler. He'd have a chance.

I ran to the window and threw back the curtains. My heart sank.

The clouds were thick, with no break in the sky. I scanned left to right. All clouds.

From across the room, I heard a low, throaty growl. I didn't know if that had been Kane or any of the other four struggling to move. To tear out his throat.

"What are you doing?" Faria said as she stood there watching me run across the room, frantic.

I went to another window, throwing those curtains open, searching the sky. Nothing. Just a thick wall of clouds above.

Faria repeated, "What are you doing?"

"I'm—I'm looking for the goddamn moon."

She came up next to me, tablet cradled in her arm again.

"Why?"

The words just poured out of me. I hadn't intended it, but I'd felt impotent, unable to do anything to help Kane. I considered grabbing my slingdart and killing each of the four but knew that unless I had perfect head shots each time, all I would do was anger them.

Or worse, awaken them from whatever fit they were suffering.

Instead, I told Faria Pental why Kane was unlike any other creature on the planet.

As I babbled on, I watched her expression change from astonishment to incredulousness to an odd look of calm.

I ran back to the screens, my fists bouncing on my thighs.

"It—I don't understand it, but the moon phases affect what he turns into," I said. "It's not full at the moment, but whatever he might transform into, it has to be better than just lying there."

Another odd sound bubbled and warbled from the monitors. Then, I realized it wasn't coming from the screens at all. It was coming from Faria.

I frowned at her. "You don't believe me," I said and turned back. "I don't care."

"On the contrary. On the contrary," she said, shaking her head as she laughed. She *was* crazy. "I mean, what you're saying is possible. Well, in the realm of creating creatures from humans, yes, it's possible. But you're trying to say he once was—?"

"A wolf!" I said, spitting the words. "Yes!"

She laughed, shaking her head. The look on her face turned my stomach. Pride.

"I carried out some animal experimentation, mice, because of—"

"Shut up," I said, wiping my eyes. "I don't want to hear it."

"Oh, but you do," she said, a queer fire in her eyes. "I just never thought. A wolf!"

I ignored her and looked at the face of my friend. His eyes just staring out. The deep, amber eyes. Pleading.

I need you.

"I may have an answer," Pental said, lifting her tablet again, thumping away. "I had to take... shortcuts, given our time frames and resources." She laughed again. "Unintended consequences. Yes. That—"

"What? What the hell are you talking about?"

She flinched but then regained her footing. "The treatment that is delivered, the one that causes the enhancing effect, would have been seen as foreign to the body. So it had to be encased in a carrier. A package that the body would, in effect, ignore. Like a car carrying a cure."

"Or an ax murderer."

"Quite so." Faria shrugged. "But what virus would I use? That was easy. A few years ago, every scientist in every country on the planet focused on just one. One virus."

"Covid."

She nodded. "Our fight against the SARS-CoV-2 virus, a worldwide effort, meant that there was more data on that one virus than any other in human history."

"The coronavirus? Your treatment used *Covid*?"

"Not as the world knew it, no. I'd weakened it so much that the body wouldn't see it as a mortal threat. No use in sending the T-cell troops out in force. Just let it waste away."

Faria explained that part of the manipulation, the therapy, required a complex hacking of the body's immune system. The SARS-CoV-2 helped, but it was also a tricky—her word—virus. Even in its weakened state.

"It fought for too much of the cell surface. The treatment was within its casing, but the virus had its own plan. Its own designs, even when weak. So I needed a type of... governor. Something to make it less effective."

"How does this explain what happened to Kane?" I shouted, pointing at the screen. "Those monsters are going to tear him apart!"

"Nicotine," she said grinning.

"What?"

"Nicotine. It was the Chinese that discovered it but wholly by accident. And not really in the lab. They worked out that those who smoked had fewer instances of Covid infection. The nicotine, it turns out, competes with the virus for surface binding. With trace amounts of nicotine, my treatment could get adequate access to the cells and do the work." She sighed, shaking her head. "Shortcuts, though. I couldn't distill it in the way I wished, so used what I had. Nicotiana sylvestris."

"Is that supposed to mean something to me?"

"The advantage of using that particular plant would be that I could force it to bloom. Easier to extract the nicotine within." She looked up at the screens. "Like flipping a switch." Pental lifted a finger in the air and traced it across the face of my friend. I wanted to punch her again. Rip her away. But something about the switch.

What was she telling me?

"In what might have taken weeks or months, I could do in a matter of days," she continued. "I got the nicotine I needed and never thought anything of it. Until now."

"Why? Why does any of this matter?"

"Because, dear Emelda. Nicotiana sylvestris is a nightshade plant." She looked up at Kane, a grin bending her wrinkled face. "It blooms by the light of the moon."

My head swam as she spoke further. Prattling on about gene manipulation of plants and people. I heard more growling on the screen.

They were waking up. Moving more now.

"I think... I can only guess," she said, her voice a whisper, "that whatever Calvin passed along to your friend... given his, well, origins... that delivery of the therapy differs some. Wolves have a relationship with the moon. It seems they are just baying at the big orb in the sky, but who knows, maybe it's more than that."

"What? How does this help?"

She looked down at her tablet, swiping and tapping again, faster than before.

"You say he needs the moon to change."

"It's overcast!" I shouted. "It won't—"

"No, no. It won't," she said and held up her tablet. "But I have the frequencies here, in my research, that I used to manipulate the nightshade plant."

Now I understood her. I looked back at the screens.

"And you think you can do that again? Shine some, um, fake moonlight down on him?"

"Yes," she said then darkened. "But they've cut the lines to my floodlights. I can make those adjustments, but you need to get the lights working again."

"How?"

She tucked the tablet under her arm, then she crossed the room and raced down the hallway. Passing three doors, all closed, we came to a bathroom in the back. Faria flicked on the light, reached down, and grabbed the spigot on the tub.

"What are you—?"

She twisted the knob then grunted and yanked. The tub lifted, and below was a ladder.

"Go," she said, speaking quickly. "This is my last-resort escape route."

"Where does it lead?"

Pushing me toward the hole, she said, "There's a tunnel. About fifty feet long. It will take you behind the carport. That's where they would have severed the cables."

"I don't—"

"Just go," she said, and I stepped onto the rungs. "You'll come out through the floor of a shed. That's where the lines are."

"How am I supposed to fix wiring? I'm not an electrician!"

"There are couplings back there. I had rats chewing through them, so you'll find a box of them. Whoever cut the lines would have made a quick, clean break. All you have to do is slip an end in each and clamp the coupling together."

I took a few steps into the dark. "What are you going to do?"

"I have to calibrate the floodlights. Moonlight is redder than sunlight—I have notes in here, but you need to get the power back on if this is going to work."

With that, I slipped into the damp tunnel below, my world turning dark. Then, I began to crawl forward as fast as I could.

Chapter Sixty-Seven

Kane

I feel my mind drifting in and out of my body.

All I want to do is sleep. Sleep and dream.

No, not dream.

I do not want the dreams anymore.

When I turn my head, I can see the dream, though. Why has it returned?

No, not the dream.

It is him. Five meters away from me, he is snarling at me. His head uneven, misshapen. This is the fist-faced man, but he is different.

Larger. Limbs longer, like Cal had been. Like Bridget Mills and Charlie Boynton.

When he glares at me, I see the eyes, deep pools of black within white.

"Y-Y..." He struggles with his words, spittle flying from his lips. "D-Do. You ag-again!"

I can only shake my head. I hate the pity I feel for him. My enemy.

Then that pity abates when I remember this is the man responsible for killing my human parents. The pity turns to resentment. Then anger. Then rage.

Forcing myself to move, I lift a leg. It twitches and flips as I do, but I am getting control back.

His eyes go wider at this, and he tries to move as well. Then he calls out. Barks something at the others, but it is unintelligible.

Around me, they begin to writhe and squirm. They are reawakening.

I must be the first to stand.

Chapter Sixty-Eight

By the time I unlatched the cover and lifted myself out of the far side of the tunnel, I was sucking in deep breaths. I never knew how claustrophobic I was.

Or just panicked.

The shed was dark, but when I stood, I felt the flutter of something against my face. I reached for it and pulled. Above me, the bulb illuminated.

Faria had been right.

I saw where the thick cable had been severed. Right next to it, an ax lay in the dirt of the shed floor. I stared up through the door but only saw the back of the carport.

If the monsters were after Kane, who cut the cables?

It didn't matter. Every second counted now.

Scanning the wood shelves, I chucked boxes to the floor, but it didn't take long. The container itself said "coupling" on it, so I grabbed one, stripped it from its plastic packaging, and knelt on the ground.

Then I paused.

One of those wires would be live. The doctor hadn't warned me about that. Had she forgotten? Or assumed I'd know that?

"Just don't touch the metal bit, Emelda," I muttered to myself. The cable was thick, and when I grabbed it by the rubber casing, my hand was shaking. I reached back for the plastic coupling, and when I turned back, a set of black eyes was waiting for me.

"What are you doing, little girl?" Gregor said then grinned wildly.

I felt an electric jolt go through me. It wasn't current but fear. Of course the tech sergeant had been the one to cut it. Then lain in wait for someone to come fix it?

Who knows?

He grinned and laughed, enjoying himself. God, I hated the guy!

"Why won't you leave us alone?" I shouted at him.

Gregor laughed. "I'm just following your lead," he said and grabbed a walkie off his belt. "Hammer. I've got the girl."

He stared at me, his black eyes dancing in milky white. Then he frowned.

"Hammer! Kane will surrender if we've got—" He looked down at the radio and banged it with his hand. "Goddamn it, where are you?"

That was my chance. I leaped forward, and he put a hand out to stop me, not even looking in my direction. But he'd given me what I needed.

I jammed the end of the cable into his wrist.

Sparks flew, and he screamed, thrown back as if I'd kicked him in the chest. Well, as if Kane had. Gregor flew out the open door of the shed, smashed against the wall of the carport, and fell into the dirt.

Now or never.

I placed one end of the clamp into the coupling and then the other. Not confident that I wouldn't electrocute myself, I grabbed a chunk of wood from beneath the shelves and used it to push the top of the clamshell casing closed.

Then I leaned down and heard a click.

The lights did not come on. Dammit! Had I done it wrong?

Faria had said she was adjusting the wavelength or frequency or whatever. Maybe she had to turn it off to do that?

Or she'd broken the circuit so I didn't fry?

She needed me to tell her when I'd reconnected the cable. But crawling down the tunnel again would take minutes Kane didn't have. I hopped up, rounded the hole, and stepped outside. I saw the windshield of the jeep.

Yes!

As I crossed, I felt a hand reach for me but easily kicked it away. Then, for good measure, and because it felt good, I put my boot into Gregor's face. He went limp again.

I ran to the jeep.

Chapter Sixty-Nine

Kane

I am up on my knees, my arms trembling. I cannot make my muscles obey.

They are awakening but too slow.

Already, two of the others have lifted themselves to standing. One stumbles over and grabs the fist-faced man, Crank, and helps him to his feet.

Why am I weaker than they?

The fourth man is now standing, and from all around me, they close in.

"Y-Y-You killed my p-people," Crank says, drool falling from his open mouth, slipping between large crooked teeth, "and you will pay in b-b-blood."

Again, I see the dream, cast over this world.

It is his face that brings it back.

The bodies of my human parents. How they lay burning in their beds. When I'd carried them into the forest, I had not been just taking them from their home.

I had been taking them to mine.

I put Mère and Père in the earth, the same that so many of my ancestors rested within. They were with my long-dead wolf family. They would be taken care of. Honored there.

But their son, their son reborn, had a debt of his own.

The strength of my love for them, the rage at their slaying, empowers me. I stand. I am just a human, not as large as these monsters, but they hesitate.

"I... I will avenge those you have taken from me," I tell the man.

This draws a laugh from Crank. A damp, coughing utterance.

He points at me, and I begin to walk forward, my legs trembling.

I cry out as I feel a tear at my back. One of the creatures has slashed at me with his claws. When I turn, another leaps forward, and another slices my shoulder. Lifting a fist into the air, I bash this second, and he goes down, but then the third and first attack in unison.

Pain and tears cover my soft man-flesh. Teeth and claws ripping my skin. But this only fuels me further.

I drive a fist across the bridge of the nose of one of the creatures biting into my side, and he falls, taking flesh and blood with him.

There are too many.

Too many of them.

Crank simply watches, laughing as nails once again rake across my back. I collapse to my knees. I feel claws dig into both shoulders and a foot in my back.

They are too strong.

Crank walks toward me, and I can see him licking his lips. I struggle to break their grip, but blood is escaping my wounds. Taking my energy with it.

I feel one of the creatures lick the blood from my side, and I shift to put an elbow into its face. He falls back. This only amuses Crank.

Laughing, he steps closer.

He barks at the other, and their grip tightens. Then Crank grips my hair, pulling his head back. He lifts his hands to strike and—

Brrrrrnnnnnnn!

We all freeze at the strange sound.

Brrrrrnnnnnnn!

What new creature is this? Even Crank is confused. Did he not know of—?

Not a creature. I recognize that sound.

Brrrrrnnnnnnn!

It is the sound Emelda makes when she is angry in traffic. And she is very often angry in traffic. It is the car horn on the jeep.

But why—?

Above us, the lights burn hot once again. And I feel the creatures holding me let go. Now is my chance! I try to stand, but something is wrong. Something is strange.

The world around me turns black and purple and red.

I know this feeling.

Above me, this is not light. Not regular light.

This is different.

This is moonlight.

I can feel the rush of strength in me, and my body twists and bends. My eyes water, and I watch as the creatures, who a moment ago held me, begin moving away. Staring up at me. They are staring up because I am rising above them.

Anger.

Rage.

Heartbreak.

I see the faces of my human parents. Not dead but alive. Then I see Emelda. It is for them. It is for them. It is for them.

It is for them that I fight.

I lift my arm into the air, extending it. I am not a dog this time. I am something more.

My blackened flesh knits together as I bathe in the strange light. I feel powerful muscles twist and enwrap me like snakes. I throw my head back and call out, a roar and howl.

I cannot see myself, but I do see what my transformation has done to the others. These creatures, these monsters, fear me. And they should.

I am the wolfwere.

Behind me, the claws scrape against my skin, but this time, they do not pierce. I turn and see the small Enhanced creature and clasp a hand upon its shoulder. Grabbing its jaw, I pull my arms apart. The head is now somewhere in the dark. The husk of the monster falls to its knees and then collapses.

The creatures stare at me, trying to regain their courage.

Their courage is wasted.

It is time to avenge my parents.

Chapter Seventy

It had taken me only a minute to crawl back through the tunnel. I'd gone slower at first, but the sounds of the battle above got my own blood up. I was terrified for Kane.

Back up the ladder, I ran from the bathroom and saw Faria watching the screen, her hands covering her mouth.

She looked at me, a queer look of pleasure on her face.

"*That* is what he becomes?" she said, her voice trembling. "He is so beautiful. How magnificent."

"What's happening?" I shouted, wiping my eyes as I stared. Then I saw.

The wolfwere had gripped one of the creatures, ripping its head right off its body and chucking it away. Faria had done it. Her artificial moonlight had turned him into the hell beast.

His clothes hung off him in tatters, exposing oil-black muscular flesh wrapped in twisting ropes of fibrous black hair. Lifting his arms like the wings of a predatory bird, his hands splayed, Kane extended hooked claws from the ends of his fingers.

The face of the man, the one I had come to know so well, had transformed into a throaty echo of his former self. A massive wolf-like head covered in coarse hair, ears set back above a recessed brow. Below that, his amber eyes were twice as they had been when human.

Standing more than eight feet tall, his body towered over the remaining Enhanced around him.

Kane bent one knee and twisted, leaping to the side and smashing into another of the creatures, off screen. When he ran, Faria adjusted the view of another camera, and just as they came into frame, there were two more creatures there.

No. Not two.

Kane had split one of them *into* two. He tossed the two halves down and stalked back to the first frame.

"How did... Can he...?" Dr. Pental couldn't even form a question. She was entranced. "He is perfection. He is what we..." Her voice drifted off when a blue indicator light above the screens lit up.

She took a step back.

Then, she looked up and around. Then, I heard it too. The *thump, thump, thump* began to rattle the fixtures of what once had been an old automaker's home.

"Why not?" I said, running to the window and peering outside. "Of course there'd be a helicopter."

Chapter Seventy-One

Kane

There are two of them left, but the fight has gone out of them.

The creature to Crank's right drops and lowers his head. Surrender? He falls to his knees and presses his face to the dirt.

I turn to the Devil's Dawn leader.

"I-I..." the fist-faced man says, trying to speak through a garble of twisted teeth. "Not ask. This. Done."

I stalk toward him. "You were a monster before they did this."

"N-No!"

"Yes. Not human. Not good. And now creature. Not any worse, only uglier."

Crank lifts his hands, first to fend me off, then turns them into fists.

I grab him by the back of the head, gripping his flesh, which bunches in my fingers. I see his skin split on his face. His eyes look up, and he begins laughing.

I turn to see what he is looking at. Only in the movies have I seen a helicopter, but here is one now. The noise is painful to the ears. The dust stirred up by the wind stings my eyes.

Then I hear Crank laughing. I turn to his face, blood trickling out of his mouth, teeth bared. Laughing at me.

I press my face to his. "Why do you laugh?"

"Th-They will... have fif-f-fifty caliber pointed at your head." He struggles for breath. "W-We were sent to dis-distract. Did-did-didn't care if we died! What a j-joke."

I squeeze the flesh of his head tighter and growl, "I have joke. My friend teaches me this."

"W-What?"

Leaning down, I whisper, "Knock, knock."

With my hand bunching the flesh at the back of his neck, Crank's mouth is forced into a gruesome grin. He laughs, coughing up blood.

"F-f-fine," he says. "Wh-Who's there?"

I grin, show him the teeth of the wolfwere, and say, "Fist."

"Fist wh—"

With all my strength, all my rage, and all my love, I drive my clutched hand through the man's open mouth, and I feel it connect with the knuckles of my other.

His head mush, I release him, and he tumbles to the ground, broken.

The remaining creature stands once more, and I move toward it, but then that feeling, that awful feeling, returns. I did not ask for this!

Pity.

Remorse.

"P-Please..." he says, his black eyes pleading. They are the eyes of a boy. This monster, creature, is only a teenager. Drawn into a terrible life. A life made far worse by this man at my feet.

I consider in a flash of time, what if I had been discovered by a man like Crank instead of my own parents? What would I have become?

Would I have been standing opposite me now?

I raise my hand and say, "Go."

The boy turns but only takes a few steps before his back explodes, pops in five, six places. Then he falls to the earth.

I look up as a spotlight from the helicopter hits me in the face, and I hold my fingers up to block the glare.

I drop my hand, and as the wind whips harder around me, I grip the earth with the claws of my feet.

The helicopter is closing in.

Yes. Yes.

I grin, baring my teeth.

I very much want to fight a helicopter.

Chapter Seventy-Two

Faria turned away from the screens and ran into the rear of the house, disappearing behind one of the closed doors.

I turned back to the screens and saw a goddamn helicopter landing in the front yard. Out the window, I saw Kane bracing, ready to fight it.

My money was on Kane.

"That bitch betrayed me," a haggard voice said behind me, and I spun. "I never liked her."

Spinning around, I saw Gregor. When I glanced at my back, he lifted his rifle higher.

"Ah, ah," he said. "Just stay there."

When I looked past him, I cursed myself. The prick followed me through the tunnel. I should have closed it and locked it when I came through! But *he* should have been dead from the shock.

Enhanced. Whatever that really means.

Trying to get some ground, I pointed at the screens. "You guys brought in reinforcements. You knew about Kane?"

Gregor looked to the screen, his eyes widening. Then, he slowly shook his head.

"No. No," he said. "Not until now. But that"—he pointed at Kane on the screen, eight feet of towering muscle facing off against the helicopter, ready for a fight—"that explains so much. Soooo much."

I stepped forward. "Get what you came for and leave him alone! He never asked for any of this!"

"True," Gregor said, stepping behind me, staring up at the screens. "But that's not my people. Well, one of them is—was. Goddamn Hammer sold out to Covenant."

"What?"

Gregor spun around, and we saw Faria Pental standing in the hallway. She said, "Ilsa is here?"

"Ilsa," Gregor said, in his singsong voice, "is a traitor. She took over the program after you abandoned us, Dr. Patel."

Faria looked at me strangely. Then her eyes flickered to the door. I shook my head, unsure what she was saying.

"I'll give you the research," she said. "I have it here."

"Of course you do." Gregor shrugged. "You're too arrogant to have destroyed it."

The doctor pointed at me. "Let Emelda leave. You don't need her."

"No," Gregor said and spun the rifle at my chest. "No, but I really, really want to kill her. You have no idea how much trouble she's been."

When he looked at me, Faria pointed beyond his head. With her other hand, she held up a palm in a "stop" motion. *Wait.*

She lowered her arms and spoke again. "I will give it to you freely if you let Emelda Thorne leave. There are passwords you will not be able to get through. And any attempt will burn the drive."

Gregor turned back to me, pointing down his sights. Then he sighed. "Fine," he said and flicked his hand at me. "Get the fuck out."

I didn't need to be told twice. I grabbed my backpack off the couch and ran for the door. Then I looked in the direction Faria had been pointing.

Beneath the readout, the red digits that sensed the enhanced chemical structure, was another number. That red number above was now down to 5.17. I guessed that once they were dead, they stopped emitting the chemical compound.

However, below that was the number eleven.

Then ten.

Then nine.

I ran for the door, threw it open, and ran outside.

The moment I passed the threshold, a steel door dropped behind me. I heard the chunk-chunk-chunk of more steel slats and looked back at the house. The windows were now gray, reflecting the flickering light of the moonlight floods.

Keeping my head low, I ran up next to Kane, standing between him and the helicopter.

I shouted over the noise of the whirring blades, "Are you okay?"

Towering three feet above me, he looked like a terrifying mesh of wolf and gorilla and hell-sent demon. When he looked down, though, his eyes were kind. "Why would I not be okay? If you are safe and I am standing, we are okay."

Tiny explosions erupted from the house, and we both took a step away. Two parts of the roof blew off, and within seconds, the entire structure was aflame.

"That's a shame," a woman's voice came from the direction of the helicopter. "So much work lost."

I stepped forward, motioning for Kane to stay behind me.

A dark-haired woman in an expensive coat stepped forward into the light. This had to be the Ilsa Hammer that Gregor had mentioned. A traitor, he'd said.

She held a fist to her mouth, staring at Kane. "You're new."

"Don't talk to him," I shouted at her.

Then she lifted her hands in the air. Her face softened.

"We are only here to undo the damage that the Organization has done." She began to take another step then looked to me with a question on her face. I nodded once, giving her permission. Slowly, she traced her fingertips across the massive, black-purple arm of my friend.

I growled at her, "You *were* working with Covenant?"

Hammer looked to me with a sad smile and nodded once.

"The government has been watching the Org for a long, long while. When someone has to step in, it's done... off the book," she said, sighing. "Covenant's job is to fix the problems the Organization creates." She looked up at Kane without any fear. "Do you want me to help fix you?"

Kane flinched and looked at me.

I shouted over the noise of the helicopter. "How?"

Ilsa Hammer took a step back. "I used to work under Faria Pental. Admittedly, I wasn't as brilliant as she was, but not half bad." She pointed to the house, totally engulfed in flames. "I suppose she's inside."

"With that asshole Gregor."

Ilsa got a small smile. "Then her research is gone. But I have notes of my own. She never knew that. And I think it will be enough to help."

"Help?" Kane finally said.

That got a bigger smile out of her. "So he does speak?"

"Of course I can speak."

She clasped her hands and put folded fingers to her mouth. "Did the virus give you a French accent?"

"He's French Canadian. Big difference."

That got a smile out of Kane, and he looked at me. A monster's face with kind eyes.

"Come with us, Kane," Hammer said, extending a hand. "Together, we can fix this. Get you back home again. I'm so sorry this has happened to you."

When he went to take a step forward, I put a hand on his arm. "Where are you going?"

He pointed at the house. "The answers we sought are in flames. If this helicopter woman has a cure, then I must go."

"'I.' What about our pack of two?"

Ilsa pointed behind her as the rotors of the helicopter sped up again. "He's too darn big. We've barely got enough room for him. We have to go before the local authorities show up. If they require us to stay, then I will. But I would rather avoid that conversation entirely."

"I will go with them," he said, his voice hitching. "And you will be safe."

"Kane, no! How can—"

"You will be safe now." He swept his arm over the bodies around us. "I have put you in such terrible danger. You have done more than anyone else ever would. Let me do this. And let me go. So that you are safe."

"What?" I said, tears spilling from my eyes. "Where am I supposed to go?"

He nodded at my backpack. "You have all the money you need. Go wherever you want to go. You wanted to work at bookstore in California? Buy one, now."

I stared up at his eyes, searching. "Is that what you really want?"

"It is."

I embraced Kane, holding him tight. Giving my friend one final squeeze, I swallowed down a sob brewing in my chest and let go. As he turned away, I caught the glimmer of dampness in his amber eyes.

Or maybe I'd seen that because mine were watery.

He started walking toward the helicopter, just outside the pool of light, then turned and looked at me. "Did you hear my joke? I did a knocking joke."

Fighting tears, I smiled at him. "I heard. Needs work. But yeah, not too bad. A real Arnie moment."

The smile on his wolfwere face was such a contradiction, I laughed.

He said, "I am happy to have had the Arnie moment my brother had wanted. And to have met you, Emelda Thorne. Be safe. You must now take care of your pack of one."

Before I could say another word, he turned away and walked toward the awaiting helicopter. Lowering his head, he stepped inside.

Ilsa Hammer startled me, placing a gentle hand on my shoulder.

"You are an amazing young woman, Emelda Thorne," she said. "Go do what you need to do. Once we get Kane cured of this wretched disease, maybe you'll consider coming to work for us?"

My eyes trained on the dark, oval doorway where my friend had stepped through and out of my life. "I just want to make sure he's okay."

"He will be. I promise."

"Fine, yes," I said, wiping my eyes. "How can I find you? I don't want any part of whatever you people do, but I want to know he's okay."

She shrugged. "Just send a note."

"Where?"

Turning, she said, "Anywhere. We'll see it." She called over her shoulder as she walked. "You won't want to deal with the local authorities," she said and pointed at the creatures on the ground. "Or have to explain any of that. The Waterloo police have been misdirected for the moment; it'll buy you about fifteen minutes. I would recommend leaving before they show up."

The moment she stepped inside the helicopter, it lifted off. In a tiny, dark window, I saw Kane for just a moment.

He waved and was gone.

Chapter Seventy-Three

I couldn't believe it was over.

Some part of me was happy to be free of the chaos of the past few weeks. Another wished I could be there when he finally got cured.

Walking back to the jeep, I had to give the home a wide berth. The home was on fire, and I wondered in some way if when Kane had seen that, he'd been reminded of when his human parents had perished. And how much he blamed himself for that.

Did he see those flames and think he would have put me in the same danger?

Hell, he had put me in danger!

But I had chosen to go along.

That was over now. And while he didn't have enough in the account to buy my fantasy store on the California coast—wolves ain't good with finances—I knew there was a big chunk of money in there. Enough to start over.

And this time, I promised myself, I'd get it right.

I reached the jeep and opened the door.

A wafting smell of fire and rot hit me in the face. When I bent down to look inside, a smoldering figure was in the passenger seat, face smearing the glass. I recoiled and walked backward, feeling the heat of the home behind me.

Gregor smiled, his teeth the only thing not burnt on his body.

"They took him, didn't they?" He coughed and chuckled. I searched for his rifle but didn't see it. His fingers were smoking and black. Blood seeped out of the cracks of his face as he grimaced in pain.

"Get the hell out of my car," I said. No anger anymore. This was a man defeated, and he knew it. "They're *helping* him. Your assholes would have only wanted to cut him up and make more monsters."

He turned to me, wincing. Then Gregor looked down to his charred fingers.

"Who do you think Covenant is?" He looked up at me. "I mean, really?"

"Get out."

Gregor smiled weakly. "They are just like the Organization. Just the other side."

"Enemy of my enemy and all that," I said, looking up at the dark clouds swirling above us. "They'll—"

"They will do the same as we would have," he said, coughing, blood dripping down from his lips. "They aren't any different. Just a different side."

"Bullshit. They're US government."

He laughed, puffs of smoke erupting from his lips.

"Did she tell you that? No. They're no more government than the Org." He sighed and leaned against the cool glass again. "Goddamn Hammer. I guess she thought she'd get what she wanted from them rather than us. After Faria left... I suspected. Should have paid better attention." He coughed again. "They won't try to cure him. They will slice and dice and experiment until they can make more like him. Kane is the perfect war machine. Even better than any of us could have hoped for. Now Covenant has him, they'll use him to make more."

I swallowed. "No. No, no. She said—"

"Ilsa lied, Emelda Thorne." He shrugged, and a wisp of smoke puffed from his shoulder. "It's what we do."

I didn't want to believe it, but standing there, watching the flames burn, I knew it was true. The Organization and Covenant weren't the bad and good guys. They were both vying for the same thing. One shitty coin, two sides.

I muttered, "What have I done?"

"Well, here's a thought." Gregor held up a charred finger then spasmed and coughed. "I can help you get him back."

"Why?"

"You want to save your big boyfriend," he said, his voice calm. He looked at me with those eyes—black coals in pools of white. "I want revenge. And the treatments they keep locked up. I *need* them, or I'm dead."

Gregor looked at me, and this time, there was no sneer. No snarky grin. I almost saw the human inside the monster.

"You'll be *dead* in minutes. There's no way you're coming back from…" I pointed at his body. A smoking husk.

"Listen, I have some doses of the Enhancement serum hidden away. My insurance policy. We just need to get there as fast as—"

"No, Gregor."

"It's the only way!"

I sighed and shook my head.

"Goddamn, Emelda!" he shouted then lifted his hands up in a weak apology for the outburst. "If you want to save Kane from years of experimentation. From pain. From the creation of an army like him, you will need my help."

Closing my eyes only made the torrent of fury and chaos in my mind worse. I opened them and glared at my enemy. "How do I know I can trust you?"

"What are your options?" He pointed at the steering wheel. "You could drive away now and be done with it. But when Covenant tears your boy apart and unlocks his secrets? There'll be nowhere you can hide from that. They will rule the world with power like that!"

I hated that I knew he was right. I should have never let Kane go.

My fault.

This was all my fault.

Why had I let him get on that damn helicopter?

"Fine. Fine," I said. "Wait here."

Gregor laughed and coughed. "Like I can move again."

"You won't need to," I said, horrified by what I was about to do. "I just hope you're thirsty, asshole."

Gregor's eyes went wide. "What the hell's that supposed to mean?"

I glanced up to the burning house then turned away and headed to the spot I'd last spoken to my friend. Where I'd handed Kane over to Covenant without a fight.

Time to start a new fight. I was going to be the most ruthless pack of one the world had ever seen.

But it was going to start off really, really gross.

I reached down and grabbed one of the bloodied creatures Kane had killed.

Then I began dragging it toward my jeep.

###

Acknowledgements

There is one name on the front of this book, but so many people played a part to get into your hands.

Okay, there are actually TWO names there, but Kane gets *plenty* of attention. Which, I would expect, he would say is exactly how it should be.

My everlasting, heartfelt thanks to my Beta readers: Myrtle The Hag. Ron Daniel. Bill Thompson, Mark Bunbury, Michael Pelto, Joe McCormick, Peggy Hackett, and Donna Cronin. You each make the book better and not just in the places where you tell me I've messed up. Thank you, thank you, thank you.

Also, much love to the kind folks at Red Adept for helping make my words more prettier and sense making.

Finally, to my lovely wife Tiffany. You are a partner in this and all things. We are, forever, a "pack of two."

Afterword

Your dear author is a serial interviewer.

I love learning about people, places, and professions.

Throughout this series, I've spoken to shopkeepers, motel workers, car show enthusiasts, military personnel, and many others.

For *Kane Unleashed*, I also spoke to a couple of amazing folks who guard our borders. For all that weight on their shoulders—the security of millions of people—I found them intelligent, delightful, and even funny! As I listened, taking pages and pages of notes on how they go about their jobs, I got a bit of a raised eyebrow down the Zoom window.

The conversation that followed, in a nutshell, was this.

Include what you need to, but where you don't need to, don't.

Ah, right. I got the message.

So I've tailored those border scenes with that in mind and even chucked in a few bits that are total fiction.

I'll leave it for you to decide which parts are which.

Thank you for reading, and I hope with all my heart you are enjoying the series.

Dick Wybrow, September 2023
Auckland New Zealand

Pre-order *Kane Unhinged* on Amazon.

Coming December 26, 2023!

Also By Dick Wybrow

THE HELL INC SERIES
Hell inc
Hell to Pay
Hell Raisers
The InBetween
The Night Vanishing
Past Life
Ride the Light
The Hangman

MELODY SUNDAY SERIES
Live Shot

Printed in Great Britain
by Amazon